Crane

MISS SEETON
ROCKS THE CRADLE

Also by Hamilton Crane
in Large Print:

Miss Seeton Goes to Bat

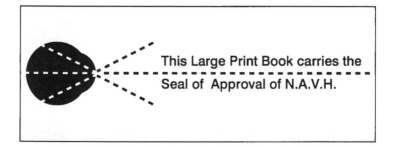

Heron Carvic's Miss Seeton

MISS SEETON
ROCKS THE CRADLE

HAMILTON CRANE

Thorndike Press • Thorndike, Maine

Published in 2000 by arrangement with Curtis Brown Ltd.

Thorndike Press Large Print Mystery Series.

The tree indicium is a trademark of Thorndike Press.

The text of this Large Print edition is unabridged.
Other aspects of the book may vary from the original edition.

Set in 16 pt. Plantin.

Printed in the United States on permanent paper.

Library of Congress Cataloging-in-Publication Data

Crane, Hamilton.
    Miss Seeton rocks the cradle / Hamilton Crane.
        p.   cm. — (Heron Carvic's Miss Seeton)
      ISBN 0-7862-2842-3 (lg. print : hc : alk. paper)
      1. Seeton, Miss (Fictitious character) — Fiction.
    2. Women detectives — England — Fiction. 3. Large type
books. I. Title. II. Series.
    PR6063.A7648 M569 2000
    823'.914—dc21   00-056823

MISS SEETON
ROCKS THE CRADLE

Chapter

1

Miss Seeton gazed at herself in the looking glass and shook her head for the umpteenth time. For the umpteenth time she removed from her head the old, wide-brimmed straw hat, and set in its place the slightly frivolous (she blushed for her self-indulgence) headpiece she had bought only that morning in Brettenden, and which was exactly the shade of yellow she had wanted. She'd recognised it the moment she spotted it in the window of "Monica Mary: Milliner" — the eye of an art teacher, even if she has been retired seven years or more, does not err. It is, however, as susceptible as any ordinary eye to glare, and dazzle, and brilliant sunshine, which, on this glorious summer afternoon, she was bound to encounter during the course of her half-mile walk along Marsh Road, from her cottage to Rytham Hall.

"My dear old straw would be so much more *practical* — so very shady," agonised

Miss Seeton, as she glanced out of her bedroom window at the cloudless sky and the crisp black shadows cast by the blazing sun. "But the colour is not quite . . . and then, what a dreadful waste it would be, not to wear this, when it matches everything so very well — and why else did I buy it, if not to match? Because it does . . ."

All Miss Seeton's earlier decisions had been made a good deal more easily. The frock: her discreet floral print with the pale primrose pattern. The jacket: her cream poplin with the neatly piped collar and the buttons — so unusual, but such a very kind thought — which Martha Bloomer (that inveterate popper into side-street shops) had found in an Ashford haberdashery and presented to her employer next day with such triumph that Miss Seeton hadn't the heart to tell her she'd managed to find the one she'd lost, after all.

"Dear Martha. Perhaps not quite the style I would have chosen," murmured Miss Seeton, her gaze drifting downwards from her hat to her buttons. "But one could hardly hurt her feelings when she offered to sew them all on — and it would have been so ungrateful to refuse the gift. One may surely be forgiven any slight suggestion of the idiosyncratic when it results from so charitable an impulse on the part of such a very dear friend . . ."

Her eyes prickled briefly with grateful tears as she remembered her first days as a resident of Plummergen, the Kentish village she was now proud and happy to call home. What a generous welcome she had received then, from everyone who wished to pay dear, kind Cousin Flora one final compliment! Cousin Flora (Old Mrs. Bannet, as the village had generally known her) had bequeathed to her young cousin Emily her delightful cottage, Sweetbriars, its entire contents, and its loyal retainers, in the persons of Martha Bloomer (goddess of domesticity) and her husband Stan, a farm worker famed for the fruit, flowers, vegetables, and fowl house he tended on Mrs. Bannet's behalf, to their mutual benefit. The arrangement had worked so well that it, too, had been included in Miss Seeton's bequest.

"A very dear friend," repeated Miss Seeton, and patted her topmost button with a fond fingertip. "But always so quick to keep one on one's toes. Dear Martha would expect me to have made up my mind long before this, I fear . . ."

Resolutely, she settled the new hat, its

brim so much narrower than she was accustomed to, firmly upon her head, skewering it with one of her remarkable hatpins. Her choice this afternoon boasted an amber bead of curious shape as its decorative feature and safety device: no danger now of piercing one's fingers and spotting blood on the crisp, bright straw of Monica Mary's latest creation.

"And this hat is, of course, almost the same colour as my necklace," Miss Seeton told the looking glass in apologetic tones, with one last lingering glance before forcing herself to collect her handbag from the bed and head for the door without further ado. If she dallied any longer, she ran the grave risk of arriving at Rytham Hall late, which would not only be discourteous, she reminded herself as she trotted down the stairs, but stewed tea had such an unpleasant taste, as well . . .

There was, however, absolutely no hesitation when Miss Seeton came to select an umbrella. The sky might not have seen a rain cloud for weeks, the forecast could be promising drought and heat and hosepipe bans, but Miss Emily Dorothea Seeton would as soon omit to settle her bills on time as to leave home without her umbrella. She had a fair selection of these in the rack beside the hall stand, but for special occasions, such as today's tea with the Colvedens, there was never a doubt in her mind. She hurried past the mirror and straight to the rack without pause, to draw out lovingly . . . "My gold umbrella," said Miss Seeton, with pride.

Not *solid* gold, she was always quick to add, when people admired this prize possession. But not plated, either — one could see the hallmark, could one not? "Hollow," she would explain, "because of the weight, naturally. And the cost as well, no doubt, for I cannot believe they are paid so much as that, although of course there are greater rewards than the monetary. For doing one's duty as they so splendidly do — policemen, that is. Job satisfaction, I believe it is called, and then, of course, promotion, when it comes, must be a reward, as well. For he was only a detective superintendent when we first met . . ."

Indeed he had been: Superintendent Alan Delphick, CID, New Scotland Yard — otherwise, the Oracle. Now one of the most highly regarded chief superintendents in the Metropolitan Police, he was generous enough to attribute to Miss Seeton her due share in his success. Her first case — when she had laid it on the line for the

11

Force and they'd followed meekly along behind, mopping up this and that as they went, while she didn't even seem to realise what she'd done for them — had left an indelible impression on Delphick's mind. One gold-handled, black silk umbrella had been a small price to pay for the privilege of having worked with her: part gratitude, part apology for not fully appreciating at first Miss Seeton's unique qualities as a catalyst for solving crimes. She never knew how she did it — indeed, he suspected that most of the time she never even knew that she was doing it — but once Miss Seeton, now retained (at his instigation) as a consultant to the Yard, had connected with a case, no matter how peripherally, then solved — by methods unorthodox and by methods unforgettable — that case would undoubtedly be.

"My gold umbrella," said Miss Seeton again with a smile, hooking it over her arm and giving it a loving pat. She picked up her keys from the hall table, shot one guilty glance in the direction of the corner clock, and made haste to fulfil her eagerly awaited engagement for afternoon tea at Rytham Hall with Sir George and Lady Colveden.

"And dear Nigel, too, if he can be spared

from the farm, of course," she murmured, as she hurried from the front door down the short paved path, pausing only for a moment to savour the rich summer perfumes of the flowers which lined it in their neatly weeded beds. Thanks to Stan Bloomer, and to the chapters she studied in that invaluable reference book *Greenfinger Points the Way*, Miss Seeton was at least sure now which were weeds, and which weren't, when she settled to rooting them out. She hoped. Greenfinger had been pointing the way for her since her first days as owner of Sweetbriars — and Stan had been interpreting the sage's printed words, when she couldn't make sufficient sense of them — once, that was to say, she had finally managed to make sense of Stan himself. An interesting accent, but on occasions, well, not entirely lucid . . .

"A true Man of Kent," mused Miss Seeton, making her way along Marsh Road at a steady pace. "Or do I mean a Kentishman? Oh dear, he would be so offended at my ignorance — the Medway comes into it, I know. East or west — where one was born — and he must surely have been born to the east of the river, which I *think* makes him a Kentishman, although . . ."

She carried on towards Rytham Hall, still pondering the puzzle of Stan's birthplace, then found her thoughts drifting to Kentishman's Tails, those mythical congenital appendages having in mediaeval times, she recalled from school history lessons, been the supposed punishment for the murder of Thomas à Becket, Archbishop of Canterbury. "Canterbury Bells," murmured Miss Seeton, remembering her garden, and Greenfinger's month-by-month recommendations to the novice in that most useful of books. "Bell, book, and candle," Miss Seeton announced to the gatepost of Rytham Hall as she began to turn into the drive, and was extremely surprised when the gatepost answered back.

"Good heavens, Miss Seeton, are you planning to exorcise something?"

Miss Seeton forgot all about candle auctions, stopped in her tracks, and dropped her umbrella. She blinked and shook her head, peering about her. She blinked again, but then the bewildered crease between her brows vanished as, from the shadows behind the gatepost, a young man, smiling and mopping his brow, emerged.

"Gosh, I'm sorry, Miss Seeton. I didn't mean to startle you, only — Here, no, let me pick that up for you —"

But Miss Seeton, with a quick smile of recognition for dear Nigel and a blush for her own absentmindedness, bent with easy briskness to grasp the crook handle of her fallen brolly — how she silently blessed the yoga which had made such a difference to her knees — and rose, neither breathless nor creaking, to return her young friend's greeting.

"How kind of you to come to meet me," she told him, as he fell in at her side and began to escort her up the drive. "I do hope I'm not late — that you haven't been waiting too long, I mean — but I was wondering, you see, where he might have been born — east or west — and ended up puzzling over the pins — for the auction, that is, when they drop out as it burns. Stan, that is to say — and candles, of course. If one were to ask him where, no doubt he would say that it was Plummergen, which is true, but not particularly helpful in indicating which side of the river is which — and it made me rather distracted, I'm afraid." With one of her loving pats on the umbrella handle, she blushed again.

Nigel had been acquainted with Miss Seeton for several years now, so that her thought processes were not always the complete mystery to him that they were to people meeting her for the first time. He missed only a very few beats before managing to frame what he regarded as the correct reply to her inarticulate question.

"Stan Bloomer? He's a Man of Kent, the same as me, born east of the Medway — though the Bloomers must go right back to the days of Hengist and Horsa, I should think. They were those Saxon thugs who turned up here, er . . . oh, way back in history, ready to bash hell out of the marauding Picts. Oh, I do beg your pardon, Miss Seeton."

But Miss Seeton had not noticed Nigel's language: she'd been too busy thinking. "Vortigern, was it not?" she asked, to Nigel's dismay: he'd already amazed himself by being able to recall even so much of his school days. Fortunately for him, she continued before he had time to confess his ignorance. "The White Horse of Kent, I suppose," she said, referring to the traditional badge of her dear adopted county. Nigel, with a loud clearing of his throat, said that his mother was sure to know, and delivered Miss Seeton thankfully to the front door of Rytham Hall, which stood open and welcoming in the hazy summer heat.

"Miss Seeton, how delightfully fresh and cool you look," said Lady Colveden, emerging from the kitchen at the sound of their arrival. She had a teapot in her hand, which she waved under Nigel's nose with a circular, jiggling motion. "Your father should be on his way by now, or he certainly ought to be, the number of times I reminded him this morning — so I'll take Miss Seeton through to the sitting room while you make the tea. The pot's already warmed," she added, and handed it to her startled son before whisking their guest away, pausing only to relieve her of the golden brolly and place it with due reverence (for she knew its history well) on top of the carved old mahogany chest which stood beside the row of coat hooks in the hall.

"It's really too hot to sit in the garden, isn't it? If I'd only thought," said Lady Colveden, as she and Miss Seeton settled themselves beside the low tea table pulled across in front of the unlit fire, "I'd have sent Nigel down to fetch you in the car, if your nerves could stand the strain, rather than have you walk when the sun's positively blazing. Though your lovely new hat must have spared you the worst of it," she added, with an admiring look. "That must

17

be one of Monica Mary's specialities, I imagine."

"I'm afraid it is." Miss Seeton blushed for her extravagance, her hand drifting unconsciously to the yellow necklace whose unusual tones were mirrored almost exactly by the straw of her latest purchase. "When it caught my notice in the window as I happened to pass by, I . . ."

"I know exactly what you mean." Lady Colveden's lovely eyes twinkled with fellow feeling. "George refuses to let me walk that way by myself, and whenever we pass the shop together he always manages to end up between me and the window, though normally he's such a stickler for walking on the outside. And, talking of outside," she added, as Nigel entered with a tea tray in his hands, "*would* you rather sit in the garden? Only we do seem to have a great many wasps this year — I've been asking and asking George to spray them with poison or whatever you're supposed to do, but he keeps telling me he's far too busy —"

"And he doesn't trust me with poison, of course," Nigel said, depositing the tray on the table with a discreet clatter and dropping into his chair with a chuckle. "I'm but a mere stripling about the place, an untried youth who doesn't know his, er, arsenic from his ergot, as one might say. You must remember, Miss Seeton, that I've only been working full-time on the farm since I graduated. What do I know about anything? What did they teach me at agricultural college?"

"Precious little," came a growl from the open French windows. Major-General Sir George Colveden, Bart, KCB, DSO, JP, long-suffering father of an irrepressible son, stood on the threshold with a battered straw hat in one hand and a large spotted handkerchief, with which he mopped his balding head, in the other. "Afternoon, Miss Seeton. Regular scorcher today — blasted bale fell on my hat, what's more." And he regarded the battered boater with some dismay. "Worn the thing for years," he lamented. "Nothing to be done with it now, I suppose," he added, gesturing with his behatted hand hopefully in his wife's direction. He sighed, loudly.

"Nothing at all," replied Lady Colveden, sounding far too cheerful for her husband's liking. "I've been trying to tell you for ages that you wanted a new one —"

"Wanted, be damned," muttered Sir George. Then, looking uncomfortable: "Sorry, Miss Seeton. Forgot myself."

As his guest smiled her sympathy for the baronet's predicament, his wife continued as if she'd heard nothing:

"And you needn't roll your eyes at me like that, George, because now you'll have to admit that I was absolutely right — so you may as well come in, sit down, and let me pour you a cup of tea while Miss Seeton tells you how splendidly simple it is to buy a new hat nowadays . . ."

As he obeyed his wife's instructions, Sir George cast a doubtful look at Miss Seeton's exclusive headgear. She made haste to reassure him. Too much haste, perhaps. "This, of course, is hardly the hat for you, Sir George. But when the weather is so hot, and one works long hours in the sun, it seems to me only prudent to protect oneself when one is, er, perhaps in more need of protection than . . . er, than . . ."

Nigel, choking over his tea, took pity on her anguished expression. The junior Colveden had inherited thick, wavy brown hair from his mother, and only wore a hat to shade his aristocratic young nose from the sun's glare; it could not be denied, however — even by those most blinded by affection — that a far larger expanse of his father's person was at permanent risk of

20

peeling. Nigel suppressed his chortles, and grinned encouragingly at Miss Seeton, whose heightened colour resulted from a cause far different to that which had troubled Sir George.

"Miss Seeton's perfectly right, Dad. Protection, that's what you need, or you'll be down to the bare bones before the week's out. I mean" — he gestured wildly with his teacup in the direction of the French windows — "you only have to look at what's happened to all the paint work over the last month or so."

Sir George grunted, and blew into his moustache. His cup rattled crossly in its saucer. Lady Colveden, knowing how he had treasured the old straw boater, thought it time to change the conversation.

"Yes, the whole house needs a thorough overhaul, George, but I've been thinking about that. Or rather, it was something Alicia Eykyn said which gave me the idea — you know how many windows there are at Mungo Hall."

Nigel pricked up his ears on hearing the name of one he had admired devotedly, though from a distance, since his first sight of her at a Hunt Ball. The young countess was generally known to be as practical as

Nigel knew himself to be a hopeless romantic, and her ideas were always worthy of attention. He reached for a scone, buttering it with a lavish hand, and inspiration struck. "Paint twice as thick, to last twice as long? I refuse to believe that she's decided to go for metal frames . . ."

"Don't be ridiculous, Nigel." His mother didn't even bother to look shocked at the suggestion, though Sir George had blinked once or twice before realising it was his son's little joke. Lady Colveden glanced at her husband before continuing, in a voice she tried to make reassuring:

"You needn't look so startled, George, it's nothing like that, truly."

"But?" supplied Nigel, with a grin, as Sir George fixed his wife with a suspicious gaze, and Miss Seeton's air of polite interest quickened. Lady Colveden blushed.

"But nothing, Nigel. Not really. Though I suppose you could call it metal, if you were in a nit-picking mood, but that seems rather, well, infra dig for gold leaf. Does anyone," enquired Lady Colveden smoothly, lifting the teapot in a hand that barely trembled, "want another cup?"

The diversion failed to work. Her words had sunk in. "Mother!" burst from Nigel, at exactly the same time as Sir George uttered a choking cry. "*Gold leaf?* You're pulling our legs — say you don't mean it!"

Now that she'd finally dared to broach the subject, Lady Colveden found herself able to enlarge upon it with comparative ease. "Yes, Nigel, gold leaf is precisely what I meant — no joke, I assure you. Alicia says it lasts easily three times as long as paint — the Devonshires at Chatsworth put her on to it in the first place, she told me. You can imagine what a time it must take to paint all of those windows: the place is enormous."

"And," supplied Nigel with a grin, as his father began to turn slowly purple, "what's good enough for dukes and earls certainly ought to be more than good enough for a baronet — if only he can afford it. We could always pawn the family silver, of course. It has a nice ironic touch about it — using silver to pay for gold —"

"Nigel," said his mother in warning tones, as his father gasped and seemed ready to explode. "That's quite enough. George, please don't pull such dreadful faces. You'll put poor Miss Seeton off her tea."

"Indeed, no, Lady Colveden," returned Miss Seeton earnestly. "Not stewed at all, and such a delicious scone — and the butter, so delightfully rich. Is it from your own cows, perhaps?"

"Rich," groaned Sir George, thinking of gold-leafed window frames, and his overdraft. "Hah!"

"George," said his wife, using exactly the same tone as she had used to her son not two minutes earlier. "Miss Seeton, I hope you don't mind my admiring your necklace. Such an unusual design, all those different yellows in the glass. Is it" — her eyes twinkled — "another little treat?"

Miss Seeton explained that it was part of dear Cousin Flora's legacy, which — not being much given to jewellery, such a worry in case one lost or damaged it — she only wore on special occasions. But, as it was always such a pleasure to visit the Hall — or rather she meant the Colvedens themselves, for, picturesque though the building might be, any house without its inhabitants lacked, she thought, a certain charm . . .

The clearly intended compliment was becoming so convoluted that, in a suitable pause as she drew breath, Nigel came rushing to Miss Seeton's rescue. "What a teatime conversation!" he remarked, stirring sugar briskly. "From poison to gold,

and from gold to the attractions of inheritance . . .

"Anyone would suppose," he said, "that
we were right in the middle of a mystery
novel . . ."

Chapter

2

The milliner's in which Miss Seeton bought
her yellow straw hat is situated in nearby
Brettenden, a favourite shopping centre.
Anyone wishing to purchase items out of
the ordinary — anyone wishing merely for a
change of scene — will take a bus (the
county service once a week is supplemented
by the twice-weekly bus run by Crabbe's
Garage), or drive (Miss Seeton, on occasion, is known to bicycle) six miles in a
northerly direction from the village, there to
have almost every wish fulfilled. Ashford,
larger, fifteen miles to the northeast, fulfils
most other wishes, and, if it fails to do so,
there always remains — viewed with suspicion by much of the village, because Miss
Seeton takes frequent trips to (she claims)
its art galleries and museums — London.

But Plummergen shops in Plummergen
itself for the basic necessities of life, and is
only too glad to do so. These necessities
being not merely staple supplies, but (to

many, rather more important) the gossip, rumour, and scandal without which at least half the village would be unable to survive. Plummergen has developed tittle-tattle and surmise to the only sort of fine art it understands: not for the clacking tongues of this tiny Kent community the echoing vaults and marble floors of aesthetic London — the village shops, all three of them, are all the populace requires for its survival. And the post office, having marginally more floor space than either the draper's or the grocer's, is the shop most favoured for the exchange and discussion of whatever item of news is most pressing on any particular day.

It was little Mrs. Hosigg who set the ball rolling on a sunny morning two days after Miss Seeton's visit to Rytham Hall. Lily Hosigg and her husband, Len, Sir George's farm foreman, were a quiet young couple living in the old Dunnihoe cottage at the lower end of The Street, Plummergen's main thoroughfare — not far, as village sceptics were wont to point out, from Sweetbriars. The Hosiggs, though they kept themselves very much to themselves, were known to be staunch supporters of Miss Seeton, about whom opinion in Plummergen could never make up its mind, with the inevitable result that about her supporters, too (and even more so when they were the incomers the Hosiggs undoubtedly were) opinion was always sharply divided.

The recent arrival of Dulcie Rose Hosigg had made Lily's retiring nature still more obvious. The birth had been both premature and difficult. Lily, barely out of childhood herself, took longer to recover full health and spirits than either Len, or Dr. Knight — summoned from his private nursing home in the middle of the night by a panic-stricken Len — would have wished. Dulcie Rose spent the first month of her life in a hospital incubator, with Lily (when permitted) vigilant at her side, and, once she had been taken triumphantly home, spent subsequent months wrapped round with blankets, anxiety, and tender loving care. All Plummergen had seen so far of the minute Miss Hosigg was, on particularly sunny days, the tip of a tiny nose, or a pale pink starfish hand fumbling from beneath a shawl . . .

"Which nobody could say's *natural*, not with it being her first, could they?" was the opinion of young Mrs. Newport, proud mother of a quartet of under-fives and sister to Mrs. Scillicough, whose triplets were a village byword. "Stands to reason there must be summat for her to keep hid, instead of letting everyone see, smothered up in that great old pram the way the poor kiddie always is."

"And for all it was a seven months babby, it's not growing so well, is it?" remarked Mrs. Henderson darkly; whereupon Mrs. Skinner, who had fallen out with Mrs. Henderson some time ago over who should arrange the flowers in church, came straight back with:

"Which is what everybody knows is nonsense, if they've any wits about 'em. Seven months babbies is after folk have got wed in a hurry, finding out it's needful to tie the knot — but them Hosiggs've bin married four or five years, and not a sign of a babby before this, poor things."

"They should have come to me," proclaimed Mrs. Flax, who held her head high as Plummergen's Wise Woman. "I could've give 'em herbs enough to help — ah, *and* to spare her the torment and trouble when her time came, but they wouldn't heed me in their pride . . ."

She allowed her words to fade away into a slow, ominous silence. Everyone shuddered, and looked over their shoulders, and crossed nervous fingers: not that they really (they told themselves) believed Mrs. Flax to have ill-wished the Hosigg baby out of spite at being rejected . . . but it did no harm to be on the safe side, did it?

Everyone, that is, except Mrs. Scillicough, who had lost faith in the purported powers of Mrs. Flax when they failed to assist in the suppressing of her triplets' insatiable — not to say unnatural — high spirits. Mrs. Scillicough snorted at the sinister hintings of the Wise Woman, and tossed her head scornfully.

"Young Lil just ain't the type to bear children easy, being so small and everything. No mystery in that. But she's not had to see the doctor for weeks now, has she?"

"That we know of," somebody pointed out. There came a general muttering, and a thoughtful pause. "Course," somebody else added, as inspiration struck, "she'd keep quiet about seeing him, wouldn't she, if there was anything not rightful to be shown — like bruises from young Len bashing the kiddie when he's taken with the drink, say."

At which point, speculation ran riot around Mr. Stillman's post office, and an excellent time was had by all — or rather, as excellent as it could be when two of

Plummergen's most noted speculators were absent. But everyone knew that, as it wasn't a day for the Brettenden bus, Miss Nuttel and Mrs. Blaine would doubtless soon be with them . . .

The Nuts, as they are commonly known in the village, can shop and gossip with the best. Their plate glass–windowed home, Lilikot, is almost directly opposite the bus stop and neighbouring post office: they therefore miss none of any Plummergen comings or goings, and are always busy with finding new twists for old, or not-so-old, tales. Erica Nuttel tends the garden, Norah Blaine (Bunny to her friend) the house; in any spare time, the ladies listen, inevitably, to the news from wireless or television.

And it was just after eleven o'clock when a breathless Bunny, string bag in hand, appeared in the post office doorway with Miss Nuttel close behind. From their air of muted excitement, it was clear to seasoned observers that they had news to impart, but, in true Nutty fashion, they approached their notificatory task in a roundabout way.

"Two boxes of caraway biscuits and a tin of soya chunks, please, Mr. Stillman." Mrs. Blaine pretended to consult her shopping list while Miss Nuttel paused by the revolving book stand, browsed briefly, then came to her senses with a start as she noticed the animated little group beginning to congregate about them.

"Looks as if we've jumped the queue, Bunny," she remarked, as Mrs. Blaine began hunting through her purse for the correct change. "Sorry," to the shoppers at large.

As they murmured that it didn't matter, Mrs. Blaine could hold herself in no longer. "Well, it's hardly surprising, is it, Eric, with my being so upset by what we've just heard — too dreadful, it really is. Those poor parents . . ."

Ears pricked; interest quickened. "The Hosiggs," came from one or two quarters. "In here just now, weren't she?" As the Nuts must know, from the customary net-curtain watch they maintained across the road. "Buying its dinner, so she were — and now summat's happened to the babby!"

Mrs. Blaine turned to Miss Nuttel, her blackcurrant eyes gleaming. "Oh, Eric, you don't think . . . surely not! To have laid their plans so carefully, and so far in advance — too positively wicked, that's the only word!"

"Could never have thought of it by themselves, though," opined Miss Nuttel. "Could they? Hardly seem that bright — or that devious," she added, driving the inference partway home while leaving Mrs. Blaine to finish the job.

And Bunny duly obliged. "Oh, Eric!" she breathed, plump hands clasped in anguish. "You don't — you *can't* mean . . . even for That Woman it would be going too far!"

The draught from flapping ears could have driven a fair-sized yacht. Everyone clustered close about Miss Nuttel as she left the book stand and went to help poor Bunny, so very distressed, carry the shopping. What were the Nuts hinting that Miss Seeton had been up to now?

"That it should come to this," moaned Mrs. Blaine, turning as pale as she could. "Our dear little village the home of a cruel, criminal mastermind — too shaming to think of!" And she allowed her voice to quaver on the final words, ending with a sigh and a sorrowful shake of the head.

Miss Nuttel frowned. "No good brooding, Bunny — actions speak louder than words. Take a good look at that baby next time we see it, and then —"

"But that's just it!" burst from Mrs.

Blaine in a voice of thrilling dismay. "Too mysterious, haven't I said so all along — nobody ever sees the Hosigg baby! She keeps it *very* well wrapped up, even though it's the middle of summer" — a chorus of *that's what we were saying not a moment since* came from her eager audience — "and now we know, only too well, why she does! How could anyone ever be sure whether it's really the Hosigg baby — Dulcie Rose, too ridiculous — or —" her voice sank to a whisper just loud enough for everyone to hear — *"Lady Marguerite MacSporran!"*

A bewildered silence greeted this bombshell, followed by an equally bewildered babble, as the listeners gazed from one Nut to another and clamoured for enlightenment. It was obvious, of course, now it had been brought to their notice, that Lily Hosigg's reluctance to let anyone take a good look at her baby could be for no good purpose — but why should it have anything to do with a Scottish heiress? Or, a vociferous minority appended, with Miss Seeton? Hardly what you'd call the motherly type, was she . . .

"On the wireless just now," said Miss Nuttel, as soon as she felt she could make herself heard above the hubbub. "No clues at all — nanny unconscious in intensive care . . ."

As she paused for effect, drawing breath to make the final announcement, Mrs. Blaine was unable to resist the temptation. *"Kidnapped,"* she informed Miss Nuttel's audience, with a sideways look to see how her friend responded, and a smirk she struggled to suppress. Miss Nuttel scowled, but did not try to compete as Bunny continued:

"Just think — those poor parents, waiting so many years for a baby — the title and everything bound to disappear if they didn't have one — all the fuss in the newspapers when she was born, and now this! Too, too dreadful!"

Fifty miles away, in London, a telephone rang in an office on the umpteenth floor of New Scotland Yard. There were two men in the office. Both were tall, though one was far taller (and far larger) than the other, who was older, with greying hair and an air of distinct command which was borne out when he glanced across from his paperwork to the younger man at his desk, and said,

"Answer that, would you, Bob? If I don't finish this report before I go up to see Sir

Hubert, he'll be tearing the carpet into little pieces even as I'm standing on it."

Detective Sergeant Ranger grinned. Sir Hubert Everleigh — Sir Heavily — didn't often pull rank, or lose his temper, but on those few occasions when he did, his subordinates (even those as high in general esteem as the Oracle) knew they'd better toe the line, and pretty fast, too. If the paperwork was important to a case, "I just haven't had time to write it down yet, sir, but I assure you I know exactly what's going on" would cut no ice at all with the Assistant Commissioner (Crime). And if there was one thing the Oracle hated, it was paperwork . . .

So Detective Sergeant Ranger grinned as he reached for the telephone and prepared to pull his superior's irons out of *his* superior's fire. An irresistible force and an immovable object, he supposed the pair of 'em must be. And on balance, he'd back the Oracle to win — he was still used to thinking on his feet, whereas the deskbound commissioner —

"Chief Superintendent Delphick's office," he said into the receiver, preparing to commit perjury by assuring Sir Heavily that he'd no idea where the Oracle might be. He was so certain it was Sir Hubert on the other end of the line that he was left gasping when a crisp female voice in his ear demanded,

"Where's the Oracle, Bob? That *is* Bob, isn't it?"

"Mel! Yes, it is. Hello." Bob looked across at Delphick, wondering whether the chief superintendent was willing to forgo the pleasures of paperwork for the chance to chat with Amelita Forby, demon reporter of the *Daily Negative*. Then his grin grew even broader. Silly question. To avoid having to read reports and report on *them,* Delphick would be willing to talk to a paranoid Trappist monk with an inferiority complex, and persecution mania to boot. Bob didn't even bother asking. "Yes," he said, "he's here," and waved the receiver in his superior's direction. "Mel Forby, sir, asking for you. How are things, Mel?" he added, and Delphick permitted a smile of relief to flicker briefly in his eyes before pushing his pile of papers to one side and picking up his telephone.

"Things," retorted Mel Forby, "could hardly be worse, as you and your boss know only too well, Bob Ranger. Have you any idea how *humiliated* I feel right now? *And* furious — and it's entirely the fault of you and your precious Oracle! Oh yes" —

above their attempted protests at the unjust and unexpected accusation — "with just a *little* help from the head of the Grub Street rat pack, of course!"

As her bitter tones rang in their puzzled ears, Delphick and Bob exchanged looks, shrugged, and mimed bewilderment. Bob put his hand over the mouthpiece, hissed, "You're the chief superintendent, sir, not me. Over to you!" and leaned back, preparing to savour every syllable of the coming row. Mel certainly hadn't sounded like somebody calling just to pass the time of day . . .

Chapter

3

With the obligations of rank weighing heavily — he couldn't help smiling at the word — upon him, Delphick sighed, rolled his eyes, and addressed himself cautiously to the telephone. He was, after all, a detective; he could understand at least part of Mel's complaint.

"And what exactly has Thrudd done to upset you, might I ask?" It was a fair bet that she wouldn't have been so insulting about anyone other than her close personal friend and professional rival, Thrudd Banner, freelance ace, star of World Wide Press. "If he's pipped you to a good story, Miss Forby, well, that's life, I'm afraid. You can hardly call it theft — and anyway, this office only handles serious crimes —"

"Like kidnapping?" snapped Mel. Delphick choked over his final words. He looked across at Bob, who was grinning. He spoke earnestly into the telephone receiver.

"Mel, I'm sorry, but the MacSporran business isn't one of our cases, and even if it were we couldn't —"

"*Why* isn't it?" demanded Mel. "Banner tells me" — there was a wealth of scornful envy in her voice — "that the nanny was bashed over the head and left for dead in the park. You don't call grievous bodily harm a serious crime?"

"Of course I do. Everybody does — which should hardly need saying, Miss Forby, as you well know. But, strange as it may appear, I'm not the only chief super-intendent at the Yard" — she muttered something he thought it wiser not to hear — "and it just so happens that someone else is handling this case. The first I heard about it must have been around the same time you did, so I hardly think —"

"Yes, from Banner, of all people! Mel Forby, the *Daily Negative*'s white hope, and that louse strolls into the flat with one of those crummy World Wide rags under his arm, and tells me to take a look at the front page! Me, with what I thought was a hot line to high places . . ."

"Be fair, Mel. Just because we've known one another for some time doesn't mean Bob and I feel obliged to leak every item of news to you first — even if we know about it, which in this instance, I repeat, we did not. Policemen have a professional code as well as pressmen, Miss Forby."

"And presswomen," she retorted, though not as sharply as he might have expected. She sighed. "Sorry, Oracle, and Bob too, if he's still hanging in there. Guess I lost my temper. It isn't really fair for me to pick on the pair of you because Banner beat me to it. To be honest, it's this damned broken ankle of mine I should be blaming, not that it's broken any longer, of course, but it still isn't what it was — which is entirely Banner's fault, and you'd think he'd realise he owes me" — Mel didn't know whether to curse or giggle at the memory of what she and Thrudd had been doing when she tumbled out of their king-sized bed — "but just catch him admitting it. And the doctor keeps telling me to rest when I can. So who was obeying doctor's orders like a good little girl when the first hint of the MacSporran story was breaking? Amelita Forby, that's who!"

"I'm very sorry, Mel," said Delphick, after a pause. It seemed a most inadequate response, but for once he was at a loss. He scowled at Bob, who was stifling a chuckle.

"I heard that snigger, Bob Ranger," came Mel's voice in the sergeant's ear.

41

"You ought to feel sorry for me, being scooped like that — after all, the three of us go back quite a long way. I'd always kind of regarded you two as people who'd be glad to keep me up-to-date with what was going on." Her tone perceptibly altered. "To keep me, as you might say, in the picture . . ."

There was a long, thoughtful silence. Mel said, "Pardon me, Oracle, but aren't you forgetting something when you say you've got no possible connection with the MacSporran case? Or maybe I should say — some*one?*"

The silence this time was even more thoughtful. Bob was sure he could hear the Oracle's brain whirling — and he knew he could hear Mel's gleeful giggle at the other end of the line. Delphick drew a deep breath.

"If you're planning to involve Miss Seeton in all this, Miss Forby, I feel I ought to warn you —"

"Miss Seeton? Why, Oracle, the idea never even entered my head! Miss S. must be about the last person in the world to muddle herself up in anything so sordid as kidnapping. No, it was the Finchingfield business I was referring to — surely you realised that?"

Delphick uttered a curse — two curses — one for himself, for having forgotten the Finchingfield case, and another for Mel, who had trapped him so neatly. He'd go down fighting, of course, but he saw no ultimate escape from the inevitable — Amelita Forby was noted in Fleet Street for much more than just her pretty face.

"Finchingfield?" he said, trying to sound casual about it. "Of course, *Bernard* Finchingfield." As if there could be two people he'd met with such a memorable surname. "Well yes, Mel, but that was a long time ago. I haven't had any dealings with bigamy for ages — you can't wonder that I'd forgotten about it."

"There aren't too many families called MacSporran," Mel said in a dry tone, and waited. The Oracle was right; it had been years back — she'd had to dig it out of the *Negative*'s morgue after numerous cross-references. She couldn't really blame him for forgetting, but she wasn't going to let him off the hook by telling him so. After all, Bernard had been the most celebrated lady-killer of his day. Delphick, with the girl's parents, had arrived in the nick of time to stop him tying the knot with that madcap whisky heiress . . .

"Artemis MacSporran," said Mel, when

it became clear the Oracle wasn't going to say anything himself. Sergeant Ranger, who knew his chief to be surprisingly modest about past achievements — and one of the least reminiscing men on the force — sat up at her words, and requested full details.

"Later, Bob." Mel and Delphick spoke together. Delphick then went on:

"A very distant cousin, Miss Forby. No immediate reason for me to connect the two cases. And I hardly think they'd thank you for dredging all that up again now, when they've a far more serious matter on their minds —"

"And no real clues, as yet," Mel broke in. "Say, Oracle, you've given me an idea." Delphick groaned. He'd seen it coming. Bob grinned: so had he. "Talking of not having any clues . . . I never even thought of it until you mentioned her first, but — well, I can't help wondering, somehow, whether anyone's thought of asking Miss S. what she thinks about all this. I know kidnapping's a pretty sordid crime, and she's bound to be kind of shocked and disapproving about everything, but you know what she's like, she'd probably consider it was worth the upset, if she was able to help. Just make an appeal to her sense of duty, and . . ."

Delphick said nothing. There was nothing to say. "We, I mean you," Mel continued, as if inspired, "could just try *asking* her, couldn't we? It might not upset her too much — and besides, she always bounces back, does our Miss S. And think how much she knows about kids, with having taught 'em art for so long . . ."

"Schoolchildren," pointed out Delphick, drawn into the argument against his better judgement, "are hardly the same as infants in arms. I doubt if Miss Seeton knows one end of a baby from — Well," as Mel and Bob exploded with mirth, "perhaps not quite that, but you know perfectly well what I mean. And, even if she did, it's not for me to propose that the investigating officer avails himself of her services. For some reason, MissEss is regarded with a degree of, well, of caution by many of my colleagues, and I can hardly force them to . . . Mel, stop laughing. And if you don't wipe that grin off your face, Sergeant Ranger, you'll be back on the beat by lunchtime. Traffic control around Marble Arch would be the most apt placement, I fancy . . ."

"So the boys in blue are scared of Miss S.," remarked Mel brightly. "I'd never have guessed it. And you're not going to jeopardise your working relationship with the rest of the Yard by insisting. But you could always *suggest* it . . ."

"I could indeed, though I have a fair suspicion of what the response might be." Despite himself, Delphick chuckled. "However, Miss Forby, you should not jump to conclusions and assume the Oracle is losing his touch: for your information, I was thinking along the same lines as you not ten minutes before you called. Devoting, I may add, rather too much time to the matter for someone who has a mound of paperwork to process, and an assistant commissioner demanding results — when it isn't, I repeat, my case . . ."

Mel dismissed Sir Hubert with an airy phrase, and then added, "So does that mean you'll be going down to Plummergen to see her? Will there be another Battling Brolly success in the news before long?"

"Unfortunately, I think not yet. You know as well as I do the, er, unique working methods employed by Miss Seeton; and I'm sure you remember that, in order for her instinct to take over and switch her to automatic pilot, or whatever you care to call it, she requires at the very least a witness statement before she can produce any drawing that may be of help in a police enquiry. But, as you yourself pointed out, the nanny is still unconscious. The hospital expects she'll remain unconscious for some time . . ."

"So as soon as she comes round," said Mel, "you'll be on your way to Plummergen, I take it — but not before. I see."

"You see more than is good for you at times," Delphick told her, trying to sound stern but not succeeding. He had a decidedly soft spot for Amelita Forby, whose determination to be a Fleet Street star, coupled with her ruthless honesty and her insistence on playing fair — with everyone except, of course, Thrudd Banner — had won his admiration. She'd have earned her success, when (not if) it came. She never seemed to stop working or it . . .

"You're scheming, Mel — I recognise the signs. What's more, you sound rather too cheerful for my liking. I hate to cast a damper on your enthusiasm, of course, but you know the sort of thing that can happen when Miss Seeton becomes embroiled — or is embroiled by an outside party — in a case, don't you? Be warned by a wiser man —"

"Like your pals at the Yard? They sound

a pretty feeble bunch," sniffed Mel. "Tough-guy cops running like rabbits from one sweet, harmless little old lady . . ."

Bob Ranger, who'd been listening to every word, couldn't help spluttering at that. Delphick cleared his throat, and rolled his eyes in despair. It was a free country. If one of Miss Seeton's friends took it into her head to make a day trip to Kent, there was nothing he could do to prevent her. And he'd known Mel long enough to be certain that she'd had it in mind right from the start — that there was no way he could deter her from whatever she'd intended to do, because once Amelita Forby's course was set, set it duly stayed.

He just hoped it wasn't likely to lead her, and Miss Seeton, over the edge of a preci-pice.

Mel Forby considered herself, after all these years, an old Plummergen hand. By now, she knew the bus timetable almost as well as the locals. Having caught her train from Charing Cross and arrived safely at Brettenden, she knew there was no need to risk the aged and asthmatic car driven by equally aged Mr. Baxter, plying for hire outside Brettenden station. She'd worked

48

it out neatly: the bus was due in ten minutes, and it was almost always, she knew, reliable.

As it proved today. Without too much recourse to the elegant walking stick she'd bought herself — better safe than sorry — Mel disembarked from the bus at the stop outside Crabbe's Garage, paused to pull a face in the direction of Lilikot's windows in case either of the Nuts happened to be watching, then limped into the post office. Here, she selected a not-too-heavy box of chocolates, asked Mr. Stillman if he'd be kind enough to help by popping it in a carrier bag, and made her way carefully southwards down The Street in the direction of Sweetbriars.

"Mel! I say, Mel — hello!" The greeting came just as she was passing the George and Dragon, preparing to cross at an angle to Miss Seeton's front gate. There was a tootle on a car horn, and she recognised Nigel Colveden's little MG.

"Need a lift anywhere?" he enquired, gesturing towards the walking stick. Mel thanked him, but said she didn't. Nigel nodded. "Are you staying — or merely passing through? And where," he added, "is Thrudd?"

Mel's eyes narrowed. "Don't breathe

that name near me, Nigel, if you want us to stay friends. Right now, Banner and I aren't exactly speaking to each other — or rather," as Nigel looked decidedly startled by this information, "it's me who's not speaking to him, the louse."

Nigel had known the Forby/Banner partnership for some years. He grinned. "Beaten you to a story, has he? Oh!" His gaze flickered from her remarkably fine eyes, which even in moments like this couldn't help dancing at the thought of Thrudd, to the cottage across the road. "You've come to ask Miss Seeton for her advice about something," deduced Nigel, feeling pleased with himself. "I won't ask what — I'm all for a quiet life, you know. We busy farmers . . ."

And, after a few more pleasantries, he was gone.

Mel waved after the little red car as it turned right into Marsh Road and chuntered off towards Rytham Hall, emitting discreet puffs of dark blue smoke as it went; then once more she prepared to cross the road to Sweetbriars.

And once more she was accosted by a voice she knew.

"Why, good gracious, surely — Mel dear, that *is* you, is it not?" The well-known accents came from behind her, and Mel spun round in some surprise. Talk about telepathy, or second sight or whatever — there she was, the very woman Amelita Forby had come to Plummergen to see.

She was making her way down the steps of the George and Dragon and, like Mel, carried a parcel, though hers was wrapped in brown paper, and instead of a walking stick she had, of course, an umbrella. As she drew nearer, Mel observed that Miss Seeton's parcel did not remind her of her own conventional box of chocolates: it was irregular in shape, for one thing. A shape Mel thought she recognised — and it gurgled — and Miss Seeton had just come out of the pub . . .

Chapter

4

Mel was quick to brush off Miss Seeton's anxious enquiries over her walking stick, saying that it was more by way of insurance than a necessity. Besides, she felt it lent her a stylish air which would do her budding reputation as a Fleet Street original no harm at all.

She made no comment on the purchase her old friend had obviously just made. Very little surprised a world-weary hack like Amelita Forby, but the idea that Miss S., of all people, had turned into a secret tippler was one of the very few things she was simply not prepared to believe.

"I was just about to make myself a cup of tea," remarked Miss Seeton, the welcoming courtesies having been concluded. "In the garden, you know — such a delightful afternoon — and you'll join me, won't you, my dear?"

For one wild moment, Mel was unable to dismiss a vision of herself and Miss

Seeton knocking back highballs together on the patio, *tea* being merely a euphemism covering anything from sherry to illicit hooch. Then common sense prevailed, and she accepted with thanks; much better for Miss Seeton's vibes, or however she did the trick, to have her sitting relaxed in her own back garden. "Though I regret," continued Miss Seeton, leading the way, "such a pity, but I cannot extend my invitation to the whole afternoon, as I have oiled it already, and pumped up the tyres, and she is expecting me — my bicycle, that is, although not at any particular time, because she understands that one can never be sure of the state of the traffic. And I have bought myself," said Miss Seeton with pride, "not only a new bell, but a basket, too." She brandished her brown paper parcel, which gurgled again. "So much safer than clipping it in a rack, I thought, which was all I had left once my old basket collapsed, and really it was too far gone, Stan assured me, for repairs. He is so very clever at mending things — just as she is, of course — although whether one should call them 'things' when they are still attached to the birds — their wings, I mean, and their legs — yet one

53

hesitates to anthropomorphise . . ."

As she chatted, she led the way up the front path and fumbled in her bag for her key; she ushered Mel into the hall, smiling as she set her brown paper–wrapped bottle on the table just inside the door. "So much better, she tells me, than brandy or whisky. For shock — some property of the juniper berries, I understand, which they eat in the wild. The birds, that is. When they are unwell." She led the way through to the kitchen, and switched on the waiting kettle.

"Mrs. Ongar knows a great deal about them," Miss Seeton continued, hunting out milk, sugar, and crockery, while Mel, with the privilege of friendship, retrieved a cake tin from its cupboard and set out the contents on a plate. "And she speaks, you know." Into Mel's mind flashed, unbidden, the image of Harpo Marx. "To Women's Institutes, for instance." Miss Seeton was warming the teapot. "And similar groups of interested people — as I am, as well. Interested, that is. In preserving our birdlife. I have paid several visits to Wounded Wings since we first met, although happily not on my own behalf. Dear Stan takes excellent care of mine — they have been laying so well recently, you know, that if you cared to take half-a-dozen home with you, I would be happy to let you have some. For how long will you be staying in Plummergen? They should be as fresh as possible, you see."

"Heading back to Town later today, more's the pity," Mel told her. "New-laid eggs are a kind thought, Miss S., but a bit awkward to carry, on a train — especially now. I'd hate to have them scrambled before I even reached home."

Miss Seeton nodded sympathetically. "And how *is* dear Mr. Banner?" she enquired, ignoring Mel's efforts to pick up the tea tray. "What a long time it seems since our last meeting, although . . ."

"Can't be too long for me, right now," Mel informed her briskly. "That louse has scooped himself a really big story — so where does that leave me? Asking for your help, that's where!" The teapot wobbled in Miss Seeton's pouring hand. Her eyes blinked a question in Mel's direction. "You're the tops when it comes to those drawings you do, Miss S. Could you manage to work the trick for Amelita Forby — if I asked you nicely? I'd love to take that Banner down a peg or two, and if I could beat him on his own story . . ."

"But Mel, my dear, I know nothing

whatever about — about stories, or scoops, or the life of a newspaper reporter," came Miss Seeton's anticipated protest. "I am always glad to be of assistance to a friend, of course, but living such a quiet life as I do . . ."

Mel hid a smile as she allowed the rest of Miss Seeton's little apology to float past unheeded. Over the years, the Battling Brolly must have encountered more newspaper reporters than she, Amelita Forby, could number, but Miss Seeton herself genuinely seemed not to recall such encounters. Essentially a private person, she regarded herself and her affairs as of no consequence to any other than her immediate circle; and whenever, innocently assisting Scotland Yard, she resolved yet another mystery, she noticed neither that she had done so, nor the immense public interest such resolutions invariably awoke.

Mel suddenly realised Miss Seeton had stopped speaking, and roused herself from this reverie. "Well, okay, Miss S., I know about all that, but I'm not asking you to take notes in shorthand or yell 'Hold the front page' — what I want's one of the good old Seeton Specials. Easy as falling off a log, for you." Miss Seeton looked doubtful. Her services as an art consultant were, after all, retained by the police — her first consideration was surely to Scotland Yard; might they not be annoyed with her if she produced one of her little IdentiKit drawings — which was plainly the burden of dear Mel's request — for one who could not, in all honesty, be regarded as an official? Might it be thought a breach of confidence — a lapse (and Miss Seeton blushed) in common courtesy? One had one's professional obligations . . .

"What was that, honey?" Miss Seeton had, blushing once more, murmured a name. The ears of a good reporter are ever acute. Mel said: "You're worried about Mr. Delphick? Don't be. Why, I told him only this morning I was coming to talk to you, and he practically wished me good luck. He sends you his best wishes, by the way." It was near enough true as made no difference, and it would serve to stop Miss S.'s conscience going into overdrive.

By a judicious mix of coaxing, cunning, and a résumé of the facts of the kidnap, Mel persuaded Miss Seeton to study the photographs she had brought with her: the MacSporrans' Town residence, Lady Marguerite at her christening (culled from the Society Page files, a loss Mel hoped to be able to make good before the editor found out), and — the reporter's longest shot — a panoramic view of the London park in which the attack upon the stolen heiress's nanny had taken place. Mel displayed this selection with some pride, and waited for Miss Seeton's reaction.

And waited. Miss Seeton, shocked and dismayed by the sad story, was not responding as Mel had hoped. No nervous dance of the fingers, no sign that one of the famous Seeton sketches was on its way; she seemed bewildered by the whole affair, unable, for once, to work her normal magic. "Guess the Oracle was right, after all," muttered Mel; then, at the expression on Miss Seeton's face, she was stricken with remorse.

"Don't take it to heart, Miss S.; you can't pull a rabbit out of the hat every time." Perhaps she was just too upset, on this particular occasion, for her inspired artistic skill to begin flowing. Not that Miss Seeton could really be considered the maternal type, but anyone was bound to be distressed by the abduction of a helpless infant. She looked so worried and tense — perhaps a complete change of scene, to take her mind off things for a while . . .

"You're bothered about being late for all

your feathered friends, aren't you, Miss S.?" Amelita Forby, Sherlock of Fleet Street. "Well, how about if I come along too? Always provided you don't mind, of course. Maybe I could write a piece for the *Negative* about this Mrs. Ongar. Animals always make good copy," said Mel, with a knowledgeable air; and she was surprised to observe that even this suggestion did not meet with Miss Seeton's approval, for she looked (if anything) rather more anxious than she had before, and murmured again, so that Mel strained to catch the words.

"Your bicycle? Have a heart, Miss S.! Do I really look like the 'Daisy, Daisy' type, even at the best of times?"

At the vision of Mel on a tandem, Miss Seeton couldn't help smiling. "I regret," she said, "that mine is not 'a bicycle made for two' — nor, unfortunately, does it have a step, even if I felt confident" — now she frowned — "of my ability to ride so far with a passenger, though they have made truly remarkable progress, over the years. My knees, I mean, with the yoga — not, of course, that I am suggesting for one minute that your weight — that is, I hope you do not think my remarks impertinent, but —"

"Never even crossed my mind," Mel assured her, grinning. "But I'll tell you what *did*. Amelita Forby, Fleet Street Genius! How about I ring for a taxi, and charge it to the good old *Negative*? Professional expenses," she added, when Miss Seeton looked like protesting. "I'll be working on my story, don't forget. And in a taxi, there'd be plenty of room for us both . . ." Miss Seeton still looked doubtful. "Room for us both," repeated Mel firmly. "Which is more than I could say for Nigel Colveden's car," and she giggled, remembering her last sight of the little MG as it chugged up Marsh Road towards Rytham Hall.

"Dear Nigel." Miss Seeton was smiling again. "He was teasing his poor parents the other day, about painting the windows of the hall with gold leaf — my umbrella, you know, is so very much more practical than wood, as he pointed out. But Sir George, I fear, deplored the expense — just as, dear Mel, I feel sure your editor may. About the taxi . . ."

It took Mel longer than she might have expected to calm Miss Seeton's doubts, but in the end she succeeded, and took it upon herself to look up the number of Crabbe's Garage in Miss Seeton's telephone directory, ignoring the protests of her anxious hostess and dialling to ask whether Jack Crabbe, or one of his family, could drive them both to the Wounded Wings Bird Sanctuary, just outside Rye. Jack said he'd be delighted to oblige; Mel asked him to pick them up in about ten minutes, and she sent Miss Seeton off to put on her hat and collect her umbrella.

And she silently resolved to return with the taxi, once the visit was over, to Plummergen; she would take a room in the George and Dragon, if necessary, but Amelita Forby did not intend to lose touch with Miss Seeton just yet.

There was still that drawing to wait for . . .

Barbara Ongar welcomed Miss Seeton and her unexpected companion with obvious pleasure, and accepted the bottle of gin gratefully. "The best pick-me-up I know," she told Mel, "though your paper will probably get letters arguing about it — but I don't care. As far as I'm concerned, it works."

Since there were no other visitors, Mel and Miss Seeton enjoyed Babs Ongar's undivided attention on their tour of Wounded Wings. Mel, who had never been to a bird sanctuary before, scribbled furiously in her notebook, wishing she had brought a camera.

"Striking looks, haven't they?" Barbara surveyed a convalescent gannet with pride. The bird was white, apart from its black wing tips and, set in a yellow head, greyish-blue eyes, which surveyed its audience with great interest. "Oil, poor thing," Babs explained. "Some damned ship passing by — but I shouldn't say too much, I suppose, with my husband in the Merchant Navy. If I thought he'd ever be this careless I'd have his guts for garters. The state this poor chap was in when he was found — but he's well on the mend now, thank goodness."

"How on earth do you treat something that size?" asked Mel, as the gannet opened a powerful bill and yawned. Daft though the idea was, she couldn't help feeling that, if it had teeth, that bird would have bitten her.

"With extreme caution and woolly pullovers," Mrs. Ongar replied, then laughed at the look on Mel's face. "Seriously. They're the most comfortable and least distressing method of soaking off surplus oil. We clean the head and wings with detergent, then wrap the birds in knitted woollen tubes with wing holes — ribbed knitting, so they can move and breathe — and pop them in a nice quiet basket, somewhere warm. It all helps to relax them; shock and stress can be bigger killers for a sick animal than anything else, you know. And they're beautiful creatures — such strength. You should see them after fish. When something with a six-foot wingspan folds itself up like an arrow and dives from one hundred feet, you certainly know about it."

"I bet you do." Mel viewed the gannet with increased respect. Miss Seeton sighed.

"I fear I must apologise yet again for my repeated lack of success with the pullovers, Mrs. Ongar. Knitting appears to be another of the skills for which I have no aptitude — yet I know how useful it would be, given the sad numbers of oiled seabirds you have in your care . . ."

"Not just seabirds, unfortunately. Just take a look at this swan, will you?" Barbara led the way to another cage, which held a bedraggled bird with weary black eyes. "It was touch and go with him for a while, though he's well on the mend now — I don't think I need to touch wood. It's seabirds who try to fool you by picking up nicely and then keeling over just when you think they're ready to leave. But swans don't seem to suffer from wet-feather the way seabirds do — oh, they can catch pneumonia from the chilling just as easily, but there's something in their makeup which means they don't lose their buoyancy and drown . . ."

They moved from cage to cage, surrounded by the sounds of recuperating birdlife: whistles, coos, yarps, piercing shrieks, trills. Babs checked drinking water, scratched the tamest heads, spoke of the idiosyncrasies of her charges. Here was a widgeon who refused to eat anything but cheddar cheese grated into bread-and-milk; this song thrush was even more nervous than the rest of its kind; the tawny owl over in that corner had lost its way down someone's chimney, laid an egg and broken a wing while trying to find her way out.

"Two years ago," Mrs. Ongar said, laughing. "Try telling her she's better, though — she won't listen. She refuses to leave: she stays in her corner during the day, and if I omit to feed her every night the way I did when she was ill, she bombs me with her wings. And it's difficult to ignore something which insists on roosting in your back garden."

"What happened to the egg?" enquired Mel, remembering her professional curiosity. But Babs, still chuckling over the tawny owl's flattering attachment, misheard.

"Oh, scrambled is much better than hard-boiled. Fledglings don't have robust digestions, you know. But when they get bigger, some species . . ." She opened a biscuit tin as she spoke, and held it out. Mel peered inside.

"Brown porridge," she said, bending for a closer look. "Ugh! *Wriggling* brown porridge — what on earth is it?"

Babs and Miss Seeton smiled. "Mealworms layered in bran," Mrs. Ongar said, closing the lid with a shake. "Tasty and tempting to the growing bird — and to some adults, too. Now, what do you make of this chap here?"

"A blackbird," said Mel at once, eager to redeem herself after the show of weakness. Babs looked at Miss Seeton, and waited. Miss Seeton studied the dark plumage with its hint of blue, the curved beak — the curved red beak . . .

"Surely — a chough?" she ventured.

"It doesn't looked particularly chuffed to me," said Mel, daughter of Liverpool. "Downright miserable, in fact."

Barbara chuckled. "Chough, not chuff, Miss Forby. They may sound the same, but they're entirely different words. The chough is our only black bird with red beak and wings — unmistakable. There's an old Cornish superstition that King Arthur will return as a chough, and it's bad luck to harm one. I'm taking particular care of Lancelot here — plenty of wood lice and earwigs, lots of sunshine — but, talking of blackbirds . . ."

Once she could compare them, Mel admitted the difference was obvious. The blackbird's bill was orange-yellow, not red, its legs were dark brown, and it was smaller than the chough, as well as far less striking in appearance.

"But a lovely bird, once he's in full health again," Mrs. Ongar said, regarding the blackbird with sympathy. "They're nothing like as nervous, you know, as other members of the thrush family, blackbirds — but there's a funny thing about this one, talking of nervous. The young couple who brought him in the other day were far from happy, believe me. They were arguing right the way up the path, and I think that if the husband, or whatever he was, had won the argument they'd never have come in at all. It was obvious, from the way she kept looking at him, something wasn't quite right." A shake of the head, and a sigh. "I couldn't help wondering whether he'd been the one who hurt the bird in the first place. It might have been a cat — but it could as easily have been a man who did it. Those tail feathers will take a month to grow back, and until they do he'll be a sitting target for any cat, with no proper sense of balance. The wife might well have threatened to report him to the authorities if he didn't let her bring the poor creature here to me . . ."

And that poor creature the blackbird blinked at them all from its cage with a sad, glittering eye.

Chapter

5

Jack Crabbe, explaining that he had a dead-
line to meet, did not accompany Mel and
Miss Seeton on their tour of Wounded
Wings, though he expressed an intention to
visit at another time. He stayed outside in
the taxi with his pencil, paper, and reference
books — a dictionary and a well-worn copy
of Roget's Thesaurus — compiling another
of the cryptic crosswords for which his
name was a byword in cruciverbalist circles.
By the time his passengers reappeared, he
had not only completed his current grid,
but was working on the next; he was
delighted to have made such progress and,
though happy to accept the fare when Mel
offered it, firmly refused any tip. "You've
brought me good luck," he told her, with a
wink. "Good luck to my blackbird, eh?"

"I thought it was the chough you were so
interested in," said Mel. On the journey
back to Plummergen Jack had questioned
his friends about what they'd seen, offering

to fit a chough into his next puzzle in their honour. *Bird's cough sounds rough despite inhalation of hydrogen* had been his off-the-cuff attempt at a clue, which had deeply impressed Miss Seeton; Mel had asked if she might write one of her "pieces" on him one day.

"Th'old chough?" he said now. "Well, so I was, but it's a blackbird for luck, Miss Forby — leastways, so they used to sing in Jacobite times. Reckon it must have stuck in my mind, being as it's one of my clues today. *Patriarchal patriot, 45, follows it to the east,* see?"

Mel, once he'd explained it, saw, and Miss Seeton was as impressed as before. Their praise made Jack mutter with embarrassment, and he drove off with the tips of his ears turning red. Mel waved after him, then turned eagerly to Miss Seeton. "Well, Miss S.? How about it? Suppose we go on in and have another cup of tea, and sit in that garden of yours — and wait for inspiration . . ."

Miss Seeton, having settled Mel in the reporter's favourite garden chair, sat watching the flicker of the apple tree's shade dance across the sketching pad she had rested on the table. Peeping over the edge of the pad, she could see the photo-

69

graphs Mel had laid out neatly in a row, sure they would be of help; but nothing, Miss Seeton sighed to herself, seemed to prompt her to draw even the quickest of doodles. She put down her pencil, sighed again, caught Mel's eye, and glanced away guiltily.

"You thirsty, Miss S.?" Mel thought her friend's glance had fallen on her empty cup. "The pot's almost dry — I'll make us both another, if you like. No, I can manage, honest — and if I don't know where everything is, by now . . ."

As she loaded the tray and prepared to leave Miss Seeton alone with her sketch pad, Mel hid a smile. Good thinking, Forby — could be all Miss S. needs to get her going is a spot of privacy. That weird drawing ability of hers always makes her uncomfortable, goodness knows why. The Oracle generally has to coax her, and what's good enough for Delphick is good enough for me . . . And she resolved to spend twice as long making a fresh pot of tea as anyone could rightly require.

She risked one quick look back as she headed for the kitchen door, but Miss Seeton was sitting just as she had left her, motionless, staring, thoughtful . . .

And when Mel could keep herself away

no longer, and came out into the garden with Earl Grey she feared would stew if it wasn't drunk soon, Miss Seeton was still sitting staring at her sketch pad, unmoving. Mel's heart sank. The Oracle *had* been right — they'd have to wait for the nanny to regain consciousness. If only she'd been able to find a picture of the girl, instead of trusting to one of the park . . .

Then she arrived at the table. The chink of china woke Miss Seeton from her apparent trance — and Mel gave a little cry of delight. Crumpled sheets of white paper were a clear indication that Miss Seeton had indeed drawn something — the sort of quickfire, instinctive, clue-bearing something for which the police valued her services, and of which she was so unaccountably ashamed, assuring everybody they were the merest scribbles, impressions, worth nothing to anyone save herself.

But she was wrong. "Attagirl, Miss S.!" Mel dumped the tray on the table without ceremony, and seized the crumpled sheets before Miss Seeton could voice a protest. "Great!" enthused Mel, spreading out her treasure trove and ignoring Miss Seeton's muted offer to pour the tea. Amelita Forby was going to gloat: Miss S. had come up trumps once more . . .

Except that, as usual — how many times had she heard the Oracle moan about it? — the drawings didn't make sense. Oh, they were bound to, once the case was solved and the entire picture was before her — whenever it was, they always did. But if you wanted to be one jump ahead of Miss S. and her inspiration, you had to interpret what her subconscious tried to tell you, which you were always just that little bit slow in working out . . .

The first picture was almost a still life. On a lump of rock, granite-grey, perched a stately bird with bright eyes: a bird with gleaming black feathers and its head held high. Beneath one claw, draped down and coiled about the base of the rock, was a necklace, formed of smooth, round stones set in an ornate arrangement of fine metalwork; equally fine was the working of the coronet which rested to one side of the rock's base, balancing the coils of the necklace. "Um," said Mel, and passed on to the other sketch.

She looked at it, looked at Miss Seeton, sitting in all innocence with her teacup in her hand, and looked back at the sketch. A slow smile of dawning enlightenment curved her lips, and she nodded to herself.

Eat your heart out, Banner! Move over, Oracle. Amelita Forby wouldn't let the men think they knew it all, by any means.

"Miss Seeton," said Mel, very gently, "you know, I think it would be rather a good idea if you'd let me take these drawings up to London . . ."

In an office at New Scotland Yard that evening, two tall men faced each other across an enormous desk. From the depths of his maroon-leather stud-backed captain's chair, Sir Hubert Everleigh, Assistant Commissioner (Crime), glared in turn at Detective Chief Superintendent Delphick and at the document he had set before his superior on the blotter.

"This," pointed out Sir Heavily, "is a photocopy, not an original, Delphick."

"It is indeed, sir. Or, to be strictly accurate, it's a photocopy of a photocopy — the original staying in my own files. For, er, safety." Delphick fixed his chief with an oracular stare, and watched the gleam appear in his eyes.

"You have the original?" The Assistant Commissioner was leaning forward over the blotter, the despised photocopy-of-a-photocopy ignored beneath his elbows. "Where, exactly?"

Delphick cleared his throat with energy. "My apologies, sir. I appear to have, er, unwittingly misled you. What I meant was that the original photocopy, if I may be permitted the oxymoron, remains in my safekeeping. The drawing from which it was taken is not, after all, official property, and we have no possible claim on it; but Miss Forby — to whom it was entrusted, as you have no doubt forgotten in the stress of the moment — will, you may rest assured, take admirable care of it. You need have no worries on that score."

Sir Hubert narrowed his eyes in a scowl, and the hiss of his breath was audible above the slow grinding of his teeth. "Don't try me too far, Delphick. There are limits beyond which even you should not attempt to pass."

"Sorry, sir." The Oracle neither sounded it, nor meant it. He'd been waging this war with Sir Heavily for years, ever since the assistant commissioner had come to realise that the lightning sketches of Miss Emily Dorothea Seeton, the Yard's unique Miss-Ess, possessed their own rare and indefinable quality which any speculator in art investments should not ignore. Sir Heavily had always been successfully deflected, so far, when he'd made his roundabout requests for a Seeton original; the Oracle saw no reason why the game shouldn't continue indefinitely, provided that he kept his wits about him.

"I think Mel Forby's put us on the right track now, with Miss Seeton's help, of course. I can't think why I didn't think of it myself, except that it hasn't been my case. But once MissEss was shown Mel's photographs — well, if the Forby byline doesn't head a scoop of the first water within a very few days, I'll be extremely surprised." And a brief smile of sympathy for the future astonishment of one Thrudd Banner flickered in his eyes. "I think somebody should have a word with this Mrs. Ongar at the earliest possible moment, sir, in the circumstances."

Together they inspected the two photocopied sketches on the assistant commissioner's blotter. One, the still life with blackbird, they had already agreed — Delphick passing on the suggestion as received from Mel — gave Miss Seeton's general opinion of the MacSporran kidnap, being of little use except as background. As for the second drawing . . .

This showed another blackbird, but far less proud in its plumage, for it had no tail. It did not perch, but rather lurked in the neighbourhood of a young couple — the man with a sullen face, the woman's eyes wary and anxious — who stood huddled together in the shade of a tall tree: a tree with a domed crown and large, spreading branches, on the topmost of which a few leaves were clearly drawn — five-pointed leaves. "A plane tree," Mel had insisted, when she'd appeared in the Oracle's office earlier the same night, hotfoot from Plummergen. "A London plane, that's what that tree is — and they grow in every park in Town!"

"It might be a sycamore, or a maple. Their leaves —"

"Come off it, Oracle. I know you're meant to exercise a bit of caution when a clue ups and clumps you on the head, but this is ridiculous. Why start Devil's Advocating now? This is a five-star, twenty-four-carat, guaranteed Seeton *certainty* I'm showing you here — at great professional risk, I might add. If Thrudd finds out before my story goes in — well, he'd better not, that's all I can say."

"Mel, have I ever let you down in past cases? If Thrudd should happen to learn of your inspired guesswork —"

"Utter brilliance," interposed Mel, with a grin.

"— then it won't be from me, I promise you. Apart from anything else, I'll be far too busy organising somebody to follow this up," and he tapped the drawings with the tip of his ballpoint pen, "to have time to chat to any reporters I may happen to meet."

"Except me, of course. You'd better let me in on the ground floor with this one, Oracle, or I'll never — Hey, I'm going crazy here! It's me who's let *you* in on the ground floor, this time!"

"It is, and we're more than grateful to you, Mel. Just to be on the safe side, though, you'd better not print anything until we've arrested the kidnappers — and before we can arrest them, of course, we have to find them — always assuming you're right about what this drawing means —"

"Oh, I am, Oracle, I am." Mel winked, taking her notebook from her handbag. "The story's all written and ready to roll, right here. Remember, it's not me you're betting on, is it? It's Miss Seeton to the rescue again . . ."

Chapter

6

Once Mel had left for London, taking the two sketches with her, it was hard for Miss Seeton to settle back into her usual routine. She tried her best, clearing away the tea things and busying herself in the kitchen, but her thoughts kept turning in sympathy to Lord and Lady Glenclachan, the parents of the missing Lady Marguerite Mac-Sporran. Such a romantic story surrounding her birth, reflected Miss Seeton, whisking bubbles in the washing-up bowl with the long-handled mop. Dear Mel had held her quite spellbound as she explained how the original grant of title and arms had come from Mary, Queen of Scots, that misguided and headstrong monarch. Whatever service the first Lord Glenclachan had rendered to Mary Stuart (Miss Seeton silently blushed, and scrubbed a stubborn stain with vigour) had made it appropriate for the grant, failing any direct male heir, to descend through the female line: in almost four hundred years, this had happened only twice before. Until now.

"Of course," Mel had said, "it was a gift to the likes of me — the Silly Season's in full swing, and editors are always on the lookout for something they can work up into a regular splash. Only this time — well, I can't help wishing they hadn't. I sort of feel it was partly our fault they snatched the poor kid, putting the idea in their heads in the first place . . ."

But when Mel returned to Town, she had seemed happier about everything, Miss Seeton reminded herself as she rinsed the mop and dishcloth under a running tap and hung them to dry on their hooks beside the sink. The tea things drained silently in the rack; it was too early for even a light supper; she did not feel in the mood for gardening, though her fingers felt restless. She must do something to quiet them.

It was inevitable that she should find herself once more taking out her sketch pad and pencils. That still life she had drawn earlier — the composition had been rather striking — she might be able to re-create it from memory, as long as she did not leave it too long before trying. Memory, as she knew only too well, was a fickle, fleeting thing, though one was thankful that the yoga exercises seemed to have done as much good to her mental powers as they had to her physical. It could not be denied that one was growing older — one had, indeed, been retired some seven years now, but there was no hint, she was thankful to observe, of the approach of dotage and debility. Her knees and her mind, Miss Seeton told herself with some pride, might well be said to flourish.

Indeed, her mind might be considered as being, tonight at least, *too* flourishing and restless. Images of birds and babies and leafy trees kept crowding before her eyes, clamouring to be set down on paper. Miss Seeton shook her head, trying to make them go away. She wanted only that one bird which had perched so proudly on the rock, with the pearl necklace beneath its claw —

"Now, why do I think it was a pearl necklace?" wondered Miss Seeton. "I would have supposed . . . dear Mel's talk of seeing Nigel — my recollecting the visit to Rytham Hall and his teasing of poor Sir George about the windows . . . I had my gold umbrella, of course, and wore Cousin Flora's yellow beads to match my hat, or was it the hat to match the beads — yet I feel sure in the picture they were pearls . . ."

She frowned, and shook her head. Perhaps her memory wasn't all she'd prided herself that it was . . . and she doodled on the sheet of paper beneath her pencil, allowing her eyes to go blank as she tried to recapture the still life . . .

And she was surprised to find, when she focussed her eyes again, that she had drawn a large and blubbery creature with a huge moustache, and next to it a man in overalls, a pencil stuck behind his ear, a ruler poking out of his top pocket, and an air of capability about him. "A walrus and a carpenter," said Miss Seeton, after only a moment's thought. "And, good gracious, these must be the poor oysters by their feet — but not yet being eaten, I am pleased to say." She reflected on Lewis Carroll's poem, which she had learned at school in the days when learning by rote was something for which one could win prizes. There had been one girl, she recalled, who had recited all of *Casablanca* and astounded even the teachers.

She shook her head. Oysters. So it *had* been a pearl necklace and not her dear beads — but why? Mel had simply said "Um," and later "Oh, yes," which was hardly . . .

"Lady Marguerite," exclaimed Miss

Seeton, delighted to have solved the mystery with the help of her school-day memories: for there had been a fashion for such things as the language of flowers and the meanings of names. Emily, her friends had told her, meant *industrious,* and was related, she thought, to Amelia, which was dear Mel's real name, she having added the "t" to make it more noticeable. "For the newspapers," murmured Miss Seeton, smiling. Emily, Amelia — variations on the same name for two such different people — just as Marguerite was a variant of Marguerite was a variant of Margaret, and Margaret, Miss Seeton reminded herself in relief, meant *pearl.* "And the coronet, of course, would have been because she is the daughter of a peer," said Miss Seeton, "while the blackbird, poor thing, is obvious . . ."

And, to her satisfaction, before she trotted back into the kitchen to prepare her supper, she managed to achieve a second version of the still life which seemed exactly like the one Mel had taken away to London in such a hurry.

The events of the day had obviously had a more lasting effect upon her than she'd realised, she thought as she prepared for bed. First, of course, she must practise her yoga routine. For some reason, tonight she added several of her newer poses, such as the Peacock, or *Mayurasana,* and the Cockerel or *Kukkutasana;* and, though she calmed her mind at the end, as she always did, in the *Shavasana,* or Dead Posture, as she fell asleep, her closing eyes beheld images of flying birds, one after the other.

In the middle of the night, she awoke. How unusual: she was normally an excellent sleeper. Something had probably disturbed her — a passing car, perhaps, or the cry of a nocturnal animal or bird after its prey . . .

The cry of a bird, certainly, mused Miss Seeton, as she cuddled back down beneath her bedclothes. She could hear a sea gull faintly mewing somewhere: it must have alighted on her roof before flying onwards, its cry waking her from —

"How strange," murmured Miss Seeton, her eyes drifting to the luminous figures of the bedside clock. Hardly time yet for the dawn chorus, and seagulls were not, so far as she knew — though she had to admit that her knowledge was by no means extensive — birds of the night. But there it was, wherever it was, mewing and crying and . . .

"In pain, poor creature," said Miss

Seeton, unable to shut out the sound once she realised what it must mean. One quick movement, and she had seized her torch from its place beside her bed — one never knew, living in the country, when the electricity supply might fail — and was trotting to the window. Plummergen's absence of street lamps meant that she might not be able to find the bird easily, in the dark, but seagulls, she knew, were generally white-feathered, except the young, of course. She would hope that the wounded bird was older rather than younger . . .

Miss Seeton shone her flashlight out of the window and peered hopefully for any glimpse of white within easy reach. There was no moon. The circle of light showed nothing untoward, and, with a sigh she could not entirely stifle, she pushed her feet into her slippers, pulled on her dressing gown, and headed down the stairs, pausing only to pick up her umbrella en route, and out of her cottage in pursuit of those pathetic cries.

Which grew louder as she came out of her front gate and stood listening in the road, trying to work out from which direction —

The telephone box, directly opposite, on the corner. It sounded as if the cries were coming from there, but she saw no sign of —

Miss Seeton hurried across the road, shining her torch up to the gently domed roof, sure that there she must see an open beak and a bright and hopeful eye — even though from her bedroom window she hadn't. And still, to her surprise, she noticed nothing . . .

Nothing on the roof, that was to say. But surely there was something white, faintly moving, emitting little mews of distress . . . *inside* the telephone box? How on earth had a wounded sea gull managed to get in there?

"It must be a cat," said Miss Seeton, struggling to pull open the heavy, many-panelled glass door with her umbrella hooked over her arm and her torch tucked under it. "Tibs has no doubt been fighting again, and this poor creature —" The door was finally open. "Oh. Oh, good gracious me . . ."

For the light from her torch had fallen, not upon one of young Amelia Potter's infamous feline's victims, but upon a wrapped white bundle which wriggled, and whimpered, and, with the torch beam playing on its face, blinked, and smiled . . .

"A baby," breathed Miss Seeton.

There was a note safety-pinned to the baby's wrappings, but Miss Seeton was too startled to read it just now. What did one do in the middle of the night with an unexpected baby? She gazed round wildly. Not a single house within reach showed a light, which was hardly surprising. Plummergen is not noted for riotously late hours. Miss Seeton and the baby would have to fend for themselves, for some time, at least . . .

Miss Seeton was reminded of Aesop's fable of the fox, the goose, and the bag of corn as she contemplated the baby, and the baby, quiet now that someone was taking an interest in it, contemplated Miss Seeton. The torch, without which one would be unable to make one's way safely home; the baby, which was, after all, the object of the entire exercise; the umbrella, her very best, which she had seized without thinking as she passed the rack, and which she would hate either to damage or to lose. Dear Mr. Delphick . . .

Thoughts of the police made her wonder about telephoning PC Potter for assistance, but to do so from the box would require money, which naturally she hadn't brought with her. Did the discovery of a baby constitute an emergency — could she, perhaps, dial 999? She felt herself turn pale at the very idea. Evidently she couldn't. And her cottage, after all, was a matter of yards away . . .

"It is clearly my duty," Miss Seeton informed the infant with a gulp, "to take you home with me until — until other, more suitable care may be found for you. Unfortunately, my acquaintance with babies is limited. If you had been older . . . however, one cannot shirk one's duty." She gulped once more, then braced herself. One remembered from one's anatomy classes that the human frame was more strongly built than it seemed; one knew from one's own experience of yoga that bones and joints need not be fragile; one hoped, therefore, that the simple act of picking up a baby with inexpert hands would do it no lasting harm. Miss Seeton gazed about her once more in the forlorn hope that one of Plummergen's young mothers might manifest herself out of the dark. Lily Hosigg, perhaps: so shy, but with such a quiet, contented child. The Hosiggs lived only the other side of the canal, in the old Dunnihoe place . . . past Martha Bloomer's cottage. Could she — Miss Seeton brightened — disturb dear Martha to ask for help?

An owl hooted overhead, reminding her

that it was still the middle of the night. She couldn't. Oh, dear . . .

The note, written in thick black capitals, said, "CHANGED OUR MINDS SO HOPE FOR THE BEST." Miss Seeton did not find this altogether enlightening, though her immediate guess was that the baby's parents had for some reason (money or ill health, probably) come to regret having had a child, and had left it in a telephone box as being the most likely place for somebody to find it before it suffered undue neglect. She had to suppose this was a reasonable method of ensuring that an abandoned baby did not go undiscovered: in the olden days, unfortunate (as they were known) mothers deposited unwanted infants on the steps of a suitable church. Perhaps these parents felt that the absentminded bachelor Reverend Arthur Treeves and his sister Molly would lack sufficient knowledge to care for a small baby . . .

"Although goodness knows," Miss Seeton informed the wide blue eyes blinking up at her from the depths of the big armchair in her sitting room, "they could hardly know less than I. Miss Treeves, moreover, is such a splendidly practical person, I feel sure she would be so much better able to . . ."

She cast one wistful look through the sitting-room window in the direction of the Victorian vicarage next to the church, across The Street, beside the George and Dragon, but of Molly Treeves there was, of course, no sign. Miss Seeton had hoped, as she struggled with the baby (scooped up under one arm), umbrella (tucked under the other), and torch (held in one nervous hand to light her way back to her front gate), that someone — anyone — might wake from slumber and help her in her nightmare. Which was perhaps being rather impolite to the baby, but was, for the moment, how Miss Seeton felt.

But nobody had come; she had coped by herself; and now, though she was breathless and bewildered, she knew there was nothing and no one to help her but her own good sense. One could hardly communicate with a baby which was, apparently, only a few weeks, maybe months, old . . .

The baby, however, could communicate with Miss Seeton — and suddenly proceeded to do so, going red in the face and clenching all its tiny muscles before wriggling once and, from an open mouth, emitting a piercing wail. And emitting — Miss Seeton's nose twitched — something else, as well.

As a means of communication it was a complete success. No words had been exchanged, yet Miss Seeton and the baby each knew what the other wanted as if they had spoken on the subject at great length. Miss Seeton gulped. Her thoughts turned to the airing cupboard, and old sheets, and safety pins in her needlework basket — but, before that . . .

"A bath," said Miss Seeton, her nose twitching again as the baby writhed in its wrappings. Her wrappings? His? It seemed discourteous to continue referring to the poor little thing as neuter. At least some part of her problem would be easily resolved. Miss Seeton squared her shoulders, and thought of fire watching during the Blitz. A gentlewoman who had faced doodlebugs and falling masonry without flinching should be able to manage to bathe a baby . . .

Chapter

7

It hadn't been, Miss Seeton reflected, one of the, well, *cleanest* experiences of her life. She breathed a silent word of thanks to the long-handled dish mop, with which she had warily polished the baby — a girl, she'd soon discovered — in the washing-up bowl in the kitchen sink. (What Martha would say when she found out, Miss Seeton dared not think. And as for what she would say when she looked in the kitchen waste bin . . .) Nor had it been one of the *driest*. She'd never realised how much energy even a small baby possessed, or how little water it took to make a great deal of damp. Once the excitement was all over, she felt very weary.

The baby was obviously far from weary. She had suffered the tentative ministrations of Miss Seeton with barely a yip or a yelp of protest, and towards the end had seemed almost to enjoy them. Miss Seeton had tipped bubble bath into the bowl with a generous hand, and had frothed it up with the mop before inserting the baby so that — well, so that things wouldn't be quite so *visible*. The little girl couldn't help herself, of course, but there were some sights Miss Seeton felt she needed time to prepare for — and on this occasion, she hadn't had it. At the thought that she might have to go through all this again, her heart quailed within her; she kept an anxious eye on the clock, and an ear listening for the dawn chorus.

The only chorus it could hear, however, was that of the baby. Warm milk, Miss Seeton supposed the solution to her charge's cries must be: her mouth had certainly been open wide enough for Miss Seeton to know that she could not wish for solid food. Warm milk — but *how* warm? Babies had such delicate digestions, she understood. Did one boil it first and allow it to cool, or . . . and surely the baby was too young to drink from a cup? Was there anything in the house from which a rudimentary bottle could be manufactured?

Suddenly, inspiration struck. This was an emergency, as anyone must agree; perhaps it would only be once, or (if she was unlucky) twice — and it wasn't as though the little girl had any teeth to lose . . .

Within five minutes, the baby was propped up by cushions in one corner of the big armchair. Beside her, Miss Seeton balanced, grateful to the yoga which had made her limbs so . . . adaptable. Miss Seeton smiled. In one hand, she carried an open tin of condensed milk, creamy and thick and sticky with nourishment; in the other, she held a spoon, which from time to time she dipped into the tin and held to the baby's mouth so that she could catch the sugary drops as they treacled from the tip. Miss Seeton was not the only one to smile. The baby smacked her lips and gurgled her appreciation of this diet, and Miss Seeton only hoped she hadn't encouraged the little girl on a self-indulgent course which would ruin her eating habits for years to come. But what else, in the circumstances, could she have done? Secretly, Miss Seeton suspected she'd coped rather well . . .

Lord and Lady Glenclachan thought so, too, once they had been joyfully reunited with their daughter. When Martha, summoned by Miss Seeton (truly thankful that dear Stan was a farm labourer, and used to rising early) realised the implications of her employer's midnight discovery, she was on the phone to PC Potter even before she offered to check the baby for — well, Miss Seeton knew what babies were, didn't she? Just let her tell Potter about the unexpected visitor to Sweetbriars, and then she'd —

With mingled modesty and pride, Miss Seeton informed her that everything about the baby's nether quarters was, at the latest time of checking, in good order. Martha stared, then nodded, pleased. Her dear Miss Emily was equal to anything, hadn't she always said so?

PC Potter — who had come hurrying down from the police house with his wife Mabel — was equally impressed by Miss Seeton's handling of the situation. Superintendent Brinton, Potter's Ashford superior, was astonished, but allowed himself no more than two minutes to recover from his astonishment before telephoning Scotland Yard. It was inevitable that he should ask for Delphick . . .

Thus it came about that Lord and Lady Glenclachan were joyfully reunited with their infant daughter. Miss Seeton, whom they insisted on meeting to thank in person, told them she was proud to have done no more than her plain duty, and shyly confessed that she couldn't remember being quite so nervous in her life before. Delphick, whose presence at the meeting had been urgently requested by his Scotland Yard colleague ("Heaven knows what makes the Battling Brolly tick — like a bomb, so I've heard. Over to you, Oracle, and welcome."), suppressed a yelp of amazement. In the seven years since he'd first met her, MissEss had encountered almost as many villains as himself; she'd been gassed, abducted, hit on the head, and threatened with knives, guns, and death by incineration. Yet none of these adventures, she seemed to be saying — and he knew her to be one of the most truthful persons of his acquaintance — had caused her as much anxiety as the Lady Marguerite MacSporran, all eleven pounds of her in her terry-towel nappy . . . Delphick found his lips pursing in a silent whistle. He looked forward eagerly to telling Chris Brinton all about it later. His old friend's blood pressure wouldn't have had such a shake-up for years.

The romantic return of the lost heiress gave the scoop of her dreams to the *Daily Negative*'s Amelita Forby. Thrudd Banner, brooding on Mel's good fortune, promptly went out and bought her a new hat, claiming that her head was sure to be too large now for any of the old ones. Mel, basking in her editor's praise and the envy of her colleagues, ignored the insult and accepted the hat (which was large enough to do duty as a wastepaper basket) with one of her sweetest smiles. She graciously permitted Thrudd to study the pages of her notebook . . . but not until after the *Negative* had been safely put to bed.

Thrudd, of course, knew who was really behind such headlines as "Found in a Phone Box" and "Missing Marguerite: Glenclachans Gleeful," but he had long ago become a member of the discreet conspiracy which strove to keep journalistic interest in Miss Seeton to a minimum. The columns he wrote for World Wide Press were as unexpansive on the subject as anything Mel might have produced. The Battling Brolly angle could not, in the circumstances, be ignored, but Miss Seeton's protectors saw to it that their newspapers never enlarged upon the nickname.

Other reporters, however, were less considerate of Miss Seeton's desire for privacy. "Pandemonium in Plummergen" was one headline, referring to the first occasion on which hordes of pressmen, camera-toting and inquisitive, rubbernecked their way about the village in an attempt to interview the heroine of the hour. Miss Seeton, however, had been strictly coached by Mel; she stayed either indoors or in her back garden, sheltered by the high brick wall. Her shopping was done on a daily basis by a resolutely mute Martha Bloomer, while Stan tended the flowers in front of the cottage so that no photographs could be snatched.

"Anne's parents say it's been pretty grim down in Plummergen over the last few days," Bob Ranger informed Delphick one morning. The nursing home run by Dr. and Mrs. Knight was at the far end of the village from Sweetbriars, yet they nevertheless managed to keep a kindly eye on Miss Seeton for the benefit of their son-in-law's nerves — and those of his superior. "Flashbulbs popping all over the place, cars parked on the verges ruining the grass — if the Best Kept Village Competition wasn't over, I think someone would have been lynched by now — and traffic jams as bad as Potter's ever seen them."

Delphick sighed. He'd just returned to the office from a meeting with the inspector in charge of the kidnap case. "And we must, I fear, expect things to become rather worse: that pair in Miss-Ess's drawing have been seen. A copy was circulated with the PhotoFits Mrs. Ongar managed to put together, and the like-nesses were good enough for a beat bobby to spot them both during a routine check of after-hours drinking — trying to recover their lost nerve, no doubt, in some pub just outside Hastings. Harry Furneux sent a couple of men to collar them, and they only just missed the blighters. So they're still in the area . . ."

"Poor Miss Seeton, when the news gets round," said Bob, scowling. "Apart from Mel and Thrudd — and a few of their pals, I suppose — I wouldn't trust a reporter as far as I could throw one." Detective Sergeant Ranger stood six foot seven, weighed seventeen stone, and played football for the police eleven. He was perfectly capable of throwing two reporters together, if necessary.

Delphick grinned at the vision which flashed across his inward eye, then grew serious at once. He picked up the telephone. "I promised Mel she should have first whack at any story, and it will do Miss Seeton no harm if I try to remind Amelita Forby of a few past favors . . ."

Mel was all gratitude and contrition once she realised the Oracle was on the other end of the line. "Great," she enthused, when she heard how the police net was closing in on the two people sus-pected of abducting Lady Marguerite MacSporran. "This should just make the fudges in the evening papers, and I know I'll get a decent spread in tomorrow's *Negative*, thanks to you — and Miss S., of course. But I'm sorry she's having a rough ride from those leather-hided hacks who call themselves Fleet Street reporters — she ought to get out of town for a while, till things calm down. Pity she won't take up that invitation to MacSporran Castle. The Glenclachans told me when I inter-viewed them that they were on the point of hightailing it back to Scotland, where it was a sight more peaceful. Matter of fact, if I phone them now to tell them, there could be another exclus—"

"What invitation?" Delphick had no time to observe the courtesies. Mel's perpetual pursuit of scoops, exclusives and front-page stories meant she was quite capable of hanging up on him before they'd fin-ished talking. A forceful interruption was often the only way to get through to her.

"What invitation? Hey, you mean she never told you? If that isn't typical of Miss S. — modesty's her middle name."

"As a matter of fact," began Delphick, despite himself; then he repeated: "*What* invitation to MacSporran Castle?"

"What? Oh, well, it seems the Glenclachans wrote and asked her to spend a few
days with them, once they'd calmed down
from getting the baby back. I was working
too hard to go back to Kent myself, but I
rang Miss S. and kind of apologised for the
fuss I knew there'd been once the story
broke — said to watch out when she was
answering the phone, and so on. She told
me all about it. Envelope with a coat of
arms on it, embossed writing paper — the
works, she said, and very impressive, and
she hardly felt she deserved such attention
— you can imagine her saying it, can't
you?"

"I can indeed. What I can't imagine is
that she would be impressed to the point
of becoming intimidated by such attention,
which seems to be what you're implying."

"Does it? Well, maybe in a way she is,
just a little. I've known Miss Seeton almost
as long as you have, Oracle, and I can't
think offhand of any time before when
she's been intimidated by anything — or
anyone, come to that. Mind you, there
have been the odd occasions when it might
not have been such a bad idea," and her
voice quivered with laughter.

"I happen to agree with you, but I'd

rather not waste time saying so. The sooner you've finished explaining, the sooner I'll ring off and let you go about your business . . ."

"Masterful, yet," replied Mel. "Okay, you've got yourself a deal, though I don't know there's much more to tell you, really. It was just the way she kept saying she was sure they were only being polite, and after their dreadful experience she supposed they'd rather be left alone because privacy's so important, isn't it — and in any case she'd hate to put them to any trouble, and Scotland is such a long way from home . . . It's more an acute attack of modesty, if you ask me, than being intimidated. With a little encouragement, she'd be packing her bags tomorrow."

"I wish, for her sake, that she would." Delphick paused in a meaningful way. "Mel, I don't suppose . . ."

"That when I'm talking to the Glenclachans," she said at once, "I could happen to mention that Miss S. would love to be coaxed into going to Scotland with them? Perhaps apply some of the famous Forby charm, and get them offering to send a car to collect her or something?"

"Maybe not that, exactly, but you have the general idea. Mel, would you?"

"For you, Oracle, I would. And I'll do more than that," she added, with a note in her voice that he knew of old. Amelita Forby had just had another idea . . .

"I've just had an idea," Mel said. "A brainwave, that's the only word for it. This MacSporran business may have started off as Banner's story, but it's mine now, and partly thanks to you. Don't think I'm not grateful. And, one good turn, right? Thrudd lost out, but I'm still in there — and there's more to come on this, if Miss S. is involved. That's what you've been thinking, isn't it?"

Delphick was startled. "As a matter of fact, no. Once Lady Marguerite was safely returned, and the suspects on the point of being caught, I would have hoped —"

"Come off it, Oracle — let's be realistic about this, okay? You know as well as I do that once Miss S. has started things moving, it'll take more than spotting a couple of small-time crooks to stop them. So maybe this pair are the only ones involved — and maybe they aren't. You'll want to flush the whole lot out of the woodwork, won't you? Now, you leave Miss S. by herself in Plummergen, she gets driven round the bend by Banner and his pals, and the case goes nowhere. Send her

102

off to Scotland, and she's out of the way of half the bother, for a start — and, if the other half's unavoidable, she might as well get it all over in one fell swoop . . . with me there, keeping an eye on everything that happens."

Delphick groaned. "Mel, I hate to admit it — but you're likely to be right. What was it Chris Brinton once said to me? There are four things in life you can't buck, and one of them's fate — and Miss Seeton is the other three. I only hope the Glenclachans realise what they're taking on, if she accepts their invitation —"

"She will, Oracle. You know she will."

"Yes, I'm afraid she will. Yet there seems little point in trying to prevent it, whatever *it* is — even if we knew how, which we've never known in the past. Whatever turmoil is doomed to arise is no doubt already beyond all hope of control. Like an unexploded bomb with the fuse already lit — Mel, you meant it when you said you'd go to Scotland too, didn't you?"

"You bet. With another Seeton case building up, would I stay in Town?"

Of course she wouldn't. Delphick had to smile, but then said urgently, "Listen, Mel, Scotland Yard has absolutely no legal standing north of the border, despite the name. The Scottish system is utterly different — we'd be treading on a fair number of toes if I even suggested anybody should go along to keep an eye on things." He paused. "Anybody official, that is. But . . . a friend . . . on holiday . . ."

"On business," retorted Mel. "So you needn't think I'm about to send you daily reports, always supposing they have telephones in the Highlands — which they'd better have, otherwise what's the point in my going, if I can't get in touch with my editor. Who else is going to authorise my expenses? But don't worry, Oracle," as "Damn your expenses" sounded in her ear. "I'll be right there keeping an eye on Miss S., I promise — and not just for the sake of my story, either."

"I know, Mel, and thank you." Delphick tried not to let his anxiety show. "If only I could be sure none of this is going to be necessary . . ."

But long acquaintance with Miss Seeton told him that it would.

Chapter

8

When you have travelled a long distance with someone who has until then been a virtual stranger, it is safe to assume you will know that someone far better by the end of the journey than you did at the start, and also that you will feel far more relaxed in their company than you did before.

So it was with Miss Seeton and the Glenclachans: except that they weren't half an hour out of London before everyone was talking and laughing together like old friends. Miss Seeton, who had entertained a few qualms the previous night, now felt sure that she was going to enjoy every minute of her Highland holiday.

"This will be something of a little adventure for me," she told Lady Glenclachan. "I have seldom had occasion to travel, and certainly have never been so far north in my life . . ." Then, as her innate honesty asserted itself, she added with a blush, "On the ground, that is. But I suppose —

if one is being strictly accurate, which of course I have always tried to insist my pupils should be — if it flew over your part of Scotland on the way — the aeroplane, I mean . . ."

By the time the full story had been coaxed out of her, they were all fast friends. Anyone, insisted Liusaidh MacSporran, Countess of Glenclachan, could have made the same mistake, particularly when travelling abroad for the first time. Anxieties about the luggage, difficulties in reading those television-sized indicator panels set so high from the ground; inability to speak French, Italian, or, indeed, any foreign language — it was really remarkable, when one came to think about it, that more people didn't make exactly the same mistake, flying to Genoa, in Italy, instead of Geneva, in Switzerland. She managed to say this without the slightest tremor in her voice, though her eyes danced a regular Highland fling and she was thankful that her husband, whose shoulders were (to her) visibly shaking, sat where his amusement would not be so noticeable, in the driver's seat of the old Rolls-Royce.

The veteran Silver Ghost was, after his wife and child, the dearest possession of

Ranald MacSporran, Earl of Glenclachan, just as it had been his grandfather's. Allain MacSporran, the old earl, had been one of Scotland's best-known and most enthusiastic motorists in the days of the walking red flag and the four-miles-per-hour speed limit. He took a horsewhip to the chauffeur when that unfortunate omitted to keep the plugs of his first car adequately oiled; and he allowed nobody else to drive him anywhere (the chauffeur being demoted to his original position as groom) until Ranald took and passed the driving test at ten o'clock in the morning of his seventeenth birthday, at the minimum permitted age. The earl and his grandson having spent many happy hours from the latter's infancy in taking cars to pieces and putting them back together again, so now did Lord Glenclachan take full credit for young Ranald's brilliant performance; and he acknowledged (under the influence of a celebratory dram) that, as his years now approached seventy, it might be wise for him to slow down a little. Which meant that for the first time in living memory since the sacking of the chauffeur, someone other than the car-crazy laird was to be seen behind the steering wheel of Allain MacSporran's motor.

Earl Allain died in his eighty-sixth year, succumbing to an apoplectic fit while listening to a wireless commentary on the racing from Brands Hatch. Everyone agreed that the old man couldn't have wished for a better way to go; and, his father Colin having died seven years earlier of a heart attack (brought on by exertion during the opening round of the haggis-hurling competition at the annual Clan Games), in such a manner did Ranald inherit together the earldom, the castle, and the car. Liusaidh, his wife, was not the only person to smile through her tears at his inheritance, and to wonder aloud which part of it Ranald valued the most.

Before they set out, Ranald had given the admiring Miss Seeton a guided tour of his treasure. "Bought to celebrate my father's birth," he said, stroking with a proud hand the bare water cap of the distinctive radiator. "Four years before Sykes designed the Spirit of Ecstasy, you know. One of the very first Silver Ghosts ever made — the best car in the world — although," and he sighed, shaking his head, "I can't help regretting that Grandfather sold his previous two-cylinder job to buy this one. Just think — there's a 1904 ten-horsepower on the road to this day, Miss

Seeton — and it's in Scotland, what's more. Lucky chap . . ."

Miss Seeton looked suitably impressed. The earl sighed again. "They're marvellous motors, Miss Seeton. D'you know that more than six out of ten of all Royces ever built — and that's going back seventy years — are still in full working order? There's a Royce in Moscow, in the Lenin museum — and in 1905 a twenty-horsepower was able to start in top gear up a gradient of one in six with nine men on board!"

"Good gracious," murmured Miss Seeton, understanding she must continue to be impressed, but not entirely sure why. Lady Glenclachan touched her husband lightly on the arm.

"Ranald, my dear, don't overwhelm poor Miss Seeton, will you? I'm sure she doesn't understand half of what you're telling her — any more than I did, when I first met you." She turned to smile at their new friend. "Believe me, Miss Seeton, I do sympathise if it feels as though you've been set down in an utterly foreign country whose language you don't speak. It must have been three years after our wedding before I knew what Ranald was talking about at least half of the time."

Lord Glenclachan swallowed his planned

reference to the radiator grille and its manufacture by skilled hand and eye without
the use of measuring instruments, patted
the water cap once more, grinned sheep-
ishly, and began to assist his passengers,
and their luggage, into their appointed
places. Liusaidh had made sure that the
picnic basket contained more than adequate supplies for the entire journey north,
though they had planned to make a short
overnight stay with friends — as Lady
Glenclachan so sagely said, it did no harm
at all to be prepared.

"Hope for the best, expect the worst,
and take what comes, so my old nanny
always told me," she remarked to Miss
Seeton as at last they set out. Miss Seeton
nodded approval of this sentiment. Lord
Glenclachan chuckled.

"There's nothing to worry about, believe
me. Never has been before, has there? I
promise you we'll arrive all in one piece
and all in good time — and I'm sure we
shan't need half of what you've packed. A
Rolls-Royce, you see, Miss Seeton, doesn't
break down. Why, just listen to the engine!
When the first Royces went across to the
United States, the customs chappies
thought they must be powered by electricity instead of petrol, because they were

so quiet. The best car in the world," he said again, and tootled a cheerful fanfare on the horn.

He sounded another fanfare late the next afternoon, as the Silver Ghost turned into the gateway of MacSporran Castle and his wife began to rouse her sleeping daughter. "Here we are," was all Ranald MacSporran said, but his tone said far more. Miss Seeton wondered fleetingly how he could ever bring himself to travel to London, when his heart was so clearly in the Highlands; then she blushed for her curiosity, and looked around with interest as the car glided up the drive.

The MacSporrans' home was not the castellated, moated, draw-bridged fortification of Miss Seeton's imagining. There was a plain, square, solid tower at the centre, with a step-gabled roof of slate which overhung the walls so far there was no need for guttering. At two opposite corners of the central square stood round towers, equally solid and plain; the entire building was (she was later to learn) harled, or rendered with a lime-based roughcast hurled on the wall, and coloured a characteristic light pink which blended well with the soft greens and browns of the countryside, the brooding greys of granite outcrops, the hazy purples of heather, and the pale pearly gold of a sunset sky.

"How delightful," exclaimed Miss Seeton, feeling in her fingers the old, familiar tingle which she hoped — as she never ceased to hope — would for once herald true fulfilment of her creative yearnings. How glad she was she had remembered to pack sketchbook, paints, charcoal, and pencils . . . Then, even as she continued to express pleasure at the view, her sturdy realism reasserted herself. With a sigh, she added her all-too-valuable eraser to that mental list. Her artistic ability, she knew only too well after so long, could never adequately achieve on paper the visions that presented themselves before her inward eye . . .

Once everyone was duly settled, Lord Glenclachan invited Miss Seeton to accompany him on a short tour of his estates. Liusaidh did not go with them, being preoccupied with little Lady Marguerite. While Nanny Angela remained in hospital — still unconscious, but happily off the danger list — nobody but the baby's parents or the most trusted of family retainers could be permitted to care for her, and now every member of the castle staff insisted upon coming to see that all was well with their future clan chief. Miss Seeton had been embarrassed by their welcome, by their gratitude for the part she had played in restoring his heiress to their laird, and Ranald, to spare his honoured guest further blushes, spoke of the need to stretch his legs after the long drive, and of his wish to check on the general progress of affairs during his three weeks' absence in Town.

"Oh, you'll find plenty to take your fancy for a sketch or two around Glenclachan, Miss Seeton," he told her, leading the way out into the cool, sweet air of an evening slow to turn from dusk to dark, as in all northern latitudes. The open sky arched clear above their heads; the first few stars had begun their slow appearance in the distant, darkling east. "We've any number of magnificent views — this is all MacSporran country, you know, and chock full of history, too. Tomorrow, I'll show you the picture room we've made at the top of the turret there" — he indicated one of the round corner towers — "with some of my ancestors on the walls. By all accounts they were a quarrelsome bunch, but I shouldn't suppose their portraits could get up to anything like the rumpus that place must have seen in the old days."

He went on to explain that the "Z-plan" design of MacSporran Castle was a common one in the Highlands, for with only two corner towers (round, not square) and the wise location of windows, a Scottish laird could have an uninterrupted line of sight in every direction for enemies attempting to take his house unawares. "And don't think for one minute it was just paranoia, Miss Seeton. They had to contend with caterans — robbers, that is — and brigands and raiders from other clans, not to mention the Sassenachs, if you'll excuse my saying so, and tax collectors. Not that we don't still have tax collectors nowadays, of course, but we're rather less likely to want to run them through with swords . . ."

They came to a low boulder, covered in bronze-green moss and weathered with centuries of rain. Ranald stopped beside it, resting his folded arms on the top of the low wall which overlooked it. "The Wolf Stone — one of my ancestors killed his first wolf here at the age of seven, so the story goes; and it was here that the Glenclachan of his day mustered the fighting men of the clan, poor devils, before leading them out to battle on behalf of Charles Edward Stuart." Ranald's tone was not that of one who considered this to have been an altogether wise move.

Miss Seeton ventured, "That is Bonnie Prince Charlie, is it not?"

"Unfortunately, yes." Ranald shook his head. "He was a right Charlie, true enough — and I wonder how much of a legend would have grown up around him if he'd been called by a less harmonious name. *Charles* translates nicely into Gaelic as *Tearlach* — but suppose they'd used Edward, or Louis, or Philippe, or Casimir instead? Those were his other Christian names," he added, as Miss Seeton regarded him questioningly. "Euphonic, is that the word? Bonnie Eddie — Teddy? No, he was lucky there. So now everyone remembers the romance of it all, or what they think of as the romance — Flora Mac-Donald, the white cockade, Cameron of Lochiel's heeled-in beech saplings he never returned to plant properly . . ."

He turned to scowl at the Wolf Stone, and favoured it with a brooding kick. "Oh, I suppose it's only human nature not to want to admit there was never any real chance of success from the start. Charles pawned his mother's own rubies to finance the invasion — *very* romantic, they were her dowry — and managed to have the weapons captured by the English before they'd been a week on the voyage from France. He didn't speak a word of the language when he finally landed, he didn't know how to wear the costume — more than half the clans refused to revolt on his behalf, and a great many of them actually took up arms against him. Do any of the great romantics ever tell you that?"

Miss Seeton murmured that she didn't believe they did, but Ranald was by now too wrapped up in his lament to hear her. "And of those clans that fought for Charles, an awful number were forced to it by their chiefs, under threat of having their homes burned and their families harmed — and most of the chiefs were in it for the plunder they hoped to take home with them. By the time it came to Culloden — oh, granted the English lost a few battles on the way, but that was sheer mischance — by the time they were ready to make a proper stand, it was sheer bloody slaughter of disorganised fanatics by well-trained, well-fed, well-equipped soldiers. At Culloden, Miss Seeton, when their bullets were gone, the Prince's troops dragged the very stones from the earth with their bare hands and flung them against the enemy . . ."

He suddenly recollected himself. "I do beg your pardon, Miss Seeton. The Forty-Five wasn't so long ago, in Highland terms. We have long memories in these parts — to match our long summer evenings," he added with a smile, gesticulating skywards. "Besides, there's nobody in Glenclachan or nearby who hasn't had their fill of the Jacobite Cause, these past few weeks, and I've not heard from anyone since we arrived back that things have changed . . ."

Miss Seeton was too polite to ask what he meant, but it was clearly his intention to explain before she did. "We're great ones for a cause, Miss Seeton, and to a Scot there's no such thing as a cause that's lost. There are Jacobites still in Scotland, and more than one self-styled heir to the Stuart throne hoping the nation will forget how Charles died without legitimate issue, and how his brother Henry became a cardinal of the Roman Catholic church, and not only never claimed to be Henry the Ninth, but went so far towards agreeing the rights of the Hanoverian claim as to accept a pension from George the Third — four thousand pounds a year, Miss Seeton, when he'd surely have tried for more if he thought he stood any chance. Yet there are those who firmly believe there's but the proper legal arguments to be met, and away with Queen Elizabeth and her own Prince Charles, and welcome back to the Royal House of Stuart." He snorted. "There's a pair of them, brother and sister, staying with friends an hour or so from here: Archduke Casimir Sobieski and his sister, Archduchess Clementina, come to see the sights and enjoy a Highland summer. As if they couldn't be sure of better weather for themselves by staying on the Continent! Casimir makes a great point, as I've been told, of not calling himself a Stuart for fear of disturbing the populace — as if anyone in their right minds," scoffed Ranald MacSporran, "is going to start a rebellion on behalf of a pair of foreign youngsters trying to look pretty in the tartan! I'd say the Queen can rest easy in her bed, Miss Seeton, whether it's at Buckingham Palace or Balmoral — or even Windsor Castle . . ."

And Miss Seeton, visualising at his words a sudden image of the massive grey walls and rounded towers of Windsor — so very different in size, yet so similar in purpose, from the castle of Glenclachan — said with the utmost certainty that his lordship, of course, spoke no more than the truth.

Chapter

9

Mel Forby had warned Miss Seeton not to be surprised if she noticed a familiar face in the neighbourhood once she had arrived in Glenclachan. "Oh, ye'll take the high road, and I'll take the low road," she sang down the telephone in mellow tones — she and Thrudd had been celebrating her imminent departure with a bottle of Chablis — "and I'll be in Scotland afore ye — not that I'm too sure about that, with the trains. You don't know how lucky you are, Miss S., going door-to-door — and in a Rolls-Royce, to boot. Which reminds me — talking of boots, have you packed your walking shoes? Our travel department tells me the hills round Glenclachan are famous for scenery and so forth. Right up your street, I would have thought."

Thrudd's voice might be heard in the background pointing out that The Street was in Plummergen, and on level ground, as opposed to in Scotland, among mountains, but Mel ignored him, except for a quick giggle. Miss Seeton said that she had indeed packed her walking shoes, and her binoculars, for Highland birdlife was supposed to be most interesting; she looked forward to seeing dear Mel again, and hoped she would have a safe journey. Which Mel, having entrusted herself to the tender mercies of British Rail's InterCity 125 diesel flagship, duly did.

Glenclachan, the travel department of the *Daily Negative* had advised her, boasted only one hotel: the Pock and Tang, prop. Hamish McQueest. Hamish greeted his guest with a nod, a stare, and a thoughtful tug at his curling red moustaches, before he pushed the register across the desk for her to sign. Having studied her signature, he informed her that her room just happened to be on the first floor.

"But there's no lift, unfortunately," he added, absently rubbing the base of his spine and wincing. "And my back's seen better days — early retirement, you know. I'd offer to carry your bags for you, only . . ."

"*Only* is the word, all right," replied Mel cheerfully. "Only one bag, see?" She picked up her overnight case from where she'd put it, out of sight under the reception desk, and brandished it across the counter under Hamish's startled nose. "You get used to travelling light, in my job. That's my key, isn't it? Thanks." And she whisked it out of his hand before he could utter a word, turned towards the stairs, and disappeared up them with an airy backward wave, leaving him to stare after her, tweaking his moustache.

Having quickly unpacked, Mel found herself in need of a drink to wash away the dust of her long journey north. She headed back downstairs, noticed that the reception desk was now unmanned, and decided to explore: Amelita Forby, always on the trail, with a nose for what mattered, every time.

With nobody around to give directions, a left turn, she thought, would do as well as any, but this time her nose let her down, and the corridor she chose led to the curtained double doors of the dining room. Mel wasn't hungry yet. British Rail sandwiches, she'd found as she travelled from London, were very much maligned by the popular press; she'd even made a start at an article on "The Fun of Food En Route," to be offered first to the *Negative*'s travel editor. Now, however, she had forsaken journalism for the lure of other, more pressing pleasures. She saw a uniformed female figure in the distance, but it vanished through a doorway as she called out to it. Mel shrugged and strode off in the opposite direction, opening one or two likely-looking doors as she passed, only to be disappointed, but, with the buzz of deep male voices somehow reaching her ear, fairly confident she couldn't be far out of her way.

And then she opened one final door, which proved her instincts had not lied, as a heaviness of warm, smoky air came billowing out to greet her, proof that she had found the bar of the Pock and Tang. Her glance took in the entire room as every tongue fell silent and every head was turned towards her, standing on the threshold, and not one of the crowd of assembled drinkers appeared to be female. Amelita Forby, endangered species — the only albino in a flock of blackbirds. Mel blinked. Why had she thought of herself like that? She hardly expected to be mobbed in broad daylight.

"Good evening, Miss Forby," came the voice — the English voice, it suddenly dawned on her — of Hamish McQueest. The heads turned again, still silent. Mel followed the direction of their gaze and saw the landlord's fiery face-fungus across the room behind the bar counter, his eyes gleaming, his hands busy polishing glasses. Glasses! Mel's own eyes gleamed, and, with a nod and a general smile of greeting, she made her passage through the little groups of drinkers clustered about the low, dark wooden tables, towards the bar — where, to her surprise, she found herself stifling a quick sigh of relief at having arrived in safety.

Safety? For heaven's sake, Forby, this isn't the middle of the jungle. You're just a bit jumpy because you miss the Banner more than you thought you would — or perhaps because you've just discovered you're an alcoholic . . .

"A double whisky, please," she said firmly, when Hamish asked her what she wanted. "With a treble orange juice for starters, though," she added, remembering that when she left her room she had, after all, been thirsty. Orange juice to settle the dust, whisky for her nerves — not her preferred tipple, but, since she was in Scotland, better make like the natives. Nerves, natives . . . why was everyone still staring at her in that peculiar way? Mel shrugged, grinned round at her audience, and hitched herself up on a polished oak stool to lean her elbows comfortably on the bar.

Only Hamish McQueest seemed to regard her appearance as something unremarkable. He returned her grin, leaned across the counter, and asked whether she wanted a single malt or a blended scotch. Mel's ears were sharp. Even as she responded (the good reporter's ever-enquiring mind) with a request for enlightenment as to the difference between single malts and blends, she was able to hear conversation starting up again behind her back.

And one of the most audible snippets she could make out was the muttered "Aye, there'll likely be a white sheet for yon lassie, I'm thinking . . ."

Fearless Forby, Fleet Street's Finest. Mel told herself this unexpected threat of a shroud was just the booze talking. With a further shrug — on the Street, you had to look tough, act tough, or go under — she sat up straight. Knives in the back she didn't seriously expect — too public, for one thing. Pity there wasn't a mirror, though, behind the bar, the way there always seemed to be in the movies. She'd like to know which of the Pock and Tang's clientele objected so much to her presence. What had happened to that famous Highland hospitality she'd read so much about in the travel pages of the *Negative*?

The *Negative* — the chance here for another scoop, maybe . . . Mel's pulses quickened, every instinct telling her there must be a story somewhere around, if they were all so keen to get rid of her — never mind the recent arrival of Miss S., who, even on her most cracking form, usually took more than a few hours to set things humming . . .

Though it seemed that, on this occasion, they'd already started. What was the Oracle's favourite term? *Embroiled,* that was it. Whenever Miss S. became embroiled in a mystery of any sort, it invariably made headline news — and here was Amelita Forby with a watching brief, right in the heart of the tiny village of Glenclachan. which already seemed to be doing a nice little line in home-grown mystery — and slap into the middle of it all had walked Miss Seeton . . .

Mel sipped her whisky with a secret, gleeful smile. Her expression was not lost on Hamish MeQueest. "I hoped you'd be pleased with the Lairigigh, Miss Forby. Not many of our Sassenach palates do justice to its finer points, I fear. Would you care for another?"

As he reached for the bottle, Mel said

quickly, "And one for yourself, Mr. McQueest. I'm sure your palate appreciates it far better than mine. Doubles for both of us — oh, and is there a dinner menu I could see?" Better, of course, if she'd eaten *before* starting to pump the proprietor, rather than after — all that scotch sloshing round on an empty stomach — but she didn't see how even the landlord of a Highland hotel could drink as much as certain of her Fleet Street colleagues. Mel Forby had long ago trained herself to keep up with those colleagues, if not to beat them at their own game. Her lips curved upwards as she thought of Thrudd Banner.

Hamish had been dispensing whisky with his back to her, and turned round in time to catch the tail end of what had been a dazzling smile. He smiled back, then winked as he pushed Mel's fresh glass across. "Thank you, Miss Forby, and your very good health."

"Thanks," returned Mel, raising her glass in reply, "and cheers, Mr. McQueest. You have a nice place here." Start by asking a few easy questions, and don't go for the hard-nosed stuff until he's nicely off his guard. "An unusual name," she went on. "What does it mean? Something to do with the plague, or the Black Death? I didn't realise they'd come so far north."

Hamish stared at her for a moment, then forced a chuckle as realisation dawned. "Pockmarks and the smell of death, of course. Dear me, what a grisly imagination! There were no such horrors round these parts in the past, I'm happy to say — the name's nothing more than a reference to the pearl fishing that goes on hereabouts."

"Pearl fishing." Mel regarded him doubtfully. Poking fun at the dumb tourist, it seemed — when she'd just bought the man a drink, what's more. "Oh, yes?"

"Yes," he replied at once, nettled by her obvious doubt. "Glenclachan's famous for its fresh-water pearls, and quite a number of people have made a living out of them, over the years. Not that it's any of your deep sea diving. Was that what made you suspect I was having you on? It's the flyers, you see," he continued, above her attempted protests. "They are extremely cold, and clean, and fast-flowing, which is what suits the creatures best, I gather. The cooler the climate, the slower the growth; the slower the growth, the better the pearl. Prized for centuries, the pearls of Scotland have been, from the time of Julius Caesar and earlier; traded by the ancient Phoenicians thousands of years ago, as I understand."

He absently topped up Mel's glass before continuing: "Of course, you have to know where to find them, and *how* to find them, too. They use special equipment — a forked stick for lifting the mussels from the riverbed, and that's called a tang; while the pock is the sack tied round a fisherman's waist or over his shoulder as he wades through the stream. That's for carrying the mussels to the riverbank to search them for pearls. Hence, you see, the name."

"Pock and Tang," muttered Mel. "Yes, I see." There was the chance for a Piece in all this, whether or not the Seeton story broke as expected; though she still had every hope, of course, that it would.

She had made her tone professionally prompting. Duly prompted, Hamish began to expand on his theme. "There's a specially adapted bucket they use, an old one with its bottom bashed out and a sheet of glass fitted — along the lines of an upside-down periscope — for holding the surface of the water steady so that they can peer down at the scaup, which is what they call the mussel bed. And, perhaps most important of all, waders, for going out into deep water."

He looked at Mel in quizzical fashion. "But I hardly suppose that you came here to fish for pearls, Miss Forby. You said yourself that, er, your job requires you to travel light, and I can't seriously believe you had a bucket and a pair of waders in your bag — though no doubt you could make a fine tang for yourself by cutting a long branch, and Pictarnitie's stores would sell you a bucket, and the glass to go with it, too. But it's a hard life, they tell me. The local rivers run deep as well as fast, and when they're in full spate the current is hard to withstand, especially, if you'll excuse me, for a young woman who can't weigh very much. Stones slippery with weed, that sort of thing — people have drowned fishing for pearls, you know."

As he paused to shake his head wisely and sip a libation to the departed from his glass, Mel contemplated him with an air of interest. Rather than let him learn her business in the village, it seemed a good idea to deflect him with a few friendly questions. She remembered Plummergen, and smiled. "How long have you lived in Glenclachan, Mr. McQueest? What made you decide to come to the Highlands to run a hotel?"

He was about to reply when there came the rattle of a latch, and the outside door opened. Another stranger, if Mel was any judge, stood on the threshold with the eyes of everyone in the bar turned towards him: a sallow, stooped, slit-eyed man with scraggy eyebrows and a cigarette depending from one corner of his mouth. He narrowed his eyes still more against the concerted stare of the room, studied every face as closely as his own was studied, then frowned, shrugged, and made his way warily towards the bar.

Conversation ebbed and flowed behind him as he passed, though it was clear this was halfhearted pretence, that everyone was intent on learning the newcomer's business with Hamish McQueest. Mel thought of a hundred westerns: double doors flung open at the arrival of the hero, gun by his side and challenge in his stance, glaring at the villain slouched over the poker table, daring him to a duel. She could hardly smother her giggles. Anything less heroic than this yellowy ratlike figure she never hoped to see.

She buried her nose in her whisky glass as the man drew near. Hamish eyed her sharply, then moved along to greet his latest customer. "Good evening," he said, with a smile. "And what can I get you?"

The man glanced at Mel, then obviously dismissed her as a person of small importance. "I'm looking," he said, in a tone someone far less shrewd than Amelita Forby would have recognised as pregnant, "for John Stuart Fraser. They tell me he's to be found in these parts."

"John Stuart Fraser?" The landlord's repetition of the name fell into an almost silent room. He nodded once in the direction of the farthest corner. "If you ask again over there, I dare say you'll be put on the right track . . . And you know, that's odd," he added, once the man, with a curt acknowledgement, had turned away. Mel's ears pricked, and she looked a question. Hamish frowned, and stroked his red moustache.

"I've lived in Glenclachan for nearly three years, Miss Forby, and to my knowledge there's never been a Fraser with John Stuart as his forenames, yet that chap's not the first to come asking for the man in person, and I doubt if he'll be the last. I can't help wondering what's going on . . ."

And Mel couldn't help wondering also.

Chapter

10

"Are you sure you don't mind amusing yourself this morning, Miss Seeton?" Liusaidh MacSporran regarded her guest with an apologetic air. "Only Mrs. McScurrie is" — she glanced over her shoulder: the dining-room door was safely closed — "in one of her *moods* today," Lady Glenclachan concluded, and stifled a giggle. "I'd better placate her, especially after having been away in London for so long. We're all utterly petrified of her, you know." Miss Seeton blinked at this. The house-keeper had not appeared to be particularly awe-inspiring; she had fussed in a most kindly manner over such matters as a stone-ware hot-water bottle in one's delightful four-poster bed (although one would have supposed that, in August, even a Scottish castle would be neither damp nor cold) and the contents of the bedside biscuit tin. Liusaidh laughed at her evident bewilder-ment.

"Bless her, Mrs. McScurrie is a MacSporran institution, and has been for centuries. We'd miss her dreadfully if she wasn't here to bully us." Miss Seeton blinked again, then nodded, and smiled. The aristocratic sense of humour . . . dear Nigel, who at a far-distant (she sincerely trusted) date would inherit his father's baronetcy, was also given to such amusing hyperbole. "In fact," Liusaidh went on, "she'd run the place far better than I ever could, and we both know it; but she feels duty bound to humour me by asking my opinion all the time, so I have to humour her by giving it, even if we both also know" — she giggled again — "that she'll do just what she wants in the end. She always has before!"

Miss Seeton nodded and smiled again, with feeling. "My own dear Martha is much the same, I am fortunate in being able to say. I feel sure she takes far better care of the house than I do, on the days when she doesn't come — that is to say, on the days when she does — come, I mean. Take care of it. Better than I do. When she doesn't." Oh dear. The countess was looking rather uncomfortable. Miss Seeton came flustering to a halt, and frowned. Had she, perhaps, sounded a little too boastful? Surely Lady Glenclachan realised that Sweetbriars, so suitable a home for one who was merely a retired teacher, could never even hope to approach the splendour of an earl's castle. How presumptuous — Miss Seeton pinkened — if one had given the impression, no matter how unintentionally, that one had a vast retinue of staff to do one's every bidding — although, in the interests of accuracy (and had that not always been her aim through- out her entire career?) she supposed she should explain the rest . . .

"And then there is Stan, who looks after my garden and collects the eggs, which are so much better to cook with, Martha tells me — but only, of course, when he is not working on the farm. Than those from the shops, I mean. Martha is noted in Plummergen," said Miss Seeton with pride, "for her fruitcakes."

"Yes" — Liusaidh leaped into the breach as Miss Seeton seemed to have come to a merciful end — "I've no doubt she is. We must exchange a few recipes before you go home. I'd better warn you, though, that Mrs. McScurrie's cakes are notorious, rather than noted. She drenches every last piece of fruit in whisky, and even old Lachlan Magandy, who's a very strict elder of the kirk, ended up under the table when he called to see Ranald about something a few months ago." Her eyes danced. "He kept telling us it must be heatstroke — in January! Oh, and talking of Ranald — I did explain, didn't I, that he'll be busy with the factor all morning?"

"Indeed you did, Lady Glenclachan. I had no idea that an earl was required to devote so much of his time to mathematics — and when you are supposed to be on holiday, what is more. I regret that my own teaching abilities, such as they are, incline almost entirely to the artistic side, even though one helped out with other classes, of course, should an emergency arise. But I am unable to assist his lordship, I fear. Mathematics, you see — factors, and decimals, and equations . . ."

Miss Seeton sighed, and shook her head, and thus did not observe the countess's eyes as they danced a regular reel. The note of control in Liusaidh's voice as she replied was, fortunately, barely noticeable. "Miss Seeton, I do beg your pardon for misleading you, but in Scotland a factor is an estate agent — though not," she added hastily, "in the English sense of someone who helps people to buy or sell a house. A factor manages the house and lands while the owner is away — and most of the time when he's there, too, if he's someone who can be relied upon, as we rely on Mr. Gleade."

Miss Seeton went pink once more, discreetly, and she thanked Lady Glenclachan for having explained. Any addition to one's knowledge and vocabulary was always of interest — she must remember to tell Jack Crabbe, once she was back in Plummergen, because it might be just what he was looking for as a clue. The compilers of crossword puzzles, she had been given to understand, always liked double meanings and cryptic clues, and Jack (although he was far too modest to say this himself) was one of the most skilful compilers in the country. Plummergen was very proud of Jack Crabbe.

"I shall walk down into the village," said Miss Seeton, "and see if the shop has a copy of any of the magazines to which he contributes. If, that is, you would care to look at one?"

"I'm sure we should, though I can't promise that either of us will be able to finish it. But it would make a pleasant stroll, and give you a chance to do a little exploration — though be warned by me, Miss Seeton, don't believe a word the weather vane says. It was taken down for repairs after a bad storm last winter, and I'm afraid Dougall McLintie — our black-smith — is a little too fond of a dram. Which, to be honest, isn't that unusual a weakness in Glenclachan, but most of the others save their drinking for after work. Poor Dougall, being his own boss, doesn't have anybody breathing down his neck except his customers, and he's the only smith for miles around. In any direction!" And Liusaidh laughed. "I don't suppose you've ever seen a weather vane where north and south are next to each other instead of opposite, have you, Miss Seeton? And west is next to east, too. There's been some talk, I may tell you, of leaving it just as it is, to attract the tourists — there's not much else for them in Glenclachan except fresh mountain air and wide open spaces."

"Which are delightful, and so very different from my own dear Kent," Miss Seeton assured her. "One might describe it all as *dramatic*, the grey crags and heather moors and little streams — I mean, burns," she corrected herself, remembering the brief guided tour she had taken with Ranald the previous night. "Should auld acquaintance be forgot," she found herself adding, no doubt under the influence of her surroundings. "And never brought to mind . . ."

"We'll take a cup of kindness yet," replied Liusaidh at once. "For auld lang syne — or, if you'd like another quote from the immortal bard — Freedom and Whisky gang thegither! They certainly do in Glenclachan, Miss Seeton. Has Ranald told you about the Jacobite rising we expect any minute?"

Miss Seeton was still smiling as, ten minutes later, she began her expedition to the village shop. The sun was warm and the sky was blue, though there were clouds on the horizon; but she had brought her umbrella, of course, and wore stout shoes with waterproofed uppers, as well as her favourite cockscomb hat and a sensible light jacket over her tweed skirt. One had been warned of the unreliability of Highland weather . . .

"And of Highland weather vanes," Miss Seeton murmured, smiling again, and resolved that her first sight-seeing task should be to seek out the deviating direction-finder, thinking it might be worth a sketch.

It was, when she trotted down into Glenclachan and found the church — kirk, she amended promptly — indeed an unusual sight, and attractive, with the brass cockerel at the centre gleaming like gold in the bright August sunshine. Miss Seeton doubted, however, whether her pencil — and indeed her eyesight — would be adequate to the task. "Or my neck," she added, for the height of the tower was considerable, and she had to squint upwards at an awkward angle to obtain the best view. She shook her head in silent amusement, smiling at her folly in wondering, albeit briefly, how the wind might be expected to know which direction it should blow from.

"Or, indeed, the rain," she added, her attention having drifted to those distant clouds, which seemed to be drawing ever nearer, dark and ominous. "But I have my umbrella, of course," regarding it with pride. "Although what dear Mr. Delphick would say if it were to be damaged — and Mr. Brinton as well . . ."

Miss Seeton had spent not a little time packing for her Highland holiday, a large proportion of which had been given to thoughts of which umbrella she should take. Mr. Brinton — Superintendent Brinton, she supposed she should say — had been very firm, some years back, about the need to keep her golden brolly for best, advising her, in his whimsical way, that for a working model she should keep to ordinary nylon with a steel shaft, to be replaced as necessary. Miss Seeton had never quite understood what he'd meant, especially as he'd added something about those of her hats destroyed in the course of duty — his idea of a joke, she supposed, as she really couldn't see why it should be thought anyone's duty to destroy a perfectly harmless, and altogether useful, hat. Miss Seeton put a hand to the cockscomb on her head and patted it. Dear Mr. Brinton might like to tease — it was perhaps fortunate that she had never taken him too seriously — but surely even he would admit that staying with an earl must warrant, on the part of his lordship's guest, the very greatest effort of courtesy. If MacSporran Castle didn't deserve the gold umbrella, then nowhere and nobody did . . .

Pondering the niceties of umbrella etiquette, Miss Seeton favoured the weather vane with one last look, then sighed as a drop of rain fell on her upturned face, and glanced behind her to see the bank of cloud racing towards the sun, driven by a high wind which only now began to disturb the lower atmosphere. Trees tossed their branches, birds headed for cover, Miss Seeton's skirt flapped around her knees as the rain began to fall in earnest. Long before the final patch of blue sky had been vanquished by the leaden conqueror, the gold-handled umbrella was open and doing its duty.

As she headed down the main street, Miss Seeton's eye travelled along its narrow, gently curving length, lined with low-roofed cottages, solid granite houses, and a lively selection of shops. She would, she thought, like to paint Glenclachan, when the weather was more settled. Perhaps, if the picture turned out well, it could serve as a farewell gift for the MacSporrans, who had been so very kind. Such an attractive place, though one could not help feeling a little, well, homesick for Plummergen, still full of colour from a riot of late summer flowers, while in this street one stepped from pavement to front door without even the smallest of gardens on the way. There was, after all, no place like home, but the curve of this street reminded her so much of The Street, now she came to consider it . . .

A vivid splash of colour emerged from one of the side roads, and Miss Seeton blinked. How bright. How unusual, indeed — yet, to an artist, how pleasing a contrast against the whitewashed walls and granite grey of Glenclachan in the rain: though this splash of colour could hardly remind anyone of Plummergen. She doubted whether the village would so much as dream of a tartan umbrella — why, she herself had never thought of such a thing, and, while not wishing to appear boastful, umbrellas were, nobody could deny, what one might call a particular interest of Emily Dorothea Seeton.

The tartan umbrella — such a large, cheerful, practical protection against the Highland weather — was still some way off when it suddenly stopped and disappeared into what Miss Seeton assumed to be a shop. Recollecting herself, she now realised she had chanced to stay her steps next to the very shop she herself had been seeking and, with a little exclamation, darted thankfully through the door, out of the rain. Just inside the door, she let down her brolly and shook it briskly over the mat before turning to examine the contents of Glenclachan's newsagent, stationer and general stores, prop. (she'd just had time to notice as she passed beneath the lintel) Jamesina Pictarnitie.

Mrs. Pictarnitie, who sat behind the main counter with a pair of knitting needles busy in her hands, was plump and friendly. She greeted Miss Seeton with a smile.

"You'll be the English visitor up to the castle, I make no doubt — the one who found the laird's baby." Miss Seeton, after an anxious pause during which she mentally played this sentence over at a slower rate, and with an accent less strong, warily agreed, with a blush, that she was. One knew that the staff at the castle had been more than flattering in their attentions, but really, one had hoped . . .

Jamesina's smile grew wider as she viewed Miss Seeton's display of modesty with approval. "Aye, well, then you're no stranger to the rain — though it's ragglish weather for summer, and the wind fairly raving, altogether unexpected. Bide you here in the dry," she invited. "Take as long as you like over your messages."

Miss Seeton caught at the one word she safely recognised among the welter of dialect. "Oh dear. I'm so sorry — were you expecting me to bring a message from the castle? I fear I must have left before anyone told me. If only I had known . . . but perhaps, if it would not cause too much inconvenience, you could telephone?"

In her turn, Jamesina took time to think; then she burst out laughing. "Och, I was forgetting, and knowing you were English, as well! It's what you'd call doing the shopping — only *we* say that a body's doing her messages." She laughed again. "What I meant was, with the storm upon us the way it is, you spend as long as you like looking round the shop, hen. Don't worry yourself about going outside in the rain — or about me telephoning up to the castle, either. A fine welcome to the Highlands it would be to end up catching your death of a host!"

Chapter

11

Miss Seeton blinked. The general intention of Mrs. Pictarnitie's little speech had (or so it must be thought) been a kindly one — but the accent in which she'd uttered it had been, to say the least, rather strong and, as a result, not a little confusing. One found it hard to credit, however, that Mrs. Pictarnitie, who had (as one supposed) known Lord Glenclachan for most of her life, suspected his lordship of harbouring dark designs against his guests, and one therefore hesitated to reply, for fear of awkwardness. Miss Seeton smiled in a manner she tried to make both courteous and noncommittal, but carefully said nothing. Jamesina, on the contrary, was in a mood to talk.

"A fearful thing, a host can be, and dangerous if you've not sense enough to coddle yourself when needful. Why, my own cousin Morag took to her bed and died of it four winters since, and Dr. Beltie saying he was aye minded to put a tape recorder beside her where she lay, as a warning to others. Coughing to tumble the rafters, she was, with a gey moose web in her throat, all on account of she'd a daft notion to gang out in the rain after her cat, and never a thought of boots, of course, or a hat, or an umbrella." She regarded Miss Seeton's brolly and sensible shoes with an air of approval, then sighed. "And she only eighty-two years old . . . Puir silly Morag." She shook her head over the tragedy of her cousin's coughing death, and Miss Seeton, at last making sense of what she'd heard, hurried to assure Mrs. Pictarnitie of the watchful eye she herself always kept upon the weather, and promised that, should she be so unfortunate as to catch a cough, she would retire at once to her bed and not leave it until she had recovered.

Her ear, she decided as she drifted about the little shop examining the various displays, was becoming attuned to the accent. So much richer, if that was the word, than that of the earl or his wife, who, after all, spent much of their time in London, whereas the genuine — no, that wasn't right, but she couldn't think what was — the *full-time*, perhaps, or might one say *local* inhabitants — though even this suggested that the Glenclachans weren't, which of course they were, as anyone would know as soon as they remembered the village had the same name . . .

At this point Miss Seeton arrived in front of a shelf of assorted books and halted thankfully in front of it to peruse the titles.

Mrs. Pictarnitie, whose comfortable chatter had accompanied her customer's perambulations without, or so it seemed, any great expectation of being answered, said at once, "Now, if you're by way of being a reader, there's one or two items on yon shelf could be of interest to a lady like yourself. If you're interested in birds, for instance . . ."

"*Bird Life of the Glens*," cried Miss Seeton in delight, not meaning to interrupt, but thrilled by the discovery she had just made. She darted forward and took a small hard-back from the top of a neat pile, over which was balanced a hand-written notice announcing that the book was by a Local Author. "What a lucky find, and such a splendid memento of my visit to Glenclachan, although from what her ladyship has said I understand that there might be postcards I could buy, if it is to be considered a . . . a tourist attraction, instead of trying to sketch it, which I had thought of doing —

until I realised it was rather too high for comfort, that is."

It was Jamesina's turn to puzzle, but not for long. She laughed. "Yon doitered weather cock, of course! Dougall McLintie's aye been a rare one for the drink, though mebbe for once Glenclachan will reap the benefit of his mistakes — and it's enough of them he's made, over the years, on account of his liking for the whisky, not a soul in the village would deny. But I've no postcards for you today, hen. They've been ordered, though, for Glenclachan himself saw to the taking of the photographs, and sent them away to be printed. He'll mebbe know when I'm to expect them in the shop. You could always ask him yourself, if you're in a hurry."

Miss Seeton said that she wasn't, and wouldn't, in any case, wish to disturb his lordship when he was so busy. She would purchase *Bird Life of the Glens*, which would be a fine addition to the small library of natural history books which she was gradually acquiring at home, in Kent. Which reminded her — Jamesina had no chance to ask why — of her original purpose in entering Mrs. Pictarnitie's shop. She was looking for a magazine with a cryptic crossword somewhere among its pages . . .

By the time Miss Seeton had, with the permission of Mrs. Pictarnitie, leafed through the pages of every likely-looking periodical on her shelves in search of a Jack Crabbe Special, it was raining harder than ever, as fearsome lashings against the shop's plate glass bore witness. Jamesina prophesied thunder and warned her new friend not to venture outside with her umbrella up, for fear of attracting a bolt of lightning. Miss Seeton explained that the shaft of her brolly was of gold, not steel, so that she must suppose herself to be safe. And, since she feared to trespass for too long upon Mrs. Pictarnitie's good nature . . .

Jamesina scoffed at this, and once more urged Miss Seeton to bide in the dry. Was this not an excellent chance for a good crack, with the rain pelting down and nobody else for either of them to talk to? Miss Seeton, never one to gossip, murmured something noncommittal and once more gazed out of the window. Surely the rain was not quite so heavy, the clouds a little less dark? She ventured to say so to Mrs. Pictarnitie, and reiterated her reluctance to take advantage of anyone's kindness, grateful though she was . . .

She was almost ready to tear herself away from the press of hospitality, and was by the door, fumbling with the catch of her umbrella, when a shadow — large and round and bright of hue — appeared on the other side of the frosted glass. Miss Seeton's artist's eye at once recognised this polychromatic manifestation, and she stepped back to allow its owner to enter.

Shaking her tartan brolly briskly, not worrying whither the raindrops flew, a tall, well-built woman strode into the news-agent's and greeted Jamesina cheerfully. Mrs. Pictarnitie returned the greeting, then called to Miss Seeton:

"Now, isn't this the very chance you'd have been sorry to miss, if you'd gone out in the rain as you wanted! Have you not just bought her book for yourself? And I'm thinking Miss Beigg'll be pleased to sign it for you, should you make the request of her. Staying," she interpolated to the new-comer, "up at the castle, so she is. This is Miss Seeton," with a meaningful look, adding, before Miss Seeton could start blushing once more, "and she's interested in birds, or else why did she just now buy a copy of yon book?" And Miss Seeton glanced with pleasure from the brown-paper parcel in her hand to the pile of *Bird Life of the Glens* beneath its Local Author notice.

It was now the author's turn to blush, as she introduced herself and shook Miss Seeton by the hand. "Philomena Beigg — my father's idea of a joke. He was an expert on Gaelic history and language — but I have to admit it looks good on a book jacket, wouldn't you agree?"

Miss Seeton agreed, but with a hint of query in her tone which made Miss Beigg smile. "Of course, to a Sassenach it doesn't have the same ring to it, I know. You must understand, Miss Seeton, that, after the Forty-Five rebellion, Highland dress — the *feileadh mor,* or big kilt — you'd call it a belted plaid, in English — was banned by the government in Westminster until 1782. Anyone who persisted in wearing it was sent to the colonies, with the result that, by the time the ban was lifted, the big kilt was nothing more than a memory. So the Highlanders — not the Scots in general, not yet — wore the *feileadh beg,* or little kilt, instead. Hence," with a wry smile, "Philly Beigg, at your service."

Miss Seeton responded to the twinkle in Philomena's eyes with a twinkle of her own, and a murmur that it was all most

151

interesting. She recalled having learned something of the history of the Highlands during her school days, and had been told more, of course, by her hosts. She favoured Philomena with a look of alert inquiry, to which Philomena was glad to respond.

"Unfortunately for me, Miss Seeton, there's a school of thought which credits the invention of the fillibeg, worn by Scots with such pride, to a Sassenach! A Mr. Rawlinson was the manager of a Lochaber iron-smelting works in seventeen twenty-something. The story goes that he adapted the fillimore, the Highland dress worn by his workers, so that they could work more easily. Very hot and uncomfortable, I've no doubt the full gear must have been — though another theory says that the kilt as we know it nowadays was invented *after* the Forty-Five, as a uniform for the High-landers who enlisted as soldiers to keep their rebellious brethren in some sort of order. Either way," she concluded, with a chuckle, "it was a regular pest of a name for me at school, even if I've managed to come to terms with my poor father's terrible sense of humour since then."

She nodded towards Miss Seeton's parcel. "If you're interested in birds — or in books — you might like to see my library. Come home with me now for a cup of coffee and a bun — I generally have something around this time of day, and I'd welcome the company," she added, above Miss Seeton's modest demur. "No, I assure you, the pleasure would be all mine. Why else do you suppose I would have ventured out in the rain, if not for the chance to be among my fellows? Writing is a solitary business, Miss Seeton. You'd be doing me a kindness to spare me just half an hour of your time."

Miss Beigg might well be solitary, but she was certainly silver-tongued. Within ten minutes, having pattered through the now gentle rain beside her tall new acquaintance, Miss Seeton was sitting in Philomena's neat little kitchen while her hostess boiled the kettle and made hot buttered toast — a treat, Philomena had decided after two umbrellas had been set to drain in the sink, to be followed (if they had room) by home-made shortcake, because she'd tried out a new recipe and would value her visitor's opinion.

Miss Seeton munched happily, drank coffee, and in reply to her hostess's courteous questions spoke of her life in Plummergen, and how kind the Glenclachans — or should she say the MacSporrans — had been to her, a virtual stranger, when there was really no particular reason why they should be. Highland hospitality was everything she had been led to believe it was.

"It always has been, Miss Seeton. Eat a man's salt, and stay beneath his roof, and you're his friend, or at least it won't be him that's to blame if you're not. Though people in times past have taken sore advantage of the obligation to think no ill towards a guest — oh, I'm so sorry." Philomena grimaced. "My latest book — my author's copies arrived this morning, and I'm afraid I'm quoting — I simply had to share it with someone, you understand . . ."

Miss Seeton murmured that she had never written a book in her life, but as an artist — of very limited ability, she hastened to explain with a blush — she could, she thought, understand something of the creative urge. Had someone not once referred to it as divine discontent? Speaking for herself, she could never say that she was completely satisfied with a painting or a sketch, but, when forced to be realistic, one had to acknowledge that there came a time beyond which mere tin-

154

kering with one's work would no longer suffice, and it had to stand or fall on its own merits, under the critical eye of those with whom one planned to share it — the experience, that was to say, which had been captured on paper, whether by writing or by drawing. For was that not the important part about any creative impulse — to have shared it with others? The experience which prompted that impulse, she meant. Or so — and she blushed again — she thought; no doubt Miss Beigg had her own views?

"In my case," said Philomena, topping up the coffee cups without waiting to be asked, "it was my editor who was the discontented one, not me, though I certainly know exactly what you mean about tinkering. I'd been so foolish as to promise the manuscript for March of last year, and when I failed to deliver she wasn't very pleased. It was in the catalogue, for one thing. But I made an all-out effort, and sent it off in June — and so now you must come and see the result," she said, jumping to her feet and beckoning Miss Seeton through into the dining room. "On the table — my first published work of fiction — isn't it splendid?"

Miss Seeton moved closer to the table in

response to the thrill in Philomena's voice. She picked up the topmost book of the little pile and read the title aloud. "*Grey Stone of the Glen* — a Scottish story, no doubt."

"The Massacre of Glencoe retold for the umpteenth time, but none the worse for that, I hope," said Philomena, taking the book from Miss Seeton's hands and trying not to look too pleased at the result of her long labours. "That age-old feuding between Campbells and MacDonalds — nobody knows when it began, but it continues to this day, I assure you. Glencoe was one of the most dramatic episodes in the past, however, which is why I feel the tale deserves retelling once in a while. Do you" — she fixed Miss Seeton with a bright, burning gaze — "know about the massacre?" But, before her startled guest could reply, she went on: "And to think that Ewen Campbell and Malcolm Mac-Donald ever thought they could be friends!"

Chapter

12

Miss Seeton, the perfect guest, murmured to Miss Beigg that she would be most interested to learn more, and settled herself in an armchair by the fireplace as Philomena launched into her lecture.

"When King James the Seventh of Scotland and Second of England was deposed in 1688, he fled to France with his wife Mary of Modena and their infant son James, who was to become the Old Pretender; and, though the English may have accepted as king his nephew and son-in-law Dutch William, who'd taken his place, many folk in the Highlands refused to acknowledge William's right to rule. But Scots have always been canny! They'd drink loyalty to the King loudly enough — but they'd hold their glasses over a bowl of water as they made their pledge, so that everyone knew the real king they toasted was James, away across the English Channel in safety."

As memory stirred, Miss Seeton nodded. "The King Over the Water — and the Little Gentleman in Black Velvet, of course," she added, with a twinkle. Philomena nodded.

"True enough, though the mole whose hill tumbled William's horse wasn't to play his part in history for some years after the Massacre of Glencoe. William and his wife Mary, James's daughter, weren't as sure of their claim on James's throne as they would like to have been: they insisted that the clans must swear an oath of allegiance, and gave them until the New Year to do it — but MacDonald of Glencoe waited until the very last minute before setting out to swear, because he'd wanted to ease his conscience by explaining to the Stuarts that it was to be for expediency he swore this oath, that he was as loyal to the true king as ever."

"A promise made under duress is not binding," mused Miss Seeton, wondering where in the world she could have heard or read this principle before. Philomena's eyes glittered.

"And so MacIan — the chief of the MacDonalds — thought! But he finally accepted that the oath must be sworn, for the good of his people — only, he encountered bad weather on the way, and any number of delays as he tried to reach the right official, and he arrived over a week late, though he was told this wouldn't be held against him. So he rode home to Glencoe believing no harm would come to the MacDonalds . . .

"And he still believed it, for he thought the assurances of the government as binding as his own word, when soldiers under the command of Robert Campbell of Glenlyon arrived in the glen at the beginning of February, asking for shelter." Philomena's tone intensified. "To a Highlander, Miss Seeton — you knew it yourself — a guest's place is privileged. Or, as some might say, a sacred trust — the trust even of an old enemy that so long as he remains on your land as your guest, you will do him no harm. The Campbells and the MacDonalds had been enemies for generations, but for ten days the Campbells stayed on MacDonald land, sharing the food and the fire and the roofs of the clansmen — who offered them gladly, as they were duty, and honour, bound to do. But others were not so honourable . . ."

Miss Seeton knew what was coming, yet Miss Beigg's voice and the words it uttered were so compelling that she felt an uncomfortable chill between her shoulder blades, and part of her wanted to put her fingers to her ears to block out the rest of Philomena's story as if, in some strange way, this would deny it its place in history.

"On February the thirteenth, 1692, the Campbells rose in the middle of the night to slaughter in cold blood thirty-eight men, women, and children of Clan MacDonald. MacIan was pistolled to death in his bedroom, butchered without warning; his wife was stripped naked, and the flesh bitten from her fingers by beasts in men's shape seeking to steal her rings. Government orders had been to wipe out the entire clan, as a warning to others . . ."

"Admiral Byng," murmured Miss Seeton, as Miss Beigg drew breath at the sheer horror of her own narration. "No, not that, perhaps — *pour encourager les autres* — but how very, very dreadful — when they had been shown such a great deal of kindness . . ."

Philomena was so rapt in her story that she plunged on to its conclusion without pausing to wonder whether it might be upsetting for her guest. A teller of tales wants to move the hearts and minds of those who listen, and it was clear, from her remarks, that Miss Seeton had indeed been moved. Miss Beigg's torrent of horrified indignation swept onwards.

"Those MacDonalds who had escaped the massacre fled into the mountains — but it was February, and the snow was deep. Another forty people perished during the flight across the mountains to safety — but the clan survived, and Glencoe has become a bitter memory, the Glen of Weeping for all who bear the name of MacDonald. To this day there are MacDonalds who would trust the devil himself before a Campbell, and who can blame them — and yet, Miss Seeton" — Philomena recollected herself with an effort — "even a tragedy like this may have its hopeful side. The soldiers had their orders to wipe out the entire clan, but they only killed directly thirty-eight people: over a hundred MacDonalds survived. It was rumoured there had been a warning given — given by a soldier — by a soldier, some said, who bore the Campbell name. He was duty bound not to betray even a treacherous government by speaking his warning directly, but he took aside a child of the clan to hear him address one of the boulders near his home.

" 'Grey stone of the glen,' " quoted Philomena in her most solemn tones,

" 'great is your right to be here. But if you only knew what was to happen this night. you would be up and away.' That, Miss Seeton, is what the soldier is supposed to have said, and he insisted the child should repeat these words to his father, and so, not all the MacDonalds died."

As she finished, there was a silence Miss Seeton knew it would be impossible to break for a while. She shivered, and Philomena's eyes lost their dark, brooding look at once.

"I've made you uneasy, Miss Seeton. I can't say I never meant to, because story-telling's in my blood. If I apologised for being good at it I'd be a hypocrite. But, as recompense, do let me sign a copy of my book for you — though you'd better not read it until you're safely home in Kent!"

Miss Seeton's modesty was once again ignored as she made an attempt to protest that, really, such generosity was not necessary. Philomena opened *Grey Stone of the Glen* to its title page, enquired of her guest what her full name might be, and inscribed the book "To Emily Dorothea Seeton, in memory of emotions (and coffee) stirred by the Author," then signed it with a flourish, followed by the date. She jumped to her feet. "We'll have another cup," she decided, without asking Miss Seeton's wishes. "To warm your curdled blood," she added. "Anybody dealing with Campbells has need of a strong stomach, believe me . . ."

And, as Miss Seeton followed her back into the kitchen, Miss Beigg narrated with relish an earlier tale of black treachery shown by Campbell to MacDonald, during the English Civil War, when the Campbells, supporting Cromwell, besieged the Royalist MacDonalds in Dunaverty Castle. For six weeks the MacDonalds resisted, until thirst drove them outside, to certain death. One young mother was offered amnesty if she would climb a cliff with her baby tied to her back, and she climbed, ninety feet upwards to the summit, until her hands reached out to safety — and a waiting Campbell officer hacked them both off with his sword, so that she fell, with her child, to death on the rocks below.

"And they named it the Cliff of the Falling Woman," said Philomena, above the cheerful song of the kettle; she seemed quite oblivious to the strange contrast of moods. "The next day, as the victors marched away, the Campbell's horse bolted with him. He fell from the saddle with his foot caught in the stirrup, so that

he was dragged screaming over the ground
. . . but not a soul bestirred themselves to
save him. They stood watching until it was
all over, and said not a single word."

"Oh," said Miss Seeton. She knew it was
inadequate, but — though some remark
was clearly called for — what else was
there to say? So much violence, so much
bitterness, but . . .

"But surely," she managed to bring out
at last, as Miss Beigg spooned coffee into
cups and poured boiling water, "it was all a
long time ago, was it not? For which we
should be thankful," she found herself
adding, with another shudder.

Philomena gave her a strange look, and
rubbed the tip of her nose. "You're staying
at the castle, of course, and they've been
away until recently — I don't suppose anyone's had time to mention it yet. But let
me assure you, Miss Seeton, that the
feuding between Campbell and Mac-
Donald is nowhere near over, in this part
of the Highlands at any rate. Not that they
were sworn enemies to begin with — far
from it, indeed. Ewen and Malcolm went
to school together, and were put to sharing
the same desk by a dominie with a warped
sense of humour — but despite that daft
schoolmaster, from the first they were like

David and Jonathan. Boys and young lads and then grown men together, never a cross word spoken, in defiance of every tale they'd ever heard told. Why, the two of them went into partnership, and still there was nothing amiss between them, though everyone said it couldn't last, that it was unnatural . . . And now everyone has been proved right, more's the pity."

Philomena sipped her coffee, and shook her head. "I was told, a long time ago, never to do business with my friends or relations, and there are far worse principles than that in life, believe me. Better to give money outright, and be glad and surprised at its return, than lend it and feel hard done by when you lose interest on the loan — not that they lent each other money. Fishing for pearls doesn't need any great financial outlay."

She went on to tell Miss Seeton much of what Mel Forby had learned from Hamish McQueest in the bar of the Pock and Tang. "Freshwater pearls are in great demand, you know, and have been for centuries. Mary Queen of Scots, for instance, wore a necklace of Scottish pearls before she was executed. It's kept at Arundel Castle — I saw it when I was researching a book about the Casket Letters — though that's by the by, as the book's not due out for six months yet." She accepted Miss Seeton's congratulations in the spirit in which they were quickly offered, then cleared her throat. "Well, Ewen and Malcolm didn't make their fortunes at the fishing, but they earned enough to live on and to spare — they'd said right from the start that everything they found would be shared equally, which it was, and the pair of them were perfectly happy with that arrangement for years . . . until one day they found one particular crook. Which, Miss Seeton, meant trouble."

Philomena sighed. Miss Seeton's sorrowful look mirrored her hostess's gloom. "When friends fall out, Miss Beigg, it must surely be one of the saddest things . . . and, though I have had little to do with what one might call the criminal classes, I believe I understand . . ."

Miss Seeton, in her own eyes and in the eyes of all when they first make her acquaintance, is a gentlewoman; gentlewomen do not have adventures, or consort with crooks: Miss Seeton, therefore, remains forever convinced that she has had *little to do with what one might call the criminal classes.*

There are those who would disagree with her.

Philomena Beigg was not one of them. She took the words of her guest at their face value, and smiled. "Oh dear, I'm sorry, Miss Seeton, but there's more than one sort of crook, and I don't just mean what shepherds use. But I must apologise for confusing you with a technicality. Pearl fishers call a 'crook' any mussel with its shell twisted to one side instead of straight — the sort of deformity which, for some reason, seems to increase the chances there could be a pearl inside. It may not be a good one, though. It could have formed too near the edge and be brown, or black: dark pearls are worthless." Her voice began once more to sound as if it was quoting. "The colours to look for are blue-white, or heather-purple, or soft pink, or cream, or silver, or grey, and, when you find one, the bigger the better, of course." She chuckled. "You might guess I researched my book pretty thoroughly, Miss Seeton! And, when all the bother between Ewen Campbell and Malcolm MacDonald started up the other day, I went back to my notes to refresh my memory."

"It is," said Miss Seeton, politely, "most interesting, indeed. Do, please, continue."

Philomena would probably have done so in any case, being intent on her tale, but she smiled absently at Miss Seeton before clearing her throat again. "Malcolm found the crook, and opened it far enough to peek inside, but not too far and kill it. He saw it had a pearl just by the edge — a brown one, more another part of the shell than a semiprecious stone. So he was all set to score it with his knife as a sign he'd already checked it, and put it back for breeding stock the way they always did, when Ewen said he'd a new theory that, given time, a brown pearl might turn white, and he'd like to take the mussel home to set in the stream near his house, and check on it in the years to come. Which Malcolm said was fair enough . . ."

Miss Seeton, whose knowledge of such matters as breeding stocks and depletion of species had been greatly increased by her friendship with Babs Ongar of Wounded Wings, nodded. "One has," she remarked, "a duty to preserve for future generations the pleasures we ourselves have enjoyed."

"And Malcolm MacDonald would have agreed with you, up to one week after the day he handed over his find to Ewen Campbell in all good faith — when he

168

learned that Ewen had never taken that mussel anywhere near a stream, but had opened it right up instead, and found a *second* pearl, buried in a sac well away from the crooked edge, under the meat. And a perfect specimen, what's more: salmon-pink, absolutely round, and weighing almost forty grains. The largest freshwater pearl ever found, Miss Seeton, only weighed forty-four and a quarter grains — a man called Abernethy, about six years ago — and it's worth thousands. Malcolm can't think how he came to miss this one, and now he's furious with Ewen for cheating him, because, instead of sharing the profits as usual, Ewen is claiming that, as Malcolm gave him the mussel as he was about to throw it away, he also gave away any right to a share in the profit of finding it — and in the glory of the find, which is almost worse . . .

"So you see what I mean, Miss Seeton. Everyone's saying Malcolm MacDonald could expect nothing less from a Campbell — because history always repeats itself . . ."

Chapter

13

"I suppose," remarked Miss Seeton, as Philomena paused, "one might say that it does, unfortunately." She sighed. "Poor Mr. MacDonald, having his friend behave in so — so dishonourable, I fear, must be the word — so dishonourable a fashion. It seems to me, Miss Beigg, that the advice you were given was extremely wise. Politics," she said, with another sigh. "Politics, and religion — and money, of course . . ."

The three subjects a gentlewoman learned from birth were likely to cause controversy. Philomena grimaced. "It's not so much dishonourable as inevitable, I suppose, speaking as an historian. Friendship between a Campbell and a MacDonald will never prosper, Miss Seeton — too much has happened over too many years, and the Campbells seem unable to live their bad name completely down. And now Malcolm's gone from one extreme to the other. Instead of being Ewen Campbell's best friend who trusted him completely, he insists he wants a proper accounting of every single pearl they've ever found, and he's hinting this isn't the first time Ewen's cheated him, just because the man drives a smarter car and lives in a bigger house — which is plain foolish. Ewen's wife's father left her ninety thousand pounds, as everyone knew full well at the time. Malcolm has no logical reason to be suspicious, only a bee in his bonnet over everything to do with the man, and he'll bear a grudge as easily as swear a friendship. He's a hot-tempered one, Malcolm MacDonald. Every time he goes to the mussel beds now, he takes a shotgun with him — which is ridiculous — and says if he sees so much as the tip of Ewen Campbell's nose peeking over the crest of a hill, he'll blow him to pieces. Which is worrying, because he just might."

"Surely not. The heat of the moment, no doubt," suggested Miss Seeton, "and Mr. MacDonald's — understandable, one must agree — disappointment over the way his friend treated him. It would be only natural to expect the language of a disappointed man to be a little . . . intemperate, in the circumstances, but one can hardly suppose him to mean it."

Philomena shrugged. "I wouldn't care to bet on that! Ewen's taking care to keep well out of Malcolm's way right now, which isn't too hard, because he's having to go farther afield to look for new pearl beds, as he's running the risk of being shot by going near the old ones he and Malcolm used to share. The hills round Glenclachan are lonely, Miss Seeton — no hikers, no campers, because there's nothing much, apart from scenery, to see — and the maps aren't as detailed as they might be. Ewen stands a fair chance of finding new beds, though he'll have to travel in odd places to find them." She chuckled. "Who knows? He could be lucky enough to find the gold mine that's been rumoured in these parts for centuries, though nobody knows exactly where it might be. I like to imagine the pearls of Mary Stuart's necklace are set in Glenclachan gold — a fanciful idea, no doubt, but there's a romantic streak in every Highlander. Why else" — her eyes twinkled — "did my father insist on giving me such a name?"

When Miss Seeton finally left Philomena's cottage, the sky was clear, the sun was high, and steam rose slowly from the pavements, after the storm. In one hand she carried her umbrella, in the other her handbag, while, tucked under one arm, she proudly carried the brown-paper parcel containing her inscribed copies of Philomena's two books. Miss Seeton had never had even one book signed for her by its author, and looked forward to reading these. Miss Beigg knew how to weave a powerful spell with her words: the shivers still ran up and down Miss Seeton's spine as she remembered her hostess's description of the Massacre of Glencoe, and the bleak horror of the Tale of the Falling Woman. The shivers reached down to the tips of Miss Seeton's fingers, and made them itch to capture on paper the images conjured up by the tales she had heard: if only — and she sighed — her talent could be as equal to the task as Miss Beigg's own talent demanded! But one could only do one's best, no more than that: everyone had different talents, differing even — her sigh this time was deeper — in intensity. Her own small ability to sketch, Miss Beigg's undoubtedly great narrative skill, Mel Forby's skill in writing well at quite another length, for a journalist and an author must surely approach their work in very different ways . . .

"Which reminds me," murmured Miss

Seeton, as, heading back to the castle, she once more passed the houses on the outskirts of Glenclachan, having walked the full length of the main street from Philomena's cottage. "She said she was planning to stay in the village, but I have not seen dear Mel this morning. I wonder where she is."

Where Mel was was in bed, with a wet towel wrapped about her head and the curtains drawn against the light.

Light in the Highlands is generally thought to be kind: soft upon heather moors, glimmering sweetly from lochs and burns, mellow where it filters through pine-tree branches to plant its pale brown kiss on the sleepy earth below . . .

People who believe this have never spent several hours in the bar of a Highland hotel drinking double Lairigighs with the landlord and listening to the story of his life, as Mel Forby had done the previous night. And what a night it had been! She thought. At least, she would have thought, if only she'd had sufficient energy for thinking. Right now, all she wanted to do was hibernate until the Lairigigh, and its peculiar effect upon her memory, wore off.

It had taken longer than Mel had

expected for the drinkers in the bar to relax, and longer for Mel herself to stop feeling like the albino blackbird who'd seemed so at risk of being mobbed by everyone else. Wrapped in a white sheet . . .

Nobody had made any further reference to her shroud, or if they had, she hadn't heard them; and she'd managed to find no easy way of introducing the topic of winding sheets into the general conversation to warn everyone she'd caught that earlier remark, and wasn't worried by it. Much. But it niggled her not to know what it might be the natives supposed she was doing in Glenclachan that made them want to stop her doing it — she might be sitting on top of the scoop of the century, if only they could be persuaded to unbutton. But it wasn't just professional curiosity that made her want to know. She had, after all, a personal interest in whether or not she was bumped off.

Or did she mean wiped out? Mel opened her eyes, moaned, gazed vacantly in the general direction of the window, and closed them again, thankful that Thrudd Banner was not there to witness her weakness. Amelita Forby, Fleet Street's own Leather Liver, hung over in the Highlands and now not sure that being wiped out wouldn't have been a better idea. At least she wouldn't have gone on feeling so grim. Toasting forks and flames didn't, as far as she knew, go up and down in such an uncomfortable way — or from side to side at the same time, either. What sadist had climbed up to hide in the rafters to ring those damned bells at her? And who in the world was playing bagpipes underneath her pillow?

Bagpipes. "It's the ghost of James Reid," groaned Mel, recalling last night's talk in the bar, and how the piper might well wish to be revenged upon a Sassenach . . .

The man who had come looking for John Stuart Fraser had taken one of the corner seats and sat nursing a single malt with an expression Mel couldn't quite recognise on his face. Gloom, mingled with gratification, was the nearest she could come to describing it — which seemed to make little sense; but the chatter of Hamish McQueest as he poured more whisky and attempted to make his guest feel at home meant she was unable to concentrate on analysing it properly. Mel sipped at her second double Lairigigh and pondered, while conversation, muted for a moment at the stranger's entrance, began to build up once more.

She caught snippets which made her wish she'd read more Scottish history before coming to the Highlands. ". . . never claimed the reward — and thirty thousand pounds was a tidy sum of money in those days!"

"Aye, they couldnae find a single soul to betray Bonnie Prince Charlie, the English with their treachery and bribes. The clans were too loyal to the House of Stuart to fall for such blandishments."

"Six months in concealment, with soldiers by the hunnert on the watch for him, and safe away to France at the end of it all, still cocking a snook at the usurper. He'd a bonnie fighting spirit, the Young Pretender."

"Oh, but he had the English on the run," someone gloated. "Lord George Murray and the rest of his fine generals forced him to retreat. If he'd only pressed on with his attack on London —"

"Panic in the streets, and the usurper on the point of fleeing back to Hanover, and the Bank of England running out of money — aye, it was a sad day indeed when they talked him into marching north again."

"December the sixth, 1745," someone said, and sighed, and shook his head. "Black Friday."

"After the glorious start at Glenfinnan," sighed someone else. "His standard unfurled by the Duke of Atholl, blessed by the Bishop of Morar — and the clans flocking from miles about to join him. August the nineteenth, when the House of Stuart reclaimed its rightful own. Glenfinnan Day . . ."

Mel jumped: five days' time! She'd never heard of Glenfinnan Day, but clearly it was a date of some importance, in these parts at least. Almost everyone in the bar raised his glass in a toast, casting defiant looks in her direction, though Hamish McQueest, presumably with due deference to her status as his guest, did not.

"We'll no forget," promised someone, as the drained glasses were set down, and people began looking to see who would buy the next round. "The House of Stuart still lives on, even in exile — aye, but who's to know what time might bring about?"

"Time will tell, true enough." Heads were nodded sagely, and Hamish grinned at Mel as she perched on her stool, her ears flapping. He cleared his throat.

"The House of Stuart may be all very well," he remarked, as everyone turned towards him at the sound. "But it's not what you'd call a sacred cause now — if, indeed, it ever was — which I take leave to doubt. You only have to think of the Chisholms, with their clan chief making sure to have a son on either side of the fight, so that no matter which king was on the throne, the Chisholms wouldn't lose. Where is the sanctity in a cause like that?"

"Ye cannae judge a cause by just one man," flashed somebody in deep indignation. "There are aye folk who'll make expediency their guide, instead of loyalty and honour . . ."

"Honour there was, and to spare," somebody else pointed out. "Thirty thousand pounds' worth, remember!"

"Flora MacDonald!" cried someone, banging on the table to the accompaniment of cheers and cries of "Aye, Malcolm, that's true!" The whisky must have primed Mel's memory, for she recalled almost at once school stories of how the Bonnie Prince had been disguised as Flora's maid for his escape over the sea to Skye. She wasn't going to cheer, though.

Neither was Hamish. He pulled a face: perhaps he didn't approve of men in drag. But when dark looks were cast at him, and people seemed ready to leave rather than fill their glasses again at his bar, he conceded that yes, it had been a stirring time, and Flora MacDonald certainly deserved the name of heroine.

"Although," he added aside to Mel, under the cover of much bustling as people came up to order fresh drinks, "what you're never told is that Flora, with her husband and sons, went to America and fought *against* the Yankee rebels *for* the Hanoverian side — the same Hanoverians whose claim to the throne had been the whole reason for this fine Highland rebellion thirty years earlier . . ."

The bustle was insufficiently loud: fresh looks of disapproval were directed against Hamish as he accepted payment for the last of the refills. It occurred to Mel that the landlord had an excellent sense of timing.

"Loyalty and honour," proclaimed one of the drinkers, in resounding tones. "Thirty thousand pounds!"

"Yes," said Hamish, "to our shame" — with an apologetic look at Mel — "the clansmen knew how well they could trust the empty promises of the English. We have to assume they'd never have seen a penny of that money, even if they *had* told the soldiers where the prince might be hiding —"

"Which they'd never have done in any event," retorted Malcolm, supporter of Flora MacDonald, amid further cheers. "It was a matter of pride for the lawful prince to be protected by his people —"

"Even to the death!" said somebody with a flushed face, and a glass that was yet again empty.

"Like poor James Reid," agreed Hamish. "An unlucky lad, there's no denying."

"And that's the English for you," crowed another Scot, a gleam in his eye and his glass in his hand. "A toast to the puir piper, murdered at York!"

Under (partial) cover of the subsequent hubbub, Hamish informed Mel that the said James Reid had been a piper in the regiment raised by Lord Ogilvy for the Young Pretender's support, captured at Carlisle, and who used as his defence the plea that he'd been coerced into joining the rebellion. (At which point, Mel reckoned Hamish's chances of having anyone buy another round that night had reached rock bottom. She wondered through the whisky fumes how the man ever made any profit at all.) The plea, reported the landlord with great relish, was refused on the grounds that, as the clans never went into battle without a piper, James Reid's bagpipes must count, in the eyes of the law, as an instrument of war.

"Executed at York, poor man," concluded Hamish, to general mutterings and the sound of shifting feet. They'd be away back to their homes any minute, Mel decided, then heard herself giggle quietly at the infectious nature of the Highland brogue, even in her thoughts. How much Lairigigh had she drunk, without realising it?

She tried to sit up straight on the bar stool. Had the landlord plied her with whisky on purpose — to deflect her, on behalf of his clientele, from asking too many questions? "If only I knew about what," she murmured. The words echoed strangely in her head. Hamish looked a question at her, but she wouldn't repeat her suspicions to him, of all people, oh no. You didn't catch Amelita Forby out like that . . .

Nor was Mel so caught-out that she failed to remark how, at long last, everyone was indeed giving the appearance of being homeward bound. Malcolm MacDonald drained his glass, scowled at Hamish, and pushed back his chair without making any attempt to collect the empties and carry them to the bar. Hamish, with a wry grin, surveyed the other drinkers doing the same. Nobody said anything; Mel suspected she'd better not try, in case she fell off the stool. A pity that she'd never got around to checking the menu for something to eat . . .

The man who'd come looking for John Stuart Fraser was gathered up among a group of the most ardent neo-Jacobites as they hustled towards the door —

Which was suddenly flung open by a near-giant with red hair and a face almost as red, as, in a voice to bring the plaster down from the ceiling, he roared,

"So here's where you've been hiding yourself away, Malcolm MacDonald, and trouble enough I've had on your account! I'm after a word or two with you — and I'll not take no for an answer!"

Chapter

14

Even now, the memory of the red-haired man's fury made Mel Forby wince. His voice had been one of the few she'd ever heard which merited in truth the adjective stentorian: she could hear it still, reverberating round her skull as she closed her eyes and sank back on her pillow . . .

"I was speaking to you, Malcolm Mac-Donald," thundered the newcomer, taking two gigantic steps into the bar before finding his path blocked by a small group of drinkers, who'd moved there, Mel realised, faster than she would have expected, with all the whisky they must have drunk. Not that she had noticed this movement — just a blink and a shimmer, and there they were, surrounding that enormous angry presence on the threshold, trying to hold him back.

For how long they'd manage it was anybody's guess. This man wasn't just tall, and rather more than burly: he looked like someone who could toss two cabers at the same time and still break records when he did it. As he raised one huge forearm to brush aside the opposition, Mel heard the indrawn breath of Hamish McQueest beside her, presumably contemplating the damage his bar, not to mention his customers, would suffer if anyone started a fight.

"Steady on, Campbell," he said, in what must have been intended as a soothing tone. "There's no need for all this commotion. You're among friends here, you know, so —"

"There's one at least who's no friend to me," broke in Ewen, brushing the bodyguard from his arm and pointing with a massive forefinger in the direction of Malcolm MacDonald. "I see him plain enough, for all he's skulking behind those who'd keep him hid — and as it's him I've my quarrel with, Hamish McQueest, not yourself, I'll thank you to quiet your tongue and mind your business!"

Hamish opened his mouth to protest, but somebody else spoke first. "I'll not hear myself accused of skulking by anyone, Ewen Campbell!" Malcolm, standing among a group of friends, now pushed them aside, the better to face his accuser.

"You see full well that here I am — and doing my best to keep the peace, what's more, by paying no heed to your blethering. And it's all very fine to talk of trouble on my account! If anyone's had trouble brought upon him it's never you, but me, as well you know. I'm a rightful share of forty thousand pounds poorer, thanks to your crooked dealings —"

"And what about the trouble I've had myself?" Ewen took three steps forward, as if those who would keep him apart from Malcolm had been mere children. "How much farther away in the hills have I to go in my searching now, with you and your threats and your shotgun waiting for me by rivers I've fished since I was a boy? Fifteen miles I've walked around Glen Spurgie the day, and nothing to show for all the waters I've waded and the journey I took to reach them. A whole day wasted, when I've as much right as any other man to fish the mussel scaups of Glenclachan — so I'm here to give you a warning, Malcolm Mac-Donald, that I'll not waste the petrol money on you and your threats again. I'll be fishing round the old beds tomorrow, and there's nothing you can do that's like to stop me!"

"Oh, is there not?" Malcolm, stepping

forward, seemed to Mel now almost as large, and certainly as angry, as ever Ewen Campbell might be. He doubled his fists, and Ewen put up his own. With his red hair, red face, and the dangerous red gleam in his eye, he looked likely to do a considerable amount of damage to anyone who crossed him.

Hamish was not the only person who had suddenly turned stone cold sober. A chorus of warning, expostulation, and attempts at pacifying both would-be combatants arose at once from every corner of the bar — though the cries might have been no more than the distant buzzing of mosquitoes, so little notice of them did the two former friends take. Each began to forge purposefully through the crowd to reach his rival, and the crowd, in silent collusion, closed in again. With some judicious jostling, Malcolm was forced, muttering furiously, away from his target, while Ewen, whose language had grown violent as his forward intent was thwarted, found that the only route left him was the way back out through the door by which he'd entered.

On the threshold, he stopped dead, and glared round in turn at everyone in the bar. The slit-eyed stranger who'd asked for

John Stuart Fraser gulped as Ewen Campbell's gaze met his own, and said, to nobody in particular, that none of this meant anything to him, that he was merely a visitor . . . But Ewen's glance passed over him, lighting at last on Malcolm MacDonald on the opposite side of the room, in the midst of a press of protectors. His lip curled in a sneer.

"Aye, you're bold enough, MacDonald, when there's others to save your skin — but just remember it's a Campbell that you've crossed, and the Campbells never forget a wrong. You can bluster your fill, Malcolm MacDonald" — as Malcolm uttered a strangled reference to Glencoe — "but 'twill avail you nothing. I'm paying no further heed to your empty talk, and I'll not even trouble myself to challenge you to fight it out man to man. I tell you straight, you'd best keep your eyes open in the days to come, because there's to be fair shares at the fishing in future, and I've laid a claim to mine!"

After such a magnificent exit line, there was only one thing left for him to do. Ewen Campbell raked the room once more with his glittering eye, turned on his heel, and went out through the door, closing it behind him with a slam the memory of which, the next day, still brought a groan to Mel Forby's quavering lips.

Outside, a bird was singing. Inside, its bed-bound and captive audience winced. Sounded more like a pneumatic drill than a . . . than a whatever sort of bird it happened to be. Miss Seeton would recognise it at once, Mel reminded herself, or her friend Babs Ongar, of course —

Which memory made her straighten and struggle to sit up in bed. Babs Ongar — the Wounded Wings Bird Sanctuary — the young couple who'd brought the injured blackbird, who'd been such likely candidates for the kidnapping of Lady Marguerite MacSporran — Miss Seeton's sketches, and Mel's instinct that she would come up trumps again . . .

"Fresh air and black coffee." Mel announced this brisk prescription to her room with as much resolution as she was able to muster. "And the fresh air first, I guess. Better work up gradually to any sort of drink — ugh. Why do I have to use foul language like that?" She shuddered and swung her feet out of bed. She groaned again. "Serve you right, Forby. That reporter's nose of yours is going to lead you into big trouble, one day. But if you want to consult with Miss S., you need to be out and about, not skulking in your room. You're no Malcolm MacDonald — not," she brooded as she swayed across to the washbasin, and began splashing her face with cold water, "that I blame him for trying to avoid a punch-up with Ewen Campbell. They'd have made rather a nasty mess of each other if there hadn't been plenty of people around to stop them."

Despite herself, Mel giggled at the memory of Hamish's face as he brooded, presumably, on broken furniture and bits of glass flying in all directions. Then another memory made her groan again: the memory of how, after everyone had finally departed — Malcolm MacDonald delayed by his friends until last, surrounded by them as he lurched out in the wake of the slit-eyed man — the landlord had locked the outside door of the bar with a sigh of deep thankfulness and poured double Lairigighs for himself and his only guest without asking whether she wanted one or not.

Mel wished, now, she'd had sufficient strength of will to refuse his kind offer. Or — as memory prodded yet again — had the offer been so kind, in reality? Hadn't she wondered last night — and, in the cold light of day, didn't she wonder all the more — about the true nature of the landlord of the Pock and Tang?

"But if anyone knows how to get right to the heart of a person's true nature," mused Mel, through foaming peppermint as she scrubbed at fur-coated teeth, "it's good old Miss S., as always. I'll have to ask her along here before long, to take a look at Hamish McQueest. There's something about him that just doesn't seem to add up. He's enough of a local to give me chapter and verse on the juiciest scandals — though it was the least he could do, seeing as I had to listen to all that rumpus between Campbell and MacDonald — but nobody seems to like him very much." She frowned at her face in the mirror as she began to apply her makeup with a hand that lacked much of its usual steadiness and skill.

"He's only lived in the village a few years, of course. But why do I get the feeling that it's just as well there's only one pub in Glenclachan? He wouldn't have it all his own way if there was any opposition, I bet — he's hardly the most tactful landlord around. He scoffs at all the Jacobite history, which people seem to take very seriously in these parts — he says the pearl fishers are hardly better than dropouts, and he's got to be wrong about that . . ."

As Mel made her cautious way out of her room and down the stairs towards the main street, she daydreamed of pearl necklaces, and Thrudd Banner, and deep-sea divers and coral reefs, and the cold, hard reality of the life about which Hamish McQueest had waxed eloquent until the small hours, in the bar last night when everyone had gone. Although Hamish had seemed to pour scorn on the pearl fishers' chosen way of life, even he could not deny that it was hard, dangerous work. The physical effort of wading through fast-flowing streams, the risk of drowning, the icicles on a fisherman's beard clanking against the bucket and pulling him down when the melt water flowed from the ice fields, the daily despair when nothing was found, the loneliness of it all. Running away from the grown-up world, Hamish had concluded. Antisocial. Forever complaining when things didn't go their own way . . .

All of which had made Mel determined to write one of her Pieces on the pearl fishers of the Highlands, if only out of sheer annoyance at Hamish's attitude. And what about her feeling that the Jacobite angle was worth pursuing? Hamish might have told her it wasn't — but what did he know?

"What, indeed," muttered Mel, as she pushed open the door of the Pock and Tang and emerged into — ugh — the sunlight. She closed her eyes, whimpered once, then steeled herself with thoughts of Thrudd, and the editor of the *Daily Negative*, and plunged down the front steps into the street. She landed heavily on her weak ankle, jarring it. Ugh, yet again. But forge on, Forby — you're here to get yourself a story. You may have to hop on one foot to get it — so, hop. Because you're going to get it. Or them. Because you just happened to be right on the spot . . .

Mel woke from her trance to find herself several hundred feet along from the hotel's front door, and on the opposite side of the road. Evidently her subconscious had taken her across out of the sunlight and into the shade. Top marks to Freud, or whoever. She was starting to feel slightly less fragile now. Was there anywhere in this burg she might find herself a decent cup of strong, hot coffee?

She glanced over at the clock on the tower of what she guessed must be the church — kirk, she supposed she ought to call it. There was an awful lot of bright blue sky behind that stern grey edifice, and too many dazzling white clouds for comfort. Her eyes narrowed in a squint. Could that be the proper time? She double-checked it with her watch; even moving her wrist made her flinch, never mind having to focus so close. Well, so she'd missed breakfast — lunch, too, unless she hurried, which she didn't feel like doing, so —

"Why, good gracious." A voice she recognised addressed her from behind. "What a coincidence, Mel dear — I was only just now thinking of you. How very nice to see you again."

Slowly, Mel turned to greet Miss Seeton, whose smile and cockscomb hat she would have known anywhere, and whose umbrella she felt like welcoming as a saviour. How to persuade Miss S. to use it as a parasol, that was the only problem . . .

Miss Seeton's smile turned to an anxious frown. "You do not, if you will excuse my saying so, seem altogether in the best of spirits this morning, Mel dear, although perhaps we should rather call it this afternoon. One tends not to notice the passage of time when one is enjoying oneself, and I have just spent the most interesting — oh.

Mel, what is the matter?"

For poor Mel, at Miss Seeton's mention of *spirits*, had felt herself slowly, inexorably start to turn green from the inside out — and the greenness had now become all too apparent to Miss Seeton's concerned, artistic eye. Change her costume and gender, pose her on a couch, and Mel could have modelled for Wallis's *Death of Chatterton*. Miss Seeton, so sympathetic when any of the children in her class fell ill — as opposed, of course, to those who merely malingered — said firmly,

"You should be in bed, my dear. Perhaps you have taken a touch of the sun — or, as there was a heavy storm earlier, you may have caught a chill. If you were out in it, that is to say, but of course you should not be now, until you are feeling better. Out, I mean. Let me help you home . . ."

Mel swallowed once or twice, gave up the unequal struggle, and consented to accept Miss Seeton's escort back over the road to the hotel. She felt more than a little foolish, especially when Miss Seeton, clucking her tongue, opened her umbrella and held it high above Mel's supposedly sunstruck head. But with the brown-paper parcel of books tucked under her spare arm, and her handbag swinging comfortably from its crook, Miss Seeton was happily confident that she had coped to the best of her ability, in the circumstances. She would see dear Mel safely to her room, then ask the manager if she might carry up a tray of tea for her, with some dry toast and perhaps a lightly poached egg . . .

And she completely ignored all of Mel's moaning requests to be allowed, quietly, to die.

Chapter

15

When Miss Seeton returned to the castle, it was to find her hostess much occupied with rusks, bone-handled rattles, and gripe water: Lady Marguerite was on the point of cutting her first tooth. She was grizzling, red-faced, and restless. Liusaidh, Mrs. McScurrie, and one of the housemaids had been taking it in turns to walk her up and down, or rock her in the old wooden cradle that had done duty by generations of small MacSporrans, but her wails, despite everyone's best efforts, continued.

Miss Seeton uttered expressions of sympathy, wondering at the same time whether to confess to that midnight tin of condensed milk. Her blushes, amid the squalls and lamentation, went unobserved — which she herself did not. On first catching sight of the newcomer's cockscomb hat, and the way the sun glittered through the nursery window upon the handle of her gold umbrella, Marguerite's eyes emptied almost miraculously of tears, and her hitherto woeful mouth parted in what seemed to be a smile.

Everyone held their breath. Nobody moved. Marguerite gurgled. She smiled again. Miss Seeton smiled back.

"Bless you, Miss Seeton," breathed the countess, as her cherished offspring began to blow bubbles. "I won't ask if you've enjoyed your day — I'm afraid I don't care, because you've certainly made ours! She's been fidgety almost from the time you left, and we haven't been able to do a thing with her, poor mite."

"Or," muttered Mrs. McScurrie, with a dark look at her mistress, "anything at all. So will we be away back down to the kitchens the now?"

"Gracious, I hadn't realised" — Liusaidh glanced at her watch, and seemed startled by what she saw — "it was so kind of you to help, but — only I was hoping to talk a few things through with — you, and . . ."

She regarded Miss Seeton with a pleading look. "You are so very good with her, Miss Seeton. Would it be too much of an imposition to ask if you'd mind — It wouldn't? Oh, that *is* kind of you! With luck" — and she rolled her eyes in the direction of the departing housekeeper —

198

"it shouldn't be for too long."

Miss Seeton and Lady Marguerite, old acquaintances now, gazed thoughtfully at each other once the door had closed. The baby was rubbing her face with chubby hands, and might, Miss Seeton guessed, be on the verge of slumber. Worn out by all the crying, no doubt. She rocked the cradle with one gentle foot, and the baby's eyelids drooped.

A bedtime story, perhaps. Miss Seeton, proud to be thus of assistance to her kind hosts, racked her brains for the fairy tales of her distant youth: an aristocratic infant — her christening . . .

"Once upon a time," began Miss Seeton, "there was a baby princess who had three fairy godmothers, called . . . called" — the prettiest names she could remember right now — "Anthea, and Melinda, and Serafina . . ."

When Liusaidh peeped through the nursery door some time later, Miss Seeton had run out of fairy tales and was reading to Marguerite from *Bird Life of the Glens*. Both parties appeared to be enjoying the experience. Lady Glenclachan smiled, and spoke softly.

"You're a marvel, Miss Seeton! I do hope you haven't been too bored?"

"Indeed, no. Although she has never fallen entirely asleep, she has remained very quiet, which is sure to have soothed her. And what an excellent writer Miss Philomena Beigg is! A pleasure to read, in every sense. I thought, however, that the Massacre of Glencoe would be rather too violent for one so young — and, growing up as she will in the Highlands, I felt it would do her no harm to learn about the natural history of the area. Educational theorists, as I understand the matter, are unable to agree on the earliest age at which a small child will absorb what she hears, and certainly Lady Marguerite seems a very alert baby — from the little I know of babies, that is. Poor Dulcie Rose, though naturally I would never be so impertinent as to tell the Hosiggs so, does seem rather, well, slower. But of course," and she brightened, "she is generally asleep when I see her, which may account for it. Poor Lily was rushed to hospital, you know, and dear Len was so worried about them both . . ."

Lady Glenclachan expressed polite concern, then thanked Miss Seeton for taking such good care of Marguerite for the second time, and suggested that she might care to freshen up before dinner. Over which meal, Ranald added his thanks to those of his wife, and Miss Seeton blushed with pleasure.

"And what are your plans for tomorrow?" enquired Ranald, who had approved Miss Seeton's choice of reading matter for his infant daughter. "Bird-watching, I suppose?"

Miss Seeton nodded. "Miss Beigg's book mentions so many species we do not have in Kent, even as visitors, and I feel it would be a great shame not to take advantage of my stay here — if, that is, it would not inconvenience anyone in any way. But from her description it seems just possible that at this time of year I might see *Bucephala clangula* — the Common Goldeneye, you know, although I understand it to be mostly a winter visitor. And then there is *Regulus regulus*. We have gold-crested wrens in Kent, of course, but as it is particularly fond of conifers as breeding sites — and there are one or two planta-tions in the area . . ."

"More's the pity," muttered Ranald, who had strong views on the Forestry Commis-sion.

Liusaidh, not wishing to become involved in a political discussion, said quickly, "One of the dialect names for it in these parts is moonie — the goldcrest, I mean. Otherwise known as a gold-cuttie, which is odd, because an ordinary cuttie was a razor-bill, or a guillemot, or even a hare, if it comes to that. Does Philly Beigg mention all this in her book? I have to confess I've not read it."

"She writes in a most detailed and knowledgeable way," Miss Seeton replied, "but I regret I am unable to remember everything as well as you do. Moonie and cuttie, you say? How interesting."

Liusaidh's eyes twinkled. "Now, might I make a guess at another of the birds you thought of looking for? The spink, or *Carduelis carduelis,* perhaps?"

As Miss Seeton blushed, Ranald said, "There aren't many goldfinches in these parts, Miss Seeton. Oh!" Realisation had finally dawned. Liusaidh smiled at her guest.

"Men are always that little bit slower than women, don't you agree? When you said you'd spent the morning with Philomena Beigg, I simply knew she would have told you about the lost gold mine. And as soon as you spoke of wanting to see those particular birds, well . . ."

Miss Seeton murmured of her subconscious, adding that it might seem foolish, but she couldn't help, well, wondering. "*The Treasure of the Sierra Madre* — such a splendid film. Not that I would know what it looked like, as when it came to the end it all blew away as dust, did it not? Except that when it is not nuggets it is to be found as veins in certain types of rock — granite, mostly, as I recall — and in jewellery, of course, when one recognises it instantly. Unless it is pinchbeck. But one would have to crush and pan it — fast-running streams, or do I mean burns? And no doubt many people have gone looking for it, and never found it."

"Over the years, yes — including me, when I was a boy — but no one's ever found a trace. The Highlands are a wild, uncharted region, Miss Seeton. It's all too easy to lose a place that might never have existed from the start, and" — his voice grew suddenly grim — "it's all to easy to lose yourself, too, if you're not careful. People have wandered off and not been found until the corbies — the carrion crows — have picked their bones clean. You must promise me you'll be sensible when you go exploring — I wouldn't want your death from exposure on my conscience for anything in the world. That would be a fine example of gratitude, after all you did for us and the baby!"

Miss Seeton blushed again, and promised faithfully that she would observe the greatest care while walking in the hills around Glenclachan. She had always impressed upon her pupils the importance of common sense, and hoped that she — who as a teacher was supposed to set a good example at all times — possessed sufficient of this quality to appreciate her singular lack of expertise at mountaineering. Walking, whether through the streets of London or on the paths around her own dear village of Plummergen, was a completely different matter from climbing. She understood the warning his lordship had seen fit to give, and only hoped that by her presence she was not causing him particular anxiety, as she would hate to think —

"Oh, Miss Seeton!" Liusaidh was conscience-stricken at her guest's remarks. "You're not a bother — of course you aren't. You mustn't think that for a moment. Indeed, it's we who should be apologising to you, for leaving you so much to your own devices. But until the . . . the kidnappers have been caught, I'd be frightened not to have Marguerite under my eye all the time — and it isn't the easiest thing in the world to keep carting a tiny baby around with you . . ."

Ranald, his eyes showing all the horror of one man in the company of two near-tearful females, said quickly, "If you take a map, and wear sensible clothes, and don't go too far, Miss Seeton, you'll be fine. You're not to worry about it any more — mind you," he added with a chuckle, "if by any chance you *should* stray, you could end up mixing with company of the very best, you know. Balmoral's not so far from here, for a noted walker like yourself. You probably won't want to speak to anyone in Glenclachan again once you've had a chat with the Queen."

Miss Seeton beamed at him. "It is most gratifying, and indeed a matter of some relief to me, that the weather has been good, on the whole, for one would much prefer there to be no suggestion of untruth, even in the interests of etiquette, although" — and a slight frown puckered her forehead — "I confess that I am not entirely sure of the correct etiquette, when wearing tweeds. Whether or not to curtsey, that is. Martha tells me that in the popular press" — a faint sigh escaped her — "it is generally remarked that, while she is at Balmoral, Her Majesty enjoys a well-deserved holiday with other members of her family, and therefore might prefer to be treated with rather less formality. Because on the last occasion when I was so fortunate as to meet her, at a garden party, Lady Colveden had been kind enough to warn me that one should curtsey and say, 'Yes, ma'am, delightful weather.' Although, of course, not *incognito*. Which, fortunately, it has been, has it not?"

Ranald blinked, and looked to Liusaidh for assistance. The countess thought rapidly. "Delightful," she agreed at last, hiding a smile. "Most of the time, anyway, and there hasn't been as much rain as some years. At least we haven't had any thunder yet. Some of our storms seem to get trapped between the mountains, and go banging and flashing round and round the glen for hours. It's all very spectacular — huge towering clouds, and positive daggers of lightning, and the air quite electric in blue and yellow and green . . ."

Miss Seeton perked up at this description, and remarked that, though she herself had not particularly worried about thunderstorms until her house had been struck by lightning — an occurrence, she had been assured, that was most unlikely to happen again — dear Martha disliked them intensely, and suffered unpleasant headaches beforehand. "Which made it a little awkward, you know, when *The Grey Day* was overpainted, though strictly speaking one should use another term, as it was pastels on watercolour — because I had considered replacing it with my painting of the electric storm, while it was at Scotland Yard. *The Grey Day*, I mean. Or, rather, waiting to be stolen from the gallery — at least, so the chief superintendent assured me . . ." She had never been entirely certain that Mr. Delphick hadn't been teasing her, as dear Bob, who after all worked for him, so often did. Calling her aunt, which naturally one found flattering as a term of affection rather than not, for instance. Not that Mr. Delphick would ever . . .

Fortunately for the Glenclachans, their guest made no attempt to voice her thoughts out loud. Life, for the earl and his countess, had already been complicated enough by the appearance in their lives of Miss Emily Dorothea Seeton . . .

Who was otherwise a model guest. She expected no fuss; she did not plague for attention; she was pleasant and amusing company when everyone was together, but able to amuse herself when they were not. As happened again the next morning, with Ranald shut away once more with his

207

factor and Liusaidh busy with the baby. The imminent tooth had still not yet broken through, and Lady Glenclachan was adamant that Miss Seeton was to spend no more of her holiday caring for someone else's offspring. She was to take her binoculars and a packed lunch, and enjoy herself among the birds of the Scottish Highlands. She might even find the gold mine, after all. Miss Seeton smiled, and turned pink. She had to confess to being a little curious — as would not anyone be, in the circumstances?

"Oh, I agree. I'm sure Ranald and his friends must have had tremendous fun looking for it, when they were children — but of course they didn't find it. So please don't be too disappointed when you don't, either." Liusaidh's smile was kindly. "It's far more likely you'll sight a moonie, or even a spink — but, whatever you see, I hope you enjoy yourself."

And, having repeated the earl's warnings about the risks of Highland climbing, checked with her on the map where she planned to go, and promised search parties if she was not safely back by suppertime, Lady Glenclachan waved farewell to her guest in the confidetice that Miss Seeton was really a most sensible little body, who had taken in everything she had been told and would surely come to no harm in the hills.

Surely . . .

Chapter

16

Miss Seeton was relieved that her appearance and equipment had met with the approval of her hostess. She had no wish to cause anxiety to anyone, and she could now set off on her little excursion in complete confidence.

Apart from the map, and a delicious packed lunch which Mrs. McScurrie had so kindly prepared for her, Miss Seeton's capacious handbag contained two clean pocket handkerchiefs, a comb, a small mirror, some loose change and her emergency five-pound note (inflation having made this a more realistic sum than the two separate notes she'd been accustomed to keep by her), her pocket flashlight, and a selection of pencils varying in hardness, together with a pencil sharpener and — she sighed for her limitations — an eraser. And, most important of all, her sketchbook. Over her arm she carried her umbrella, and on her head she wore her cockscomb hat.

Miss Seeton smiled at the memory of his lordship's gentle teasing last night, after dinner, when he had left the room at the coffee stage and returned with a feather which, he assured her, was an eagle's, and the mark of a Highland chief. She ought, he said, to be properly dressed, just in case she met the Queen again: everyone was equal in the open air, and Her Majesty would understand the democratic significance of the new decoration on Miss Seeton's hat.

Miss Seeton had demurred, pointing out that she was, as surely his lordship remembered, neither Scottish nor of any importance in the world whatsoever — certainly not a chief. Ranald said that, in gratitude for her sterling service to his infant daughter, he was making her an honorary chieftain of the MacSporrans, as (he being the head of that clan) was his prerogative. She was to regard it as the nearest to a medal he could award, and Liusaidh added that she thought it looked rather well inside the band, and they must remember to take Miss Seeton's photograph in an appropriate setting before she went back home to Plummergen.

Miss Seeton allowed herself to be persuaded; and, having later studied the reflection in her bedroom looking glass, conceded that the addition might almost be said to suit her — or rather (modesty added hastily) the hat, anyway. One was tempted to say — a temptation to be resisted — to say, well, distinguished. Which, of course, she was not, for how could a retired art teacher expect to distinguish herself in any way? She led the quietest and most private of lives . . . but, should there be even the slightest chance that, during her little excursion, she might encounter Her Majesty, then it was plainly her duty to show every respect. Which dressing the part, she supposed, would do. If only — she sighed once more — she had remembered to ask about the curtsey . . .

Miss Seeton, in sensible tweeds and comfortable shoes, walked on under the August sun, drinking in the view and the birdsong, from time to time raising the binoculars she wore about her neck to study some passing songster as it settled on a clump of heather or the low branch of a tree. It was a beautiful day — indeed, a fine day. Miss Seeton hummed Madame Butterfly's famous aria and felt at peace with the world.

She began to feel thirsty. Mrs. McScurrie

had suggested she should carry a flask of coffee, for which kindness Miss Seeton had been grateful, though it would make one's bag rather heavier than one would wish, for a day out in the hills. Lady Glenclachan had come to her rescue, speaking with such enthusiasm on the joys of drinking from clear Highland streams that Miss Seeton had been enchanted.

"It's the finest water in the world, true enough," Ranald MacSporran, overhearing the discussion, confirmed in his most fervent tones. "Soft and pure and flavoured with peat — just a taste, no more — but it's what makes our whisky what it is, Miss Seeton. There's none better."

Miss Seeton didn't plan to take whisky with her any more than she wanted to carry a heavy thermos. She compromised by slipping the silver top of his lordship's personal flask, which he mischievously offered her, into her jacket pocket. Her original romantic notion of scooping up water in cupped hands was dismissed, on reflection, as impractical.

For this dismissal, she was to be thankful. She found a stream, every bit as bright and sparkling as Liusaidh had promised, chattering over pebbles between low green banks — banks with steep, crumbling sides. The rich peaty soil, no doubt. Stooping and scooping from such water would mean the grave risk of a tumble, Miss Seeton thought. Even for one such as herself, whose knees, thanks to the yoga . . .

Having found a little inlet where she might safely lower and fill the silver cup, Miss Seeton did so, and sat for a while on a convenient boulder, grey and glittering with what common sense told her was unlikely to be gold. She smiled for her daydreams. Hadn't his lordship said something about mica, in granite? And calcium, or had that been carbon, as well? She couldn't quite remember, but on a day like this it didn't seem to matter much. She dipped another cup of water, drank it, and decided it made her feel hungry.

She sat for a while after her modest lunch — saving some for later in case, as she recalled the warnings, anything should go wrong — with her sketchpad open on her knee and a pencil in her hand, drawing quick impressions of the various views to be seen in different directions. Consulting the Ordnance Survey map lent her by Lord Glenclachan, she identified most of the obvious landmarks, and was particularly struck by the name of a strangely shaped crag in the near distance. Quet-na-Scrabberteistie reminded Miss Seeton, as her pencil captured its remarkable outline, of a seabird — one of the auk family, perhaps. "A guillemot," mused Miss Seeton, and smiled as she remembered the talk she'd had last night with Lady Glenclachan. "Or do I mean a cuttie? When it does not look in the least," she added, surveying first her drawing and then the crag, "like a shirt, which is what I understood it to mean. Cutty Sark — a witch, as I recall, trying to lure poor Tam O'Shanter to his doom — although the ship is most graceful, and for school excursions so interesting, as well as convenient." She gazed slowly about her. "How very different all this is from Greenwich, although it occurs to me now to wonder why it is pronounced *Grennitch* and not *green witch* — most apposite, with the Cutty Sark on display there — and from London in general, of course. Different, that is . . ."

For a while she pondered her time at the school in Hampstead, and thought how glad she was that, now she'd retired, she could still be of use (albeit in a part-time capacity) to the village in which she had been so fortunate as to make her home, where she was happy to stay in utter contentment. Apart from the occasional holiday, which the kindness of friends made possible, nothing ever happened to disturb her otherwise unremarkable life . . .

She came out of her daydream to find that the sheet of paper on which she'd begun to sketch Quet-na-Scrabberteistie had now been filled by a series of sketches of birds. Which was, she supposed, understandable — or would have been, had they been recognisable as guillemots or other auks. To her surprise and dismay, they were nothing like seabirds, or at least most of them weren't, being small and perky and bright of eye, with inquisitive beaks that reminded her of finches, or wrens, perhaps. The other birds were obviously waterfowl of some sort, but ducks rather than auks — the bills were entirely different.

"Oh dear," said Miss Seeton, turning to a fresh page and wondering whether it was worth the effort of starting again. Maybe if she were to look at the crag from another angle, it might be easier to capture its strange appearance on paper; and the map showed her that, by a fortunate coincidence, if she followed the stream — Skutie Burn, she corrected herself — she would, before long, find herself at the foot of

Quet-na-Scrabberteistie.

She collected her belongings together, briefly admired the glitter of the granite boulder which had been her seat, and headed off upstream. The correct procedure when lost, as his lordship had made clear last night, was to find water and follow it *down*stream; as she did not mean to become lost, it would surely not matter if she reversed the theory in order to achieve her goal.

It took longer than she had intended, mostly because the terrain grew more uneven where what she guessed was an outcrop of the crag had shattered through centuries of rough weather, forming pebbles, stones, and scree which were partly overgrown, partly exposed, so that she could never be sure, until she was almost on top of an obstacle, how much of an obstacle it would turn out to be. Skutie Burn had taken the easiest course down from the summit, winding around and between rock or root or tree trunk gnarled with age; and Miss Seeton kept wanting to stop and sketch details of these unusual formations, which slowed her progress all the more.

She marvelled at the rainbow and the wind ripples on a small pool formed by the spillage from a waterfall, which danced and splashed and sparkled in the sun. It splashed, indeed, rather more than Miss Seeton would have liked, blowing faint spray into her eyes and, she realised, soaking her hat, with its special feather. How ungrateful of his lordship's kindness it would be to return to his home with her chieftain's token damp and bedraggled! She moved to one side, looking for some way to bypass the waterfall, but a mischievous breeze tossed spray in her face again, and without conscious thought she opened her umbrella.

With a screech and a flap of startled wings, a bird, big and black and green-gleaming in the sunlight, flew up out of a nearby clump of gorse. A crow, maybe a rook, Miss Seeton thought — no, a rook's glossiness was purple, rather than greenish. A carrion crow, then. She wondered what it had been doing. Either the sudden movement or the unaccustomed shape of the umbrella's shadow had disturbed it; and, as her new path was to take her within a few feet of the golden gorse in which the bird had been so busy, she realised with a slight sensation of queasiness — dear Mel, she hoped she was feeling better today — that it was very probable she was about to find, unfortunately, a dead or dying sheep. His lordship had spoken at some length last night on the regrettable feeding habits of the bird family *Corvus,* although his wife had reminded him that "carrion" was rather a corruption of the qualifying "corone" than a description of what the bird ate.

"Very suitable, then," retorted Ranald, going on to talk of gamekeepers, and ghillies, and living lambs with their eyes pecked out.

Miss Seeton swallowed. She looked towards the clump of gorse, then back to the waterfall, then on to the soaring strangeness of Quet-na-Scrabberteistie. She was probably now close enough to attempt another sketch . . . but suppose the lamb was still alive . . . but she had heard no bleats or cries . . . and were lambs so small and helpless this late in the year . . . but it might have been injured in a tumble down the waterfall, and crawled for shelter on broken legs . . .

Miss Seeton's imagination made up her mind for her, even as she flinched from what she was about to see. A dead lamb was beyond her assistance; a living creature, wounded, helpless, a suffering victim, was another matter. Her duty was plain.

She lowered and furled the umbrella, with some vague thought of a prod to ward off predators. She gulped, took a deep breath, and set her shoulders. Feeling decidedly shaky inside, Miss Seeton marched straight for the gorse and forced herself to walk round behind it to see what the crow had been doing . . .

And then she wished she hadn't.

Mel Forby had felt much better after a good night's sleep. The poached egg and toast Miss Seeton had persuaded her to swallow, washed down with two cups of weak tea, sent her off into a comfortable doze from which she woke in time to enjoy a lightly cooked supper in the hotel dining room. The uniformed female glimpsed fleetingly on her first night was in attendance and, after some prompting, revealed that her name was Shona. She offered Mel the wine list and asked, with a smirk, if she was to expect the pleasure of Miss Forby's company in the bar later on. Mr. McQueest, she added with another smirk, was away on one of his jaunts, so . . .

Mel loftily ignored both the insinuations and the wine list and said she'd think about it. She drank water right through her meal and, having thought, went instead for a gentle stroll among the moth-soft shadows of Scotland's summer dusk.

There were still lights on in the bar when she returned, with her weak ankle twinging slightly but her spirits — no, make that *joie de vivre* — once more high. She almost felt like throwing her walking stick away. She would be her old self again tomorrow: one day older, but a good deal wiser. No more Lairigigh, she vowed silently, and she ran up the stairs to her room two steps at a time before she could change her mind and march into the bar just for the satisfaction of proving Shona wrong.

Pride goes before a fall. Mel spent most of the next day rubbing liniment into her aching ankle, and talking with whichever of the hotel staff was prepared to spare the time. Shona, now that the ice had been broken, was good for a spot of gossip whenever Hamish wasn't around. When he was, the girl communicated in monosyllables, and performed her usual vanishing trick. She, Mel had no need to ask, was a local. Newcomer Hamish, when finally cornered, expounded on life in Glenclachan, his wish to turn the Pock and Tang into a tourist attraction, and the virtues of moderation (in a tone of barely suppressed amusement). Mel pointedly drank orange juice, feeling peeved, wondering yet again how the landlord managed to keep his clientele. He probably didn't care, she concluded: he hoped to drive them all away, so that he could go upmarket with a vengeance, and fleece the trippers in their thousands.

But he hadn't driven them away just yet. The afternoon contingent muttered when they arrived to find Mel once more perched on her stool by the bar, but by the time she headed for the dining room, they seemed to have resigned themselves to her presence. She hadn't said much; she'd been too busy listening to the accent, making mental notes for the series of Pieces she planned for the *Daily Negative*'s on "The Uniqueness of Highland Life."

Malcolmn MacDonald was not among the drinkers, and from what Mel could make out, hadn't been seen all day. Campbell, too, had been invisible, it seemed. At least there couldn't be any punch-ups in the bar while they were both absent . . .

Mel returned to her room to renew her makeup, and wished she could talk to Thrudd, whose presence she was missing rather more than she'd expected. Would the editor of the *Negative*, she wondered, permit a personal telephone call on her expenses? Except that the telephone booth in the hall near Reception wasn't all that personal, really. If Hamish was serious about going upmarket, phones in bedrooms would be an excellent place to start. But there might not be anyone around when she rang; she could always hang up, or change the subject, if — oh. No, she couldn't — or at least she wouldn't — because Glenclachan, as she'd learned among other items of varying interest from Shona, wasn't on Subscriber Trunk Dialling yet. She didn't fancy the idea of some bat-eared postmistress at the one-horse telephone exchange — they probably still had to crank a handle, for heaven's sake — being able to quote every last syllable of her London-bound badinage . . .

There came a sudden hubbub from the bar below. Mel's ears pricked up, and her eyes sparkled. Campbell, or MacDonald, maybe both of them, had come back, she'd bet on it — which meant action — which meant a story. And, where there was a story, there too was Amelita Forby. Mel jumped to her feet, winced without noticing she did so, snatched up her stick, and headed out of her room in the direction of the bar.

"Aye, it's true enough, there's no chance of a mistake," someone was saying as she opened the door. "Dead as a doornail, close by Skutie Burn, and looking for all the world at first as if drowning was the cause, they say —"

"Except," broke in someone else, "that nobody who's been drowned comes crawling oot the watter after to hide under a gorse bush . . ."

Mel's ears were out on stalks. Somebody dead — and foul play suspected, which she'd bet was the crime she'd been waiting for. Or else she'd made a big mistake coming to Glenclachan right from the start.

". . . heid fairly bashed in, on seeing the back of it," she heard someone say, "and a great stone covered with blood close by . . ."

Definitely foul play. But who was the victim? Had the kidnappers returned for another attempt at Lady Marguerite, and quarrelled? When thieves fall out . . .

". . . a corbie set to peck out his eyes," offered someone else, "if it hadnae been for that auld woman covering his heid with her umbrella to scare the creature away . . ."

Mel's ears fairly flapped. Her trip to

Glenclachan had just now justified itself, a hundred times over, because, in the context of a crime, "umbrella" could only mean one thing.

Chapter

17

Mel's ears flapped into overdrive as the animated discussion and speculation swirled about her. If it hadn't been for the accent, she could have sworn she was back in Plummergen. Poor Miss S., finding a body — yet good for Miss S., delivering the goods again, with Amelita Forby waiting on the spot to turn it all into another headline maker.

It would be a big help to know who the victim was, but if she tried asking, ten to one they'd clam up on her. They seemed to have ignored her when she walked in, which made a change from the night before last, but she couldn't count on it lasting. She remembered how they'd reacted when the rat-faced man — another one who wasn't here tonight — turned up to ask for that unknown Fraser; and as for how many of the regulars apart from Campbell and MacDonald were missing, of course she had no idea, and didn't really see how she could easily find out. Her best bet would be trying to stay as unobtrusive as possible for as long as she could, then find a telephone and risk the operator's curiosity — she probably knew more about it all than Mel would ever learn, anyway.

"Staying up at the castle, the puir wee soul, and what a sight to find when you're doing no more than look for birds, and thinking all's well with the world —"

"It's Malcolm MacDonald will be thinking all's well with the world now," someone pointed out, and there was a sudden, grim silence. Then everyone began to talk at once, expressing their shock and surprise anew, and their sorrow for (Mel was now absolutely certain) Miss Seeton . . .

Mel was almost as certain that she knew the identity of the dead — the murdered — body. Surely there could be only one explanation for the way they'd all reacted to the idea that the person most likely to be cheered by hearing the news was Malcolm MacDonald? Unless Malcolm made a habit of quarrelling with people, the victim had to be —

"Ewen Campbell," said somebody, raising a glass to toast the departed, making Mel jump. She'd heard of the

Sight, had even thought of writing one of her Pieces about it, but maybe not, on second (she frowned) thoughts. Amelita Forby, who'd always considered herself a city girl to the marrow of her bones — bones, it somehow cheered her to recall, which had so interested Miss Seeton at their first meeting — could not feel altogether comfortable with the idea that anyone might be reading her mind. As for encouraging them . . .

"Ewen Campbell," said somebody else, and another glass was raised.

Coincidence, decided Mel. She hoped. Dammit, she was a seasoned Fleet Street hack, not a superstitious, spineless country cousin. Not that any of this bunch seemed particularly spineless: tough cookies, the lot of them. Porridge and bracing mountain air, probably. Ewen Campbell wasn't — hadn't been — the only one who looked capable of tossing two cabers at a time, not by any means. But, so long as they didn't start on again about her shroud, she'd be happy left in peace sitting on her stool, listening, composing paragraphs in her head.

There was a surge of customers to the bar, every one of whom ordered double whisky. Mel winced. Hamish poured, one glass after another, passed glasses across the counter, took money, handed change. Sideways glances were slanted at Mel as she sat perched on the stool with a half-empty glass in front of her.

"You're not drinking, hen," observed someone with a less wary expression than the others, the first person, apart from Hamish, to address the albino blackbird.

Mel smiled. Maybe the Scots weren't quite as mean with their money as everyone liked to make out. "This is fine, thanks." Her fingers curled round the glass as she moved it a little closer.

"Fine?" The speaker's eyes narrowed. "So that's your opinion, is it?" And the others began to mutter.

Mel raised an eyebrow. Not that her nutritional regime was really anyone else's business, but they were all looking at her so strangely . . . "Vitamins," she said.

"You ought to be ashamed of yourself, woman. Vitamins. indeed! But then," and he gestured expressively, "what else could a body rightly expect from a Sassenach save newfangled talk and disrespect?"

The general muttering increased, as everyone decided Mel was beyond redemption and turned their backs pointedly upon her, making for their habitual tables with alacrity. Hamish shook his head, and sighed. "You could always have taken it with water," he murmured, wiping down the counter close to where her elbows leaned. "They're a touchy lot in Glenclachan, as I know better than most."

This confidence hardly surprised Mel, given what she'd seen of the landlord's attitude to his clientele. She hoped he'd be rather more cooperative in her own case, and leaned closer across the bar. "What's with this not approving of vitamins? Haven't they heard of Linus Pauling?"

Hamish shook his head again, moving to the optics at the back of the bar. He dispensed a single whisky and pushed it, with the water jug, over to Mel. "Purists might say it was just as disrespectful to weaken good scotch, but you'll find it'll make things easier all round. Compliments of the house — I'm not risking trouble tonight," he added, as she was about to speak. "You make a pretence of drinking — just a drop now and again — and they'll be happy. As happy as anyone's likely to be, that is," and he frowned, dropping his voice still more, so that she could barely hear him. "Always excepting Malcolm MacDonald, of course . . ."

"Ewen Campbell, rest his soul," someone cried, and every glass was raised.

Mel, at a look from Hamish, tipped a generous splash of water into her own tumbler, raised it, then pointedly sipped, conscious of eyes boring into her back, and grudging acknowledgement of her action. The grin which she directed at Hamish was, to her surprise, shaky.

But, now that honour was satisfied, nobody took any more notice of her; they all began to reminisce about the departed Ewen Campbell and as more whisky flowed, tongues began to loosen. The intense solemnity and shock of the first few minutes gave way to a rather more realistic evaluation of the late Campbell's character. Mel, becoming accustomed to the brogue, learned gradually that the dead man had been far from the least irascible person in the world, falling out at one time or another with almost everyone in Glenclachan — though seldom, as far as she could gather, about anything particularly serious, until the quarrel with Malcolm MacDonald. She caught tantalising snippets which everyone apart from Hamish and herself seemed to recognise at once — references to "Teeock's bagpipes" and "when Ewen used the tent pole for a caber" and "the day the mealy pudden crossed the street" left too much to her journalist's imagination, and she longed to enquire further. Ewen Campbell sounded as if he might have merited an entire Piece of his own.

Then, with a further few rounds, conversation took on a darker aspect. "But it's no more than you'd expect, from a Campbell," was the consensus of opinion when people began to speak of "Auld McPiet's savings" and "that car he sold to Hector Scremerston" and "Cheepart's tree he'd the nerve to cut down, without so much as asking" — which made Mel start to wonder what the whisky equivalent of *in vino veritas* might be . . .

They drank, and talked — and drank, and talked — and drank. Mel took care only to drink when Hamish tipped her the wink that someone was watching. The landlord's face, under its professional air of calm mine-hostery, revealed to the shrewd observer (which Mel Forby knew herself to be) a relief he was trying hard to suppress — probably about the good business he was, for once, doing. Mel shivered. Talk about dead men's shoes. The drinkers were all too busy with their fifth, or sixth, drinks to notice, but she was sitting with her face towards the bar, and the man behind it. Okay, he hadn't known Ewen

Campbell as long as the others, but it was kind of grisly to be so glad about what had happened . . .

They started to sing, quietly, slowly, a mournful tune Mel didn't recognise, in a language she guessed must be the Gaelic nobody used in everyday speech anymore. It sounded like — and most likely was — a funeral song, a dirge for the dead man. What do you know, Forby, you've landed yourself in the middle of a regular, old-fashioned wake. Maybe they aren't as keen on the guy as they tried at first to make out — but they're doing the best they can for him. No wonder they wanted you to join them, and accused you of showing no respect. As bad as wearing trousers in church . . .

Someone jumped up from his seat and headed straight for Mel's stool. The Sight Strikes Again? Should she promise faithfully never in the future to wear, or even to think of wearing, slacks, jeans, or flares either in or out of places of worship? But the man, having almost lurched against her, leaned past Mel to pick up the water jug, and continued to ignore her as he carried the jug back to his table. He set it carefully down in the centre. More drinks were ordered, and when everyone had a full glass in his hand, after the now routine toast to Ewen Campbell, a voice proclaimed,

"The King!" They all thrust their glasses forward in a circular motion above the water jug, then drank deeply.

The King Over the Water, of course. Mel nodded, pleased she'd read the Travel Pages and knew about the Jacobites and the Forty-Five. Hamish caught her eye and raised his brows in a despairing grimace: nearly two hundred and thirty years (he seemed to be saying) ought to be long enough ago for this romantic nonsense to be sensibly forgotten . . .

"Farewell to all our Scottish fame," somebody sang, and others picked up the tune in a spirited chorus. "Farewell our ancient glory./Farewell even to our Scottish name/So famed in martial story./Now Sark runs over the Solway Sands/And Tweed runs to the ocean/To mark where England's province stands/Such a parcel of rogues in a nation!"

The singers were by now so far gone with mingled whisky and emotion that nobody bothered to look towards Mel at the mention of England; nor did anyone notice when Hamish, trying to suppress a smirk, began to explain that such sentiment, from a historical point of view, was hardly accurate. "Parcel of Rogues" referred rather to the forcing through Parliament of the Act of Union, eight years before the first Jacobite uprising, than to the uprising itself, though there was little doubt (he conceded) that the Act had contributed to the general dissatisfaction of Scots with their lot, encouraging the deposed and exiled James the Second to make the attempt to regain his throne in the following year.

"And then, Miss Forby, what do you suppose the poor chap did, when his ships were on the point of sailing from Dunkirk with five thousand men? Caught measles!" he informed her, in a tone of intense disapproval. Mel didn't doubt for a moment that had the ill-fated expedition been organised by Hamish McQueest, there would now be a Stuart monarch on the throne of the United Kingdom, instead of one of Hanoverian descent. The landlord gave every impression, though he tried to hide it, of being a skilled and wily operator. "Jacobites," he concluded, "have a very romantic and grand-sounding name, but not much else, you know."

". . . were bought and sold for English gold," came the final lines of the lament.

"Such a parcel of rogues in a nation!" And Hamish, pulling a face, fell silent, making ready to pour more whisky as required.

Suddenly there came a rattle at the outside door, and it was flung open. Those who had started to speak fell silent; those who were moving towards the bar stayed still. Every head turned to see what was happening. Mel had a brief and shuddery sensation of déjà vu. Only two nights ago, Ewen Campbell had appeared, in just such a precipitate fashion — only now Ewen Campbell was dead.

"Ewen Campbell is dead," announced the newcomer.

Something cold crept slowly up Mel's spine, and stroked her neck, and caught in her throat. No way would she be visiting the Highlands again in a hurry, she promised herself: her nerves weren't up to it. Just let her get back to the bright city lights, and she'd never leave them again . . .

"Ewen Campbell is dead," repeated Malcolm MacDonald. He advanced into the room. "Someone has killed him, and left him dead on the hills — and it's me who's been blamed for it, when I never laid a finger on the man — but when I find out who did. I'll —"

"Nobody's blaming you, Malcolm." The voice that uttered this reassurance was echoed by a chorus from the whole room, but Malcolm ignored it.

"I'll deal with him myself," he finished, his face dark. "I've been spending most of the afternoon having daft questions fired at me by the police. Not by Sergeant Trumpie, though it was him sent to find me and drag me away from the fishing — sent by some jumped-up inspector from the town, Badock by name." His features writhed at the memory. "The man's a fool, but a fool with some small authority, and the notion from who-knows-where I'd be the most likely person to have beaten a stone about Ewen Campbell's heid. And I'd be glad to know" — glaring from face to face as the silent drinkers stared at him — "who I've to thank for spreading such a pack of lies to blacken my good name . . ."

"Wheesht, man, come you in and sit down. There's nobody wanting to blacken your name — it's a mistake, nothing more. What else would you expect from a town-bred fule who kens naught of the way of things around Glenclachan?" There was a note of near-amusement — amusement, of all things! — in the speaker's voice. "Just because you'd threatened Ewen

Campbell with a shotgun, there's no need —"

"You've said enough, Dougall McLintie!" Malcolm stepped even farther into the room, breathing hard, his hands balled into fists. "A man can speak in the heat of the moment, and no blame to him if he does — but to . . . take a stone . . . over and over and over again . . . to someone's heid . . ."

He choked into silence, and the mischievous Dougall said quickly, "Och, it's sorry I am indeed, Malcolm. The pair of you were right good friends, I know. You'll need to grieve properly for him, to ease your mind — so, come along and sit you down by me. If we don't give him a fine send-off among the crowd of us, it's a poor night's work."

A general murmur of agreement echoed this invitation, to Malcolm's evident relief. He looked round at everyone he'd expected to be hostile, his eyes narrowing as he spotted Mel; then he nodded, breathed one long and trembling breath, and moved jerkily across to the table where Dougall McLintie sat among his cronies. There was a shuffling of chairs as one or two people stood up to offer their seats to the new arrival. Hamish, unasked, began to pour more whisky. "A double," he said, proffering the glass. "On the house — do you more good than anything else . . ."

Everyone was too polite to ask Malcolm how, if he'd been questioned for so long and suspected (it appeared) for even longer, he was a free man now. Bail, decided Mel, or the Scots equivalent of it. And what the chances of it lasting might be, she wouldn't care to guess.

They were singing again, in a mournful chorus. ". . . me and my true love will never meet again/On the bonnie, bonnie banks of Loch Lomond."

"Sing something else!" cried Malcolm MacDonald, as they were about to start another verse. "Something else!"

"Speed, bonnie boat, like a bird on the wing," Dougall began. "Onward! the sailors cry." The others, clearing their throats, joined in. "Carry the lad that's born to the king/Over the sea to Skye . . ."

Another Jacobite song, pregnant with meaning and emotion and — Mel couldn't help but feel — undercurrents that surged in ways she couldn't begin to guess. She heard the lilting, whisky-rich voices and turned sideways to watch the faces to which they belonged. Was everyone sorrowing equally for the loss of Ewen Campbell — or did somebody have something to hide?

"Hey, Johnnie Cope," sang Dougall McLintie, as the "Skye Boat Song" died away. A smattering of cheers greeted this new offering with its tone of mockery, and everyone insisted he should go back to the beginning, so that they could start together.

"Hey, Johnnie Cope, are ye wauking yet?/Or are ye sleeping, I would wit?/Oh, haste ye, get up, for the drums do beat!/O fie, Cope, rise in the morning!"

Hamish whispered that England's unfortunate General Cope, surprised by the clansmen's dawn attack, had brought news of the English defeat to Berwick on Tweed, and never lived it down. Mel did sums in her head, and sighed for such intensity of political feeling after over two centuries.

"Good luck to my blackbird," suggested Malcolm, as the singers drew breath and toasted one another. There were tears in his eyes, a quaver in his throat. "Good luck to my blackbird . . ."

Dougall, patting him on the arm, prepared to send the first few notes rumbling into the room, then choked, and stopped. His eyes widened.

They all followed his gaze.

Without anyone noticing, the outside door of the bar had opened. A man stood on the threshold. He flinched as the gaze of twenty men (and one interested woman) fastened upon him. He cleared his throat.

"I'm looking," he said, in a husky voice, "for John Stuart Fraser . . ."

Chapter

18

Mel's headache next morning was nothing like the one she'd had two days earlier. She smirked at herself in the mirror over the washbasin as she set about her toilet: virtue, and orange juice, certainly paid dividends. The only reason she now felt as if her eyes needed props to keep them open was that she was so very, very tired. What time had she finally torn herself away from Ewen Campbell's wake? And how long had the — festivities? celebration? — no, the obsequies (one splash of cold water did wonders for the vocabulary) continued? It had been impossible for her either to write her story, or to do any serious thinking, with everyone singing, talking, and singing still more in the room underneath her own.

They'd gone at last, and she'd fallen asleep — fitfully, but better than not sleeping at all. And as she drifted off into slumber, her weary mind had made another firm resolution: to talk to Miss

Seeton as soon as she could. First things first, though. She'd file a preliminary story with the *Negative* before she headed for the castle — find herself a telephone, warn Miss S. not to leave town, then ring London to report the latest in the Seeton Saga, tell them to hold the front page — but talk to Miss S. was the next priority.

"Battling Brolly Finds Body in Burn," murmured Mel, with one eye, carefully shadowed, on her waiting notebook. "Body By Bush?" She completed her makeup and picked up a pencil. "Corpse Near Crag," she decided, and began to scribble.

Miss Seeton's return to MacSporran Castle yesterday had startled the countess, whose guests did not normally arrive under police escort — a part-time officer, as are many in remote Highland regions, of course, but wearing uniform, and with the regulation blue light on the roof of his car. The light wasn't working, but the sight was still enough to make Liusaidh almost drop the baby. Only the swift action of Mrs. McScurrie prevented a nasty accident.

"A nasty accident she's seen, puir wee soul," Special Constable Duncan Muffit informed Lady Glenclachan, after his charge, looking slightly green, had thanked him for his kind assistance and begged her hostess to excuse her, just for a few moments, while she composed herself: such a shock, even though one knew accidents could happen in the hills if one was a trifle careless, which it seemed the poor man had been — but oh, dear, if Lady Glenclachan wouldn't mind, she would so like just to slip inside for a few moments . . .

"Best make her a cup of tea," suggested Duncan, as, with a horrified clucking, Mrs. McScurrie urged Miss Seeton in the direction of the nearest door. "We brewed a pot at Sergeant Trumpie's house, but it was mebbe a bit strong for her, with the sugar and all, for the shock. At her age, too. A nasty accident she's seen, puir wee soul — or that's what she's been thinking, and your leddyship would oblige if she's left in that opinion."

Duncan met Liusaidh's startled eye, and nodded slowly. "Never mind what she did for the bairn, you've only to look at her to know Miss Seeton's no criminal. And she's such a wee body, what's more — she could never so much as lift a finger against a man, let alone the great stone it must have been, to cause such damage — there's no suspicion attached to her, for all she was the one who found the corpus. But she would have it he'd taken a tumble from Quet-na-Scrabberteistie, and happier left believing so, when there's neither sense or need for her to know the truth. An accident, as far as she's concerned, if you don't mind . . ."

"And as far as the police are concerned?"

Sergeant Muffit looked at Lady Glenclachan and shrugged. "A strange way to commit suicide. Well-nigh impossible, any reasonable man might say, to tumble off the crag and under a bush and have your head take such a battering on the way, never mind you couldn't be sure it would work."

"Murder, then." Liusaidh had turned rather pale. "It's a terrible thing, I imagine, to find anyone dead at the best of times, but poor Miss Seeton leads such a quiet life. She may never want to go for a walk again, and I can't say I'd blame her for feeling that way. I'm sure she can't have expected this to happen when we invited her for a holiday; nobody would, and we certainly didn't. Dead bodies and . . . crime — murders — simply aren't . . . aren't normal."

To Miss Seeton — Scotland Yard's MissEss — crime, if not murder, might well be considered normal. With murder she is not unacquainted, and she has watched in hospital morgues as dead bodies were dissected, laying open to her interested student gaze bones and muscles and sinews. Anatomy classes, and diagrams in books, somehow weren't the same . . .

But a gentlewoman seldom talks about herself — and her art college days are long since past — and few people ever realise that the Battling Brolly beloved by the popular press is no gamp-wielding gorgon, but rather a retired spinster schoolmarm who stands just over five feet tall in her stout walking shoes, and weighs seven stone, fully clothed. The MacSporrans had been so overjoyed at the safe recovery of Lady Marguerite that they failed to take in even the little that Chief Superintendent Delphick saw fit to tell them of their daughter's guardian angel . . .

"Poor Miss Seeton," Liusaidh said. "I suppose one could hardly suggest that she take a dram to calm her nerves? Mrs. McScurrie will look after her, though." She suddenly directed the full force of her smile towards Sergeant Muffit. "And while she's being looked after, are you going to tell me if it was anyone we know? Ranald," she reminded him, "is provost of Glenclachan as well as the laird, after all."

Duncan had no intention of keeping the local magistrate in ignorance of what he had every right to know, and said so — and did not voice any reservations about the rights of the provost's lady, though her husband was nowhere to be seen. Liusaidh accordingly heard as much about the death of Ewen Campbell as she wanted, and sent Sergeant Muffit on his way before Miss Seeton should reappear to be upset again at the sight of him, with instructions to keep the castle informed. And Sergeant Muffit was to take no particular notice of what Inspector Badock might say . . .

While the wake was being held at the Pock and Tang, Lord and Lady Glenclachan were taking pains to look after their guest. Mrs. McScurrie had prepared a light, though nourishing, supper; Ranald opened a classic wine, on which he said he would value Miss Seeton's opinion, and he begged her to take "a wee dram or two" to see what she might think of the malt. There was not one suggestion of treatment for shock. The television, an antique black-and-white model which had in any case barely been switched on throughout Miss Seeton's stay, fell victim to that mysterious signal loss which from time to time plagues the Highland regions, and everyone was far too busy to think of suggesting they might listen to the wireless news instead. Miss Seeton, who had looked after Lady Marguerite with such care, was now being cared for by Lady Marguerite's fond parents and faithful retainers . . .

So that when Mel Forby telephoned next morning with her request to speak to Miss Seeton, she did not find it an easy request to fulfil. Eat your heart out, Martha Bloomer: Armorel McScurrie could be twice as protective without even trying. Mel took several deep breaths, imagined herself eating honey by the tablespoon, and eventually persuaded the housekeeper to pass on a message that Miss Forby, Miss Seeton's friend from London, staying in the neighbourhood, would like to pay a visit later that morning.

When later, and Mel, duly arrived, it was not to be met by Lady Glenclachan or Miss Seeton, but to be confronted on the doorstep by Mrs. McScurrie, bristling with indignation. Every grim syllable of her greeting made Mel feel her mascara must be smudged. It wasn't until long after that she remembered she hardly wore any these days, since Miss S. had persuaded her to soften the Forby nail-hard image by softening her makeup . . . and that had been years ago.

But Armorel McScurrie read the newspapers with rather more enthusiasm than her employers knew, and had recognised (or at least suspected that she recognised) the name of Miss Seeton's London friend, and was now determined to test the new arrival's bona fides.

"Miss Forby?" Mrs. McScurrie's eyes narrowed. "It's an uncommon name, as no doubt you've been told. Not Scottish."

"No," agreed Mel. "Lancashire born and bred, if you ignore those crackpot boundary changes we had foisted on us. Plain Liverpool's good enough for Amelita Forby." And she thumped her stick on the ground, trying to look like some hard-working gaffer or gammer worn out by rheumatism after years of honest toil.

"Ah, yes." Armorel's smile was thin and self-satisfied. "It's you that writes for one of the national newspapers, then? As I said, you've an uncommon name."

"Christened Amelia, so what else could I do? Except add a T, that is. Not that tea's my preferred tipple — give me coffee every time. Deadlines," she explained. "Helps keep me awake." She observed Mrs. McScurrie's expression, and hid a smile. "Just the opposite of Miss Seeton, though," she continued, making the point of old acquaintance. "Our Miss S. prefers her tea weak, no sugar — and you know Miss Seeton, too polite to tell you if you've got it wrong. Hope you've been looking after her properly."

More bristles rose along Armorel McScurrie's spine, but before she could say anything else, her employer appeared. "Miss Forby, isn't it? Good morning!" Liusaidh held out a hand, smiling. "It seems an age since we met in London."

"Certainly does." Mel's eyes flicked towards the bleak-visaged form of the housekeeper, still barring her entrance. "Only — not that I'm being rude, Lady Glenclachan, but it was Miss Seeton I came to see."

"Of course, you're old friends, aren't you? Do come in. Mrs. McScurrie, would you be kind enough to find Miss Seeton, and tell her about her visitor? And would you bring some coffee to the drawing room, please?"

The nose through which Armorel sniffed was held high in disapproval as she stalked back into the hall without a word to her mistress, who looked at Mel, and sighed. "She's been giving you a hard time, has she? I'm so sorry, but you can imagine how anxious we've been about . . . about all this. Poor Miss Seeton's here on holiday — as our guest — and we felt it our job to keep away, well . . . ."

"Undesirables?" Mel finished for her, with a grin. "Oh, I guess none of you need worry too much — we go back a long way together, Miss S. and yours truly. She took me to a bird sanctuary just last week. In Kent."

Liusaidh nodded, and led the way through to the drawing room. "She was out bird-watching when . . . when this dreadful . . . when the body was discovered. Poor Miss Seeton. I'm so afraid this will distress her far more in the longer term than she seems prepared to admit. This morning she's kept insisting she feels fine, but one can't help but suspect her of simply being polite. Yesterday, you see, she was rather shaken — which is no surprise, of course — she's led such a very quiet life. For something like this to happen . . . ."

When Mel had given up the unequal struggle and permitted the bubbling laughter deep inside her to erupt in a strangled guffaw, she had to wait several

251

minutes before she felt able to explain even part of Miss Seeton's unique quality to an astounded audience. Liusaidh kept saying "my goodness" and "I had absolutely no idea" when informed that the renowned Battling Brolly was not only staying under her roof, but was the saviour of her cherished only child.

"We never read anything about it, you see," she said to Mel, who nodded. "I suppose we were cowards not to face up to what had happened, but we simply wanted to forget everything and bring Marguerite home to Glenclachan, where we felt she'd be safe. I'm sure the press had a field day . . ." Her voice tailed away. A look of strain came into her eyes. "After your visit — and you were the first reporter to talk to us, remember . . . but then there were so many . . . and I'm afraid we simply couldn't bear any more reminders of . . . of the whole dreadful business. And we certainly didn't know about Miss Seeton —"

"No need to mention it." Mel's gesture was airy, knowing, dismissive. "She'll only be embarrassed if you do." Liusaidh looked doubtful. "Honest. Besides, who's to know that Miss S. *is* that good old Battling Brolly? Nobody who's read about her in the *Daily Negative*, that's for sure . . ."

Mrs. McScurrie, striving to obstruct Liusaidh's request without positive disobedience, had by now run out of delaying tactics. It was therefore at this moment that Miss Seeton escaped from the kindly clutches she hadn't realised held her captive, and arrived in the drawing room to look for her guest. "Mel, my dear," she greeted Miss Forby with pleasure. "How much better you look than the last time I saw you — you have made a full recovery, I trust? And how is your poor ankle?" as she noticed the stick, leaning on the side of Mel's chair. Recently broken, and the sunshine, she explained to Lady Glenclachan, apologising for her public discussion of so personal a topic as someone's health; but she had been rather concerned for dear Mel, and, had yesterday's little unpleasantness not occurred to make her forget her obligations . . .

"And it was such a beautiful day," she sighed. "So very bright for the eyes when one is tired from travelling — the sun, I mean. Such a strain for the system. The day before, that is. Not that yesterday," she added, "was not. And, of course, my dear friend Martha also suffers from them. Headaches. Bright, yet not oppressively hot — perfect for walking — or climbing.

Poor man. Unless, of course, one is recovering from a broken ankle, naturally. Before a thunderstorm, that is. Not that we have as yet had thunder, but there was certainly a storm, and the principle, one has to suppose, must be the same."

"I suppose it must," murmured Mel, while Liusaidh tried to suppress the tickle in her throat. Mel did not dare to meet her eyes. Instead, she looked straight at Miss Seeton.

"As a matter of fact, it was yesterday brought me to see you, Miss S. I've been thinking about, well, what happened — the man you found, and everything — so what I thought was, how about you try to sketch me what you saw? Just the rough idea," she added, as Liusaidh seemed about to protest. "And while you're doing it," she went on, "if you could spare a few thoughts on the topic of John Stuart Fraser, I'd be very grateful . . ."

Chapter

19

"John Stuart Fraser?" Miss Seeton repeated the unfamiliar name thoughtfully, welcoming it as a distraction from her memories of the previous day. She looked towards Liusaidh, and frowned. "Fraser — no doubt there is a clan of that name, or at least a — what was the word? Sept?" Liusaidh nodded. Miss Seeton, still frowning, went on: "And surely I have heard of the House of Fraser — the department store? Stuart, of course, would be the Scottish royal family, even though I understand from his lordship that there is currently some other family with a claim to the throne . . ."

"The Sobieksis," Liusaidh said, as Miss Seeton's frown grew deeper in an attempt to recall the details. "Archduke Casimir and his sister Clementina, of all the nonsensical names." She looked at Mel. "Surely you don't want to know about aspiring Jacobite nobility! There's a brace of them staying not fifty miles from

Glenclachan right now, but they aren't worth wasting newsprint on, believe me."

Mel's eyes gleamed, but Miss Seeton hadn't heard: she was too busy thinking. "And as for John, really, one has heard so many: Prester John, John Bull, John O'Groats," she said, with a smile for her Scottish hostess.

"John Anderson, my Jo," responded Liusaidh. "And, if we feel like another quote from Burns, how about John Barleycorn? Whisky," she explained, as Miss Seeton looked puzzled and Mel looked blank. She thickened her accent to one Harry Lauder would have admired, and declaimed: "Inspiring bold John Barleycorn,/What dangers thou canst make us scorn!/Wi' tippenny, we fear nae evil;/Wi' usquebagh, we'll face the devil! Tippenny is the dialect for twopenny, ale — tuppence a pint, in the good old days."

"Really? I had always supposed," ventured Miss Seeton, "that the song referred to ale and not whisky, though the words are somewhat different, in my recollection. Another version, no doubt, as it seems to me that the final stanza I knew at school was" — she began to hum in a gentle, off-key pipe — "They pour him out of an old brown jug and they call him home-brewed ale."

Liusaidh said cheerfully, "Well, if that doesn't sum up the difference between the Scot and the Sassenach, I really don't know what does. Methods One and Two for making use of the malt . . . What do you think, Miss Forby?"

"I think," said Mel slowly, "I'm more interested in what Miss S. makes of everything. Not that I intend to drag you into all this, honey" — hastily, and with emphasis — "and I don't want you dwelling on what happened yesterday, but — how about one of the Seeton Specials, if you can bear it?" And Miss Seeton, twisting her fingers together at the intensity of Mel's tone, hesitated.

A monumental sniff at this juncture heralded the arrival of Mrs. McScurrie with a laden tray. As the tray was banged down on the low table in front of Liusaidh, the sugar lumps danced in their silver bowl, and the cups clattered on their saucers. Mrs. McScurrie sniffed again, glared at Mel, directed a scowl towards Lady Glenclachan, and remarked to Miss Seeton that her tea, which everyone (with another glare for Mel) knew she preferred, would be here in a few moments, and if there was aught else she needed she'd only to ask. She then turned on her heel, sniffed once more, and flounced out of the room.

"My goodness," breathed Liusaidh, following the furious housekeeper with widened eyes. "You've certainly won over Mrs. McScurrie, Miss Seeton — how on earth did you manage it? Silly question," she added, before Miss Seeton could reply. "She absolutely adores the baby, of course. And after what you did for Marguerite . . ."

At Miss Seeton's blush, the countess drifted into an embarrassed silence. Mel caught her eye, and mouthed *I told you so* in Miss Seeton's direction before asking if she could have her coffee black. Liusaidh smiled, and poured, and was about to turn to Miss Seeton when, to her surprise, she saw that her guest was rising to her feet, her fingers writhing, her face wearing a look of frowning abstraction.

"If you would please excuse me," she murmured and, with a vague smile in Mel's direction, hurried from the room.

"Oh dear," said Liusaidh. "You did warn me, didn't you? I'm afraid it's because of what I said —"

"It isn't," said Mel, the Seeton expert. "It's me — or do I mean I? Whichever." She shrugged. "What I said about drawing has started her up — I thought it would. I know the signs. She's popped off to her room, or wherever she keeps her sketch-book, and she'll be back in a few minutes with a certain type of drawing that's going to be, well, kind of interesting, believe me . . ."

Mrs. McScurrie's disapproval on observing Miss Seeton's absence was awesome to behold. The month may have been August, but the temperature in the drawing room of MacSporran Castle would have broken January records. "I'll be away up to her room, then, and telling her there's a fresh pot of tea waiting," she said, on learning her favourite's whereabouts. "The puir wee soul — come here for a holiday, and never allowed a minute's peace . . ."

As Armorel stamped away in righteous indignation, Mel looked at Liusaidh, and Liusaidh looked at Mel. The faces of both would have made a picture, had anyone been there to capture them . . .

Such as Miss Seeton, for instance. Who was not there, but who, before long, proved that Mel's guess had been correct. Within five minutes of Mrs. McScurrie's departure to the rescue, there came a pattering of feet along the hall towards the drawing-room door, feet which were too light for the angry Armorel, too dithery as they approached the door to be someone who felt sure of what she was doing. "Is that you, Miss S.?" enquired Mel, raising her voice. "Come along in and let's see what you've got!

"She hates people to look at these weird sketches she does," she hissed to Lady Glenclachan, "so if you wouldn't mind not noticing . . . Hi, Miss S. Isn't that your sketchbook you've brought with you? Show! Come on, honey," as Miss Seeton wavered. "Swap you for a nice cup of tea . . ."

Miss Seeton hesitated in the doorway, her sketchbook in her hand and an apologetic look on her face. "I'm afraid," she murmured to Mel, "it's hardly — that is, I cannot really suppose you will wish to see this. I'm so sorry, but — when it's so very much like the others . . ."

The drawing which Mel finally managed to wrest from the apologetic Miss Seeton was, at first sight, another copy of that still life produced after the visit to Wounded Wings. The rock, the black bird — a crow? a raven? — and the crown; the necklace, draped so artistically . . . But closer study showed subtle variations. Certain aspects were, Mel observed as she flipped back through earlier pages of the sketchbook, given a different emphasis from that which they'd been given before. The rock was craggier, more savage-looking, strangely shaped — why did it remind Mel of a sharp-beaked bird? — and there were hills in the background which hadn't been in the two other versions. This bird seemed far larger, more looming, its claws more grasping as it clutched the necklace, which was still decorated with pearls, though set not in gold, but in a metal that looked pale and sinister, as if the lifeblood had drained out of it . . . And the crown *was* a crown, no longer a nobleman's lighter coronet but the recognised emblem of royalty . . .

Mel gazed again at the still life. It was, she'd been startled to realise, not the second, but the third version Miss Seeton had drawn. She turned a worried look towards the artist, who, now that matters, and her sketchbook, had been taken out of her hands, was blissfully drinking tea and eating a slice of shortbread. Mrs. McScurrie had been so very kind as to say that she had made it especially; might it be, Miss Seeton mused, considered an impertinence if one were to ask for the recipe? Because it was truly delicious, and dear Martha, who was sure a splendid cook, would enjoy it, Miss Seeton was sure.

But Liusaidh's reply went right over Mel

Forby's head as she looked and looked again at the still life, and thought about all she'd seen and heard during the past few days . . .

Liusaidh wondered if Miss Forby might care to join herself and Miss Seeton at luncheon, but Mel politely refused the invitation, claiming with a laugh only Thrudd Banner would have known was forced that she was far too scared of Mrs. McScurrie's probable wrath to care to risk life and limb. Like many a reporter in a delicate situation, she made her excuses and left. She had a lot to think about.

By the time she'd walked back to the Pock and Tang, her head was aching, and not only her head. Despite her use of the walking stick, her ankle, released from its plaster a matter of weeks ago, once more clamoured for liniment, bandages, and rest. In her room she had adequate supplies to deal with one problem — and in the bar she knew that Hamish McQueest kept suitable restoratives for the other.

Hamish was hovering near the reception desk as she came in through the front door, something yellow in his hand and a puzzled expression on his face. "A message for you, Miss Forby," he greeted her, one hand brushing the curl of his red moustache as he held the other out to her.

Mel nodded. "Just come, has it? Guess I know who it's from." No peace for the wicked. She'd decided to risk the operator's curiosity, and had phoned her preliminary story down to London from a call box on her way to the castle. The editor probably wanted to moan about someth— "Oh."

Mel raised an eyebrow — two eyebrows — as she read what Hamish had scrawled in shaky capitals on the sheet of yellow paper: "Telephone message from Chief Superintendent Delphick, New Scotland Yard. Both blackbirds did the trick. Well done, Miss Essand Forby. Scoop."

It took a few moments to work out what the Oracle, oracular as ever, wanted her to know. Miss Seeton's sketches, which had led to Babs Ongar at Wounded Wings, had now resulted in the apprehension of the kidnappers of Lady Marguerite Mac-Sporran. Fuller details, such as how, when, and where, Delphick was obviously unwilling to tell a stranger, which explained the cryptic nature of his message. Must have been taking a leaf or two out of Jack Crabbe's book, Mel decided with a chuckle.

The chuckle was quickly followed by a decided smirk. Whose bright idea had it been, for heaven's sake, to dig those photos out of the *Negative*'s files and charge down to Kent with them? Amelita Forby, that's who! Okay, the baby would still have ended up safely at home after taking that little Plummergen detour, but the people who took her and then lost their nerve wouldn't have been nobbled. Delphick was right: this was a scoop. Hers.

Or — was it? She remembered the expression on Liusaidh MacSporran's face as she spoke of the distress the family had undergone, spoke without being so insulting to her guest as to blame her for any anguish increased by media pressure . . . And it was old news, anyway, wasn't it? A fortnight old — time for something new — from Amelita Forby, at any rate. And in the middle of the Silly Season, she doubted if too many reporters were likely to rush all the way from Town to follow up a story two weeks old . . . She hoped. She hoped, for (she was astounded to find herself thinking) the sake of Lord and Lady Glenclachan . . .

"Must be getting feeble in my old age," she told herself as she thrust Delphick's message resolutely into the pocket of her jacket — and felt there the folded shape of Miss Seeton's most recent sketch, which she had asked if she might, for the moment, keep. Now, if *this* wasn't going to make up-to-the-minute headlines, she didn't know what was.

She brushed a hand across her forehead. Still aching. She looked at Hamish. "The bar open, is it?"

"Yes, it is." He regarded her with some curiosity. "Are you feeling somewhat fragile? No doubt it's the change in the air pressure. And a drop of what the locals call the creature is the best cure I know for that . . ."

Since Mel had sworn off Lairigigh, after she had settled herself on her accustomed stool Hamish selected a blended malt which, he assured her, had far less kick and almost as many good qualities as the pure stuff, and which was (with a smile) a bargain, being just three-quarters the price.

"An argument to appeal to a Scot," he said, chuckling as he poured.

Mel returned his smile absently. She was thinking again about the sketch in her pocket: Miss Seeton's umpteenth version of that enigmatic still life. This time, though — or Mel's instincts were all wrong — Miss S. seemed to be hinting at some

Scottish connection, rather than just producing the same indeterminate view: those hills and crags had an atmosphere about them which was, after the past couple of days, familiar. The artist had seen them in real life, or such was Mel's guess — from which her next guess followed on in an enormous leap, unjustified to anyone who had never had dealings with Miss Seeton: to the effect that, with Glenfinnan Day just around the corner, Miss Seeton, and the unfortunate Ewen Campbell, had in some way become caught up in . . . Mel could scarcely credit her own conclusion, but . . . in a plot to reinstate the House of Stuart . . .

Chapter

20

The House of Stuart — whose supporters
Mel herself had witnessed creeping into the
bar of the only pub in Glenclachan, where
the locals congregated every night, asking
for someone whose name was unknown to
the newcomer landlord, but which as a
Jacobite password could hardly be bet-
tered . . .

Ewen Campbell, fishing for pearls in an
area he'd never been known to fish before,
where those locals in the conspiracy might
reasonably assume they could conspire
undiscovered, must nevertheless have discovered them. And had died for that discovery. The Jacobites might have tried to
make his death look like an accident, but
— as the Pock and Tang's drinkers had
insisted, as Miss Seeton's few memories
coaxed by Mel had confirmed — his death
had been deliberate. No victim of an accident crawls to shelter beneath a distant
gorse bush when life-giving water is close

by, in a pool at the foot of the waterfall from whose height the victim is supposed to have fallen.

"Unless," murmured Mel, "he had concussion from the fall — and wasn't acting rationally — which I refuse to believe. Not knowing Miss S. the way I do . . ."

She moved her drink to one side, took the folded sketch out of her pocket, and unfolded it. She set it thoughtfully on the bar in front of her. Hamish, who'd been keeping an eye on her, stopped polishing glasses and moved closer.

Mel spun the drawing round so that he could study it. "Those hills," she said. "Remind you of anywhere? Anywhere around here," she amended. Even for a Jacobite conspiracy, she wasn't up to hiking halfway across the Highlands — come to think of it, she probably wasn't hiking anywhere at all this afternoon, or this evening, with her ankle. She'd have to get her scoop by remote control . . .

Think this through, Forby. Miss S. seems as sure as she ever is about any of her special sketches that the hills in the background of her still life are the same hills where she found Ewen Campbell's body. So if Hamish, for all he's a newcomer, recognises them, and confirms what Miss S. thinks . . . then it only goes to prove how very powerful her vision must have been: whatever's going on around Glenclachan isn't peanuts. And, whatever it is, it'd been haunting her for days before she even got here, judging by the number of times she seems to have turned out the same drawing over and over again. An ordinary murder — a sordid domestic squabble or a bash on the head from a professional rival — *that* would never build up in her subconscious to anything like the same extent. She's been involved in far too many murders over recent years for her vibes to go into overdrive for anything ordinary.

Which was an adjective you'd hardly apply to a plot to reinstate the Stuart kings . . . "Sorry?"

But it was not Hamish who'd spoken. Mel had been brooding so hard, she hadn't noticed the door open and Dougall McLintie come in. He strode up to the bar and asked for a double Lairigigh, looking sideways at Mel to observe her reaction. He caught a glimpse of Miss Seeton's sketch and leaned closer. Mel, without thinking, casually laid a hand over the blackbird on its rock, leaving only the background hills in general view. Dougall muttered something, picked up his drink, and headed for a corner table.

Mel uncovered the sketch and looked at Hamish. He'd had ample time to think about it. "Well?"

"Well, I'd say not, at a first glance — around here, you said, didn't you? Yet there's something . . . something that reminds me . . ." With a final tweak at his moustache, he seemed to make up his mind. "Have you ever been to" — his voice held a peculiar emphasis — "Skoon, Miss Forby?"

Mel frowned. "Spelled like scone? As in the Stone of Scone that somebody pinched from under the Coronation Chair in Westminster Abbey about twenty years ago?"

"That's the place." He regarded her strangely, through narrowed eyes. "So they did. And it's generally supposed to have been found, and returned to be a sign of England's domination of the Scots — generally supposed," he repeated, fixing her with an intense look and nodding sagely. "Maybe they got the real one back — or maybe it's just a copy in the Abbey, while the real Stone of Destiny is hidden away somewhere, waiting to crown the kings again as they used to be crowned. And what's in the back of my mind . . . Have you ever been to Perth, Miss Forby?"

"In Australia?" Mel had a fair idea, though, that Hamish was about to tell her this wasn't what he'd meant.

"In Scotland." Good guess, Forby: Miss S. strikes again! As Mel had felt sure she would . . . "There's a look," Hamish said slowly, "of the hills around Perth in that picture, not that I've any claim to know them particularly well — but Old Scone and the palace are just outside the city, Miss Forby." He gazed at her once more. "Which isn't all that far from where the, er, archduke and his sister are staying . . ."

Mel felt that, considering how the bar was starting to fill with regulars, Hamish could have dropped his voice a little more, but the landlord's lack of tact was his problem, not hers. Hers, she realised as soon as she asked him where Perth stood in relation to Glenclachan, was rather more immediate. She had decisions to make, and, though of course she trusted Miss Seeton's sketch, she wasn't the Oracle. She might be misinterpreting it. What she needed was some way to check on her suspicions without having to travel miles out of her way, by car (since Hamish had warned there was no railway line) and with a wonky ankle . . .

"You know a fair bit about history —" she began, but the landlord shook his head.

"Good heavens, no. I was an engineer, before I had to retire," and he rubbed the base of his spine again. "I'm a great believer in self-preservation, you see, which is why — well, with so many people round here going on and on about the Sacred Cause . . . but I'm no expert, Miss Forby. If it's information about the Jacobites you want, you couldn't do better than consult old Philly Beigg." And he explained something of Philomena's reputation to a more-than-interested Mel, who resolved to talk to the historian before too long but, on learning where she lived, decided it would be wise to rest her ankle for a while before going to find her.

Or so she told Hamish: partly for his benefit, partly to satisfy the curiosity of any of the Jacobite clientele who might be listening. Let them think she wasn't going after her scoop today. They'd be wrong.

Because she was going to sit on this stool, saving her ankle for the important task she was going to impose on it: to follow, when he left the Pock and Tang in company with the conspirators, the next person who came into the bar asking for

John Stuart Fraser . . .

Fleet Street breeds considerable cunning. Mel, loudly bemoaning her ankle, asked if Shona could be persuaded to make sandwiches, or the Scottish equivalent of a ploughman's lunch. She had no intention of moving from the bar to waste valuable snooping time on mere food, served too slowly in the dining room: she'd take a bet that this would be the one occasion when the Fraser-hunter (if any came) didn't stay and drink with his new friends until closing time, but, as soon as he'd made contact after the exchange of passwords, went straight out again.

And, when and where he went, Amelita Forby was going to be as close behind him as she could manage . . .

She just hoped she'd made the right choice; she frowned, rubbing her forehead. Hamish looked at her. "That storm's still on its way, Miss Forby, make no doubt about it. We'll have some remarkable pyrotechnics before long . . ."

Though she restrained her drinking as much as possible, orange juice takes up more room than whisky: not for nothing are spirits colloquially known as "shorts." Mel waited for a commendably long time, but there came a moment when even she could wait no longer. She slipped out to the cloakroom.

Her return was much sooner than any of the drinkers had expected. ". . . keechin," she heard someone say, as she came back into the bar. "Wheesht! Mind the white sheet, eh?"

Somebody else choked over a mouthful of whisky, and Mel thought she overheard a muttered reference to jute. Dundee, she reminded herself as she hopped back up on her stool, was in Scotland. Vague memories of school geography, combined with what she'd read in the travel pages of the *Daily Negative*, made her think of ropes, and sacking, and hessian mats. Which latter (she supposed) somebody had thoughts of using in the decoration of their kitchen, although where the white sheet came into it, she had no idea. Unless, of course, it was the curtains, or the tablecloth. Did people make tablecloths out of jute?

"Do cats eat bats?" Mel murmured, unable to answer any of the questions she'd asked, and settled herself to listen, watch, and wait once more in the bar of the Pock and Tang.

The promised storm, when it came, was

every bit as spectacular as Miss Seeton had been led to suppose. Grey-green clouds surged out of the north, collided with the sweeter, calmer air from the south, and became trapped in the glen, piling layer upon layer until they turned from grey to charcoal, from charcoal to midnight black. "And it's not four in the afternoon yet," said Liusaidh, cuddling Marguerite as she held her before an open window to see what would happen. She was not too young, this longed-for Glenclachan heiress, to witness for herself (her father insisted) the climate which had nourished and tormented and inspired generations of MacSporrans. Liusaidh agreed, but insisted in her turn that it should be, while she was still so very young, from indoors.

"She's safe enough, now the kidnappers are caught," said Ranald, who had been in an exhilarated mood since Delphick's telephone call. One or two celebratory drams had been drunk to wet the baby's head and welcome her home, but Liusaidh, though smiling secretly for her husband's enthusiasm, stayed firm. If Ranald wanted to rush out in a thunderstorm and risk death by lightning, if not by double pneumonia, he was at liberty to do so, but she, and Marguerite, and Miss Seeton had more sense, and would watch the storm from within the stout-walled safety of Mac-Sporran Castle.

And it had been worth watching. As solid shafts of rain leached blackness from the sky, vivid spears and forks and sheets of lightning tinted the growing grey with colours not seen on any earthly palette. "Psychedelic," cried Ranald, who had decided against going outside when he saw just how heavy the downpour was. "Is that not the word for such a sight, Miss Seeton?"

Miss Seeton, sighing for her lack of talent, agreed that she believed it was, then blinked as the whole world seemed suddenly turned to purplish-green, and the castle shook to its very foundations. "Right on top of us, that one!" the earl exulted; then, a moment later: "Good God!"

A second thunderous rumble had shaken the floor, even as the first was still dying away, but there had been no lightning flash to herald it. And, as it rumbled on, it changed more to a clattering — not raindrops, not even hail, but — "The tower!" Ranald dropped his glass of whisky and ran from the room. Liusaidh stared out through the rain. "The roof," she gasped, looking where Ranald had looked, along to the farthest visible corner. "The portrait tower — it's been struck by lightning!"

Indeed it had. The clatter was the sound of slates, tumbling from their broken rafters to the ground, and above the roar of the storm and the crack of timber came the grim jangling of splintered glass. "Oh," moaned Liusaidh, as she clutched the baby to her breast, "if it catches fire . . ."

Marguerite, who until now had been a silent, interested spectator, uttered a little squawk at being so nearly smothered. Miss Seeton uttered her own little squeak of sympathy; and, as with a hasty "Hold her, please," Lady Glenclachan thrust the baby into the arms of her startled guest to rush out after her husband, from all corners of the castle came other, louder cries as the alarm was raised. People shouted for buckets, and the hose; for axes, and the pump. Mrs. McScurrie's shrill advice that she had called the fire brigade could just be heard above the slashing hiss of the rain as it pelted past the window and fell in a relentless waterfall from the gutterless roof to the ground . . .

And, as Miss Seeton watched and worried, from the top floor of the portrait tower flames began to flicker.

Next morning, only two persons in the whole of MacSporran Castle were to wake with nerves unshattered by the events of the night. Lady Marguerite, of course, had been too young to participate in any active way in the saving of her future inheritance — but everyone else had had a role to play, whether large or small.

Miss Seeton's had been limited, on Liusaidh's instructions, to taking care of the baby as she had done so well on previous occasions. "You're our guest, Miss Seeton," the countess had reminded her. "We can't expect you to start running around with mops and tarpaulins . . ." She was careful to suggest no other reason — indeed, would have felt it foolish, if not an impertinence, to do so. Miss Seeton's slight form and grey hair might indicate a person some years into retirement, but her physical agility and stamina would have shamed many half her age. Nevertheless, reasoned Lady Glenclachan, there were people in plenty at the castle capable of scrambling about in the fire brigade's wake, putting things to rights, but Miss Seeton was one of the very few who could keep the baby quiet.

By the time that the fire (mercifully

more or less under control before the engine, manned by village volunteers, arrived) had been extinguished, the tower checked for structural damage, and the portraits of past MacSporrans removed to a place of safety, it was so late in the evening as to be almost time for bed. Supper, a meal whose snatched nature brought tears of mortification to the eyes of Mrs. McScurrie, was served to all who had joined in the struggle to thwart the elements. Laird Ranald dispensed drams at triple measure to deserving clan members — which meant everybody there — thanking them in a broken voice for their loyal efforts. Blind Diarmid Pirr, the piper, roused from his cottage by all the commotion, composed a fitting lament, and played it to great approval.

And then, worn out by excitement, heroism, and physical exertion, everyone went home.

Chapter

21

Mel Forby, observing the rush from the bar when the summons to man the fire engine was given, spent an anxious hour or so wishing she'd weaselled her way up to the castle to make sure of Miss Seeton's safety: but she was enough of a realist, reporter though she was, to know she would only have been in the way, far more of a hindrance than a help. With her physical limitations, she couldn't even have carried a bucket to any useful purpose. In the normal way, a bolt of lightning and a fire would have had her struggling through the storm to get her story — but she was no longer able to think of the Glenclachans as ordinary headline material. If Thrudd ever found out how soft she was becoming . . .

But the events of the day had put paid, she thought, to any hope that the Jacobites would do anything of interest. She decided to wait for the return of the fire fighters, find out what she could, and telephone the castle if necessary — which it wasn't. Hamish poured whisky, and smiled dryly as the quality of his Lairigigh was unfavourably compared to Ranald's Rainbird; and Mel's ears caught references to the "wee body caring for the bairn as good as any nurse" who, as further comments made plain, could only have been Miss Seeton. Relieved, and resolving to telephone her friend first thing in the morning, Mel went, like everyone else, to bed — where her slumbers, like those of almost everyone else, were disturbed by further rumbles of thunder, and another burst of heavy, battering rain.

Of all the inhabitants of the glen that night, only two enjoyed undisturbed sleep: the Lady Marguerite MacSporran (whose armstocratic thumb lulled her into oblivion and kept her there for the regulation eight hours) and Miss Emily Seeton, who, before climbing into her enchanting four-poster bed, had not omitted (despite the day's excitement) to perform a single exercise of her yoga routine, and who therefore not only slept soundly, but was able to wake, fully refreshed, at seven o'clock in the morning.

Not a soul was stirring about the castle as Miss Seeton, having carried out the matutinal part of her programme, followed by her toilet, opened her bedroom door and peeked into the corridor. Really, it was not surprising — they must all be so very tired, after so much hard work — and, while one understood that the baby had to be cared for, one had felt rather . . . *guilty* might be considered self-indulgent, but certainly *superfluous*, when everyone else had been so busy — though the countess had been kind enough to say that one had been of use, but, though this was no doubt true, it had not been of such very *physical* use as the others . . .

In another's house, Miss Seeton hesitated to enter the kitchen, though she longed for a cup of tea. But it was a lovely morning, after the storm, just the day for a walk in the hills, and another picnic — for which there was, surely, no need to trouble anyone at the castle. Had she not seen a fine assortment of snack foods in Mrs. Pictarnitie's general stores? A bottle of orange squash, perhaps, which one could dilute with water from one of the burns, a packet of chocolate bisc— No, they would melt in the sunshine of what promised to be a warm day. But cheese straws, an apple or two — how fortunate that one did not have too large an appetite — a packet of plain digestive biscuits, which wouldn't melt, a plastic beaker, if one could be bought. His lordship's silver flask-top had been around the right size . . .

Miss Seeton collected her handbag, umbrella, binoculars, and sketchbook, scribbled a brief explanatory note which she left on the large oak chest in the hall, and drew back the bolts on the castle's front door, iron-banded and heavy. With a creak, it swung slowly inwards, and Miss Seeton held her breath. Despite the assurances of Lord Glenclachan that the suits of armour, one on either side of the doorway, had stood there for generations, one couldn't help wondering . . . But the arc of the opening door had clearly been calculated to within an inch by some long-ago MacSporran. The armour, be-speared and be-shielded (only had his lordship not told her that such shields were known as targes?) remained safe and shining in its appointed position.

She released her pent-up breath, and drew in another. Her nostrils were assailed by a strange, acrid smell, which she soon realised was that of water-soaked ashes warmed by the rising sun, wafted through the door by the brisk, though pleasant, morning breeze. Miss Seeton's nose twitched; her eyes sparkled. Everything seemed set to make this a perfect day for a walk, and she started out with a joyful step.

She failed to notice that the incoming breeze had caught up her careful note, whisking it from the top of the ancient chest down behind the back of the carved oak settle, where it was invisible to all but the most thorough search . . .

She would not, she decided, walk in the same direction she'd taken the other day. After all, she hadn't found the gold mine, and she *had* found . . . well, she hadn't found the gold mine. Not that one seriously expected to find . . . but it did no harm to amuse oneself with daydreams, and there was the possibility of a rare bird, at least — and the certainty of fine weather, for the sky was a vivid blue, without a single cloud. Halfway down the long castle drive, Miss Seeton turned to look back at the forlorn sight of the portrait turret's tarpaulin-covered roof, and sighed. At least there seemed to be no further risk of rain . . .

As she neared the bottom of the drive, she remembered the Wolf Stone she had seen on her first night in Glenclachan, and went to take another look. Her eye was caught by an effect of light and shadow which hadn't been there at that later hour, and she settled herself on the stone to capture as much as she could on paper. Here, she recalled his lordship as saying, the Glenclachan of his time had mustered the clan's fighting men in support of Bonnie Prince Charlie, who had tried to take the throne on behalf of his father. Claymores and kilts and bagpipes, she supposed — no, not kilts, from what Miss Beigg had said, but belted plaids, whatever they might be. A most impressive sight, none the less, she felt sure . . .

And so, to her delight, they soon were: striding across her sketchbook, shoulder to shoulder, rank upon rank of brawny warriors, bright-eyed with conviction, ready to give their lives for the Jacobite cause. Mistakenly so, as she had gathered from his lordship and Miss Beigg, but courageously — gloriously — unforgettably. Two hundred and thirty years later, even Miss Emily Seeton, English spinster, could thrill to the symbol of the white cockade in the bonnets of the foremost rows of clansmen, blazing defiant loyalty to the Stuart crown . . . the crown which she hadn't noticed herself drawing, but which had appeared, mysteriously, as the goal towards which the host was marching, a shining presence in the distant hills. Hills whose perspective made them seem much closer than common sense suggested they must be. Otherwise, she supposed (having puzzled over this for a while), it would not have been possible to make out so much of the detail in the crown. Such an unusual cross on the top . . . such, well, restraint in the number of jewels and their setting . . .

Miss Seeton sat so motionless in thought that a passing blackbird diverted from its course with a curious flick of its wings and alighted on the ground almost at her feet. With an upward flirt of its tail, it hopped a few steps, stopped, listened, and suddenly plunged its orange beak down through the moss to emerge with a worm wriggling frantically in its grasp. Miss Seeton blinked.

"Breakfast," she said firmly. The blackbird nodded, and flew away. Miss Seeton collected her belongings together and continued her stroll down into the village.

When she pushed open the door of Jamesina Pictarnitie's shop, it was to find more people there than she might have expected, at so early an hour. Or — she glanced at her watch — was it indeed so early? Days were long and nights were short in a Highland summer, she had been told, and no doubt everyone was accustomed to making the most of the extra hours before winter followed autumn, bringing shorter days and long, dark, chilly nights. Which, thankfully, were some months away.

"Good morning," said Miss Seeton, as everyone stopped talking at her entrance. She smiled. They smiled back: was this not the shy wee soul who'd found the laird's baby in a telephone box, and didn't care to have a fuss made? They greeted her cheerfully and asked how things were at the castle after all the excitement: the excitement which had been the topic under discussion when Miss Seeton arrived.

"Very well, I believe, though tired, of course, with so very much to worry about during the night — his lordship's ancestors, you see, except that they were removed early on, but it is only temporary, as I understand. And they are to come later today, I believe, to repair the turret roof properly — the builders. Because it can do such a great deal of damage, can it not? Lightning, that is."

"Aye, so it can, and that's a fact," replied Mrs. Pictarnitie. "Though there's damage and damage, of course," which cryptic remark she followed with a chuckle, echoed by everyone else in the shop except Miss Seeton, who smiled politely. Jamesina added, as the general mirth died away, how true it was that every cloud had a silver lining. It helped to find it, of course, if you knew from which direction the cloud was to come — as Dougall McLintie no doubt agreed.

Everybody laughed again. Pete Reake, one of the loudest laughers added, sometimes turned up trumps, after all; there was Dougall, being paid twice over for doing the same job of work, all thanks to the weather . . .

Miss Seeton was by now looking so puzzled that Jamesina took pity on her. "The weather cock," she explained. "Fair and square hit by a dagger of lightning last night, not ten minutes after your trouble up at the castle, and sent crashing to the ground in shivereens. 'Twas by a miracle naebody suffered hurt, for it's a gey heavy weight. Dougall, the daftie, sees it as a judgement on him for the drink — though he's not above charging to mend it, judgement or no."

"And he's all for putting it back thegither with north and south in their

288

correct place," said someone, as Jamesina drew breath. "But the minister, now, he's for having it as it was, on account of people coming frae miles to see — and good for business, of course," which had everyone laughing again. Really, thought Miss Seeton, one might almost be at home in dear Plummergen, for everyone was so friendly . . .

"And what other cause would people have to come to Glenclachan?" asked someone, with a wink for Miss Seeton. "Save the scenery, that's to say, for you're no gun, from the look of you — and besides, himself cancelled the shoot this year, on account of all the upset over the bairn."

"If you're wanting an attraction," suggested Jamesina in some haste, sparing Miss Seeton's blushes, "never forget there's the creature." A smile ran round the little shop. Miss Seeton's interest quickened, and she nodded.

"The Loch Ness Monster," she said, producing the broadest smiles so far. "Or rather — that is to say, although art is my subject and not geography, but I believe Loch Ness is rather a long way from here, is it not? If Glenclachan has its own monster, perhaps one could encourage visitors

. . ." As the smiles grew broader, she turned slightly pink. "Or there is always, of course, the Best Kept Village Competition, if these are held in Scotland as they are in England. Plummergen," she informed the shoppers with pride, "came second this year, and the results have been most gratifying — such a great many people, coming to admire, and of course we are all aware of our duty to share our good fortune. Mr. Treeves — our vicar, that is — has written with some eloquence on the subject in the parish magazine . . ."

Miss Seeton is incapable of telling an untruth. She had no knowledge, as she spoke, of Plummergen's general belief that it had been the vicar's sister Molly who originally penned those stirring lines which were copied by her dutiful brother and published over his name, but some vague memory of Martha Bloomer's brisk remarks on the topic now tugged at her conscience. She allowed her words to tail away into silence.

"We'll stick with the weather vane, I'm thinking," Jamesina said, with another chuckle. "The shelter in the glen's not sufficient for growing grand flowers so far north, even in summer — though it's fine enough scenery, nae doubt of that.

Will you be off on another walk this morning?"

Miss Seeton agreed that she would. As everybody was to be so very occupied today with builders and repairs, she explained, one felt it only courteous to remove one's presence temporarily from the castle so that no one need feel obliged to entertain or otherwise worry about her. Craftsmen, she knew only too well from watching dear Mr. Eggleden the blacksmith at home, found it disconcerting in the extreme to have unskilled persons in the vicinity, making foolish remarks — not, of course, that she was suggesting for a moment that the earl or his wife would make foolish remarks, or even that she herself would be so, well, careless, she sincerely hoped — but it seemed to her far more sensible to leave them plenty of room this morning to manoeuvre, if that was the word she wanted. The builders, she meant.

"Very sensible," approved Mrs. Pictarnitie, with a nod. "You'll take good care, though, that it's only for the morning you'll be away? By the look of things, there's another storm to come, and a wee body like you'd be drowned in no time if it's half so bad as yesterday."

The entire shop seconded this view, and Miss Seeton was pink with gratification at such kindly concern for the welfare of a stranger. She promised to be back at the castle well before lunch, and now would like to purchase some few small items for a picnic, or rather, of course, when Mrs. Pictarnitie had finished serving her other customers.

But the other customers insisted they were in no hurry; not a shopper in Jamesina's little store but threw herself into the task of selecting a suitable picnic for the Sassenach lady who'd saved the laird's baby, and Miss Seeton was on her way, with adequate provisions in her bag and a warm glow in her heart, before another ten minutes had elapsed.

She remembered to look for the broken weather vane as she passed the kirk, and saw someone she supposed to be Dougall McLintie, the smith, shaking his head over the wrought-iron wreckage at the foot of the clock tower.

Automatically, Miss Seeton noted the time. Rather later than she had thought, but still not too late for a pleasant walk, and perhaps a little exploration . . .

It did not occur to her to wonder why Dougall — if that shaker of so sorrowful a head was indeed Glenclachan's answer to Daniel Eggelden — had been the first person of the male gender she had observed anywhere about the village that morning . . .

Chapter
22

Mel Forby, risen late from her bed when Shona came knocking to service the room, encountered Hamish in the foyer of the hotel. As he greeted her, she recalled his suggestion of the previous afternoon that she should consult Miss Philomena Beigg about the Jacobites. But her brain was working slowly this morning: lack of sleep, she supposed.

"That thunderstorm last night —" she began, then broke off with a yawn. "Wow. The Scots really go in for weather in a big way, don't they?"

"Last night was certainly out of the ordinary," acknowledged the landlord with a smile. "Will you have breakfast before setting about your affairs?"

"If there's any still on offer, guess I should." She'd ignore his passing comment on her morals, thought Mel with a giggle. "I need something to wake me up properly — nothing too heavy, though. I've got problems to solve today, so I have to be right on the ball from the start. Toast and coffee will do fine, and then I'm off to talk to the local historian, if she's in."

"On a Saturday morning, she's usually doing the housework after working on her books all week," said Hamish, confirming Mel's suspicion that villages were no different the whole country — if not the world — over. In Plummergen, too, your business was as much your neighbour's as your own, even if you'd only lived in the place for five minutes. There was only one exception to this rule —

"Miss Seeton!" Mel slapped a hand across her forehead. "Hey, I forgot — I was going to ring the castle!"

Hamish eyed her strangely. "That's your friend staying with Lord Glenclachan — the one who found the baby? You've no need to worry about her — I saw her earlier on, just by the church, when I slipped out for a breath of air. She had the look of someone going out for a long time, and I can't say I blame her, knowing how the builders will be running round the castle today getting under everybody's feet. She seems the type to enjoy a walk."

"Oh, she is. You're sure, well, she looked okay?"

"She looked fine. Off for another day's bird-watching, I expect — let's hope she has rather better luck than last time. Only joking," he reassured her, as Mel still looked anxious. "She'll be fine — no reason on earth why she shouldn't be. A sensible little woman, by all accounts."

"She used to be a teacher, before she retired . . ."

"There you are, then — no need to worry! If she's anything like the school-marm who first taught me my letters, you couldn't wish for anyone better able to take care of herself. Just as you," Hamish reminded her, "should be taking care of *your* good self, Miss Forby. Breakfast, wasn't it, before you go to talk to Philomena Beigg?"

And, before Mel quite knew how it had happened, she'd been hustled by Hamish through to the dining room, seated at a table, and left while he departed kitchen-wards, calling for Shona and talking of coffee, hot brown toast, and, as a special treat, heather honey.

New Year's Eve, reflected Mel half an hour later, might be the traditional time for making resolutions — but there was always room for someone to challenge tradition. August the eighteenth would

296

henceforth go down in her personal calendar as "never eat honey with newly washed hair unless you've first tied it back with a ribbon" day . . .

And it was not until she was towelling the last sticky traces from her shoulder-length locks that the significance of that date struck her. August the eighteenth — just one day before August the nineteenth: Glenfinnan Day. One of the high spots of the Jacobite calendar . . .

The ache in her ankle was almost forgotten as Mel made her hurried way to the cottage of Miss Philomena Beigg. She hadn't bothered to telephone ahead, Shona having assured her that in and around Glenclachan it was a rare individual who could vanish for long without his or her neighbours knowing. "Except," she added, as Hamish busied himself elsewhere, "Mr. McQueest, for he aye disappears and leaves the running of this place to the rest of us — but who cares for him? He's a Sassenach, begging your pardon, Miss Forby." And Shona pressed another helping of honey on Mel to show there were no hard feelings, before explaining that if a visitor were to arrive on Miss Beigg's doorstep and she not there to greet her, then someone would not only know

297

where she might have gone, and how long she was like to be away, but would most probably offer to send to fetch her, if the said visitor seemed in a hurry.

Mel, pondering once more the complexities of country life, decided it would do no harm to trust the waitress's local knowledge. What if she phoned, and nobody answered? By the time she'd walked as far as the cottage to check, the missing Miss Beigg would no doubt be back at home . . .

Miss Beigg was, however, already at home when Mel rapped on her front door. About her middle she had tied a checked apron, in her hand she carried a feather duster, and on her face she wore a look of extreme boredom — which disappeared the instant Mel introduced herself.

"Amelita Forby of the *Daily Negative*? And my book only just out! Isn't that splendid? Do come in."

She tossed the duster into a corner, tugged at her apron in a halfhearted manner, and ushered Mel right through to the kitchen with the grubby gingham still flapping round her waist. "I loathe housekeeping," she said. "Any excuse to stop, and I'll take it. I was on the point of making myself a cup of coffee — you'll join me, won't you? And then you can tell me why you've really come — oh" — as Mel tried to speak — "there's no need to be polite, my dear. I'm enough of a realist to know that the national press doesn't come all the way into the Highlands to talk to someone like me just because of a few books on natural history and a novel or two."

Mel was charmed by this approach. So many people — Miss Seeton being one of the rare exceptions — would do virtually anything to have their names in the newspapers; most of them (and what they did) were hardly, in her opinion, worth the effort, although more than once she'd struggled valiantly to suppress that opinion as she wrote her story.

"Oh, I'm not so sure about that," she said slowly. "Not after all I've heard about you — and especially now I've met you. I reckon I could do a nice little feature on you, Miss Beigg. Once you've told me what I want to know, of course. You help me, I help you: have we got a deal?"

Philomena raised an eyebrow. "We most certainly have, Miss Forby, though I might well have chosen to tell you what you wished to know in any event. It's a lonely life, being an author. You're always glad of the chance to chat — once you're finished your work for the day, that is." She tugged again at her knotted apron strings, muttered what Mel took to be a Gaelic imprecation, and snatched open the drawer of the kitchen table. As she took out a wicked-looking pair of scissors, she sighed.

"Yet what my poor dear father — an idealist, Miss Forby — would have said if he'd ever dreamed I would become not only the victim, but the perpetrator of even such a gentle blackmail, heaven alone can say." She brandished the bright steel blades under Mel's startled nose. "Would you mind?" And promptly turned her back. "I am quite unable to think straight with this abomination about my midriff."

Mel shrugged. She didn't much care for the domestic life, either. "With one bound, our heroine was free," she said, snipping cheerfully. "What do you plan to do with the pieces — a patchwork quilt, or something?"

Miss Beigg snorted. "Your sense of humour, Miss Forby, may yet lead to a breach between us before you have achieved the object of your visit. Suppose you sit down and tell me all about it, while I boil the kettle?"

When you decided to tell everything in due order, mused Mel as she obeyed Miss

Beigg's command, it sounded rather, well, unlikely. Unless you knew Miss Seeton, and, since she was a person whose privacy must be respected, it wasn't easy to explain just why you felt as strongly as you did that something odd was going on. Careful now, Forby . . .

"I've heard you know pretty much all there is to know of Highland history," she began, waited for Philomena's modest disclaimer, and then continued. "So suppose you give me some sort of condensed Jacobite background? Modern times, I mean — not the two-hundred-years-ago stuff — fanatics of the nineteen-seventies sort of thing."

"Modern Jacobites?" Philomena frowned. "There's always the Seventeen Forty-Five Association, but nobody could call them fanatical. Scholarly, intelligent — but that's not" — as Mel stirred — "what you want, is it? You're looking for a bunch of dreamers who think all they have to do is supply an heir — Archduke Casimir, as he calls himself, for example — and Queen Elizabeth will bow gracefully out of Balmoral and off the Scottish throne. Right?"

"Right. I'm staying at the Pock and Tang, and the other night, at Ewen Campbell's wake, there seemed to be an awful lot of Jacobite-type songs floating around — at least, the landlord said that's what they were. Nobody else was willing to talk to me." Mel smiled. "So I wondered . . ."

Miss Beigg smiled back. "August is indeed the silly season, Miss Forby, if reporters are reduced to the writing of stories based on the visit of a pair of minor European royalty — self-styled royalty, at that — and the maudlin music of whisky-sodden songsters." She paused. "Dear me. Not bad, for an impromptu effort! But, seriously, to answer your question — I know of no such group of persons, nor can I credit that any could flourish without falling by the wayside before too long. Oh, there might be a burst of initial enthusiasm, if someone sufficiently — I dislike the debased modern meaning of the word, but *charismatic* will have to do — if someone of that nature should put him or her self forward as a leader . . . but whoever it was would soon find that stirring the populace to rebellion is far easier said than done. The momentum would have to be maintained, and there would need to be even the least chance that something would happen — which is improbable in the extreme — to keep the general interest. We Scots are romantic, nobody is going to deny that fact, but" — switching suddenly to a strong brogue — "aye canny wi' it. There's a solid ground of guid common sense beneath all the kilts and the singing and the bagpipe laments, ye ken." She chuckled, and returned to her normal voice. "I honestly don't believe you'll find much to write about in Casimir and Clementina, I'm afraid."

Mel hesitated. Would it be betraying a confidence? But unless she said who'd drawn the thing, she didn't think . . .

"What do you make of this?" she enquired, drawing Miss Seeton's sketch out of her pocket and unfolding it. "Looks awfully like a crown, to me — and they were singing 'Good luck to my blackbird,' which Hamish McQueest assured me —"

"Hamish McQueest!" Philomena dismissed the landlord of the Pock and Tang with a toss of her grey head. "That man's borrowed more history books from me, and caused more trouble with the borrowing, than anyone else I can think of. Goodness knows why he seems to take such delight in trampling on the finer feelings of his customers, but he does. I'm not a frequenter of the hotel myself, but I've heard about Hamish McQueest."

"Oh, yes?" Mel cocked her head to one

side, her eyes as bright as any blackbird. She knew professional rivalry when she saw it: Thrudd Banner, for one. "Have you also," in her crispest tones, "heard about John Stuart Fraser?"

Philomena Beigg stared. Mel's smile was triumphant. "John *Stuart* Fraser," she repeated, with emphasis. "There's an awful lot of people interested in him — including yours truly. What do you know about him? Where's he hiding out? Nobody seems to know anything about him . . ."

Philomena continued to stare. She blinked, and shook her head. "John Stuart Fraser," she repeated. "Well, if it weren't for the fact that you seem so very sure he's alive today, I could have told you a little about him, but —"

"Alive today — you mean he's not? He's dead? Was he murdered, like Ewen Campbell? When?" But then Mel noticed Philomena's expression. It was a mixture of amusement and apology — for bursting the bubble, Mel suddenly guessed. She said slowly, "So . . . he was in history . . . not recent?"

"He was indeed, if he's the one I'm thinking about. One of the last great Highland heroes, in many people's opinion; not that of my father, I hasten to add, for he wasn't only a romantic at heart, he was a strict elder of the kirk. Which made it easier for him than for many Scots to pay his taxes to the government with hardly a murmur, though I'm sure it hurt him every bit as much. Whereas your man Fraser . . ."

Mel said nothing, but her look was eloquent. Philomena might almost have been said to smirk. "Why, he was one of the finest whisky smugglers who ever gave the Revenue men a run for their money — the last of the big-time boys, by all accounts. The first quarter of the nineteenth century, as far as I recall. In earlier days, Miss Forby, the distillation of whisky had been more or less a cottage industry for centuries — but then authority tried to muscle in, as it always does. John Stuart Fraser, who was obviously a canny fellow, used to smuggle the stuff south in coffins, up to thirty gallons a week — pure malt, what's more. Until the government reduced the excise duty and forced distillers to store the spirit in warehouses, there were around fifteen hundred illicit stills in the Highlands."

"Oh," said Mel. "Then — if anyone came along asking for John Stuart Fraser . . ."

"I'd suspect," said Miss Beigg in a dry tone, "that he — for any woman would have more concern for the state of her liver — was dropping a coded hint that he'd been told about a secret still, somewhere in the area — and wanted to sample a dram or two before committing himself to buy. Because, of course, there'd be a risk. He'd be worried about breaking the law . . ."

"And the people running the still," said Mel, "would be breaking it too. Wouldn't they?"

But were they likely to be worried about it — worried enough to kill?

Chapter

23

Miss Seeton had not been walking for very long, and was wondering in which direction she should strike out across the moor — her map had shown that the nearest suitable burn was half a mile away — when there came a rattle and a toot from behind her. Turning, she beheld a ramshackle single-decker bus, khaki and dark green in livery, drawing in to the side of the road.

Though the sun was in her eyes, she could see the driver beckoning to her through the windscreen. "You'll be wanting a ride, hen," he said, as she trotted up in response to his summons. "Hop in now, and save your legs. Where had you a mind to go?"

Miss Seeton replied that really, she had no idea; she'd simply thought that it was a lovely day for a little exploring — she produced the map — although she had no intention of going too far, as she had promised to be back in time for lunch. The driver, with a chuckle, advised her in that case to give Balmoral a miss, for today. Miss Seeton smiled, and replied that perhaps — if it would not trouble him to do so, of course — the driver might be kind enough to suggest a few places of interest — a view worth sketching, the habitat of some unusual birds — that she could reach without having to travel too far?

The driver rubbed his nose, and asked to study the map, which made Miss Seeton a little anxious lest his passengers might complain at being delayed in this fashion, when she'd only meant him to make a few suggestions; but, standing on tiptoe and leaning on her umbrella as she craned her neck, she could make out only one other person in the body of the bus: a white-haired old gentleman bent over a gnarled stick, nodding in apparent slumber. Since he said nothing — and the driver was holding out his hand — and she would be so grateful for any advice, Miss Seeton passed her new friend the map, and stood waiting while he pondered and the engine idled.

"Aye," he said at last, rubbing his nose again, "there's no problem, if it's birds you're wanting. Three or four miles further on there's a wee loch, a matter of a few hundred yards from this turning" — he leaned out of the window to indicate the spot on the map — "and a shelter put up a short while since that's not shown here, on account of being new. You could settle yourself for an hour or so to watch the birds, then come back to the main road to hail the next one of our buses that comes by. It's a regular route, and the driver's sure to stop, just as I did. How does that sound?"

It sounded splendid. Miss Seeton asked how often one might expect a bus to come by, and learned that the Saturday service ran once an hour, which was sufficiently reassuring to make up her mind for her. She hurried round to the passenger door and quickly climbed the steps.

"And be sure to wait on the other side of the road from where I'll set you down," said the driver, taking her money with a smile. "About quarter past the hour — och, no, you may as well make that twenty past, today." He sighed, and shook his head. "We cannae be so sure of running to time at present, I have to tell you, on account of the traffic being held up Larick way while some fancy film director's taking what they call location shots — for the cinema, ye ken."

"How very exciting," interposed Miss Seeton, inveterate film-goer. The driver stared at her.

"Exciting? Aye, well, mebbe it is, if you're not fashed by living with all the commotion. Three days, it's going to take, they told us — starting yesterday. Market day! Local colour, the man called it." He sighed again. "But it's not just the damned disruption, if you'll excuse me, while they close the roads: it's the way everyone's gone rampaging mad. Dressing in costume as extras, if you can credit anything so daft." He chuckled suddenly. "The director, or whatever he calls himself, asked my cousin Jamie if he was interested, so Jamie said he might be, if there was money in it. Twenty pound a day, says the man. But Jamie's aye canny. 'And how much is the star being paid?' he wanted to know — never one at a loss for words, isn't Jamie. There's some folk think a Scotsman will do anything for money, and near enough a whole town willing to make believe it's the time of the Highland Clearances and go prancing around like a pack of fules!"

His final words woke the sleeper halfway down the bus, who jerked himself upright, blinked, and remarked in a loud voice that he couldn't agree more. Whereupon Miss

Seeton, feeling guilty at having delayed proceedings with her questions, made haste to take her seat near the front, while the driver stamped on the accelerator and sent the bus jolting down the road.

He set her down at the junction with what she had expected would be a side road, but was in reality a rough track. "Sure you'll be all right, hen? Twenty past the hour, dinna forget now!" And tootling a farewell blast on the horn, he drove the old bus away in a rattle of blue smoke.

How restful everything about her was, mused Miss Seeton, as she watched the bus disappear around a bend in the road, leaving her by herself among the sheep, the heather, and the wheeling birds above. Of course, one would hardly describe one's setting as deserted, when there was so much movement, so much life all around: the calling of birds, the bleat of sheep, the rustle of grass as the breeze tousled its scrubby tufts into elflocks . . .

"Deserted," she said aloud, as she checked once more on the map before setting off along the track towards the loch. "No, perhaps that is not quite the word, although certainly there was almost nobody on the bus . . . but it does seem perhaps a little strange . . . though no doubt everyone has gone to Larick to assist in the making of the film — but I would nevertheless have supposed . . ."

She broke off, because, now she came to think of it, she wasn't sure just what she' had supposed, except that whatever had caught her attention had seemed, well, a little strange. "Earlier," she remarked, as she walked with care, her eyes fixed on the ruts and potholes of the track rather than on the scenery. She would be glad when she'd reached the shelter by the loch, so that she could catch her breath and take her bearings; it was so much farther from anywhere than she had at first realised. "Yet not exactly deserted," she told herself, frowning. "Although earlier . . ."

But she was so busy concentrating on not twisting her ankle that the thought drifted away again. It took a little while for her to remember how strange it had seemed — except that it hadn't, at the time, because she'd only just now thought of it — but, now that she *had* thought of it, surely it must be unusual for the main street of Glenclachan to have been almost totally devoid of masculine presence, only half an hour ago.

"Unbalanced," said Miss Seeton, retired art teacher, who was not bothered by empty spaces and lonely places, but who found other forms of irregularity . . . disconcerting. Life, she felt, should as far as possible imitate art: with shape and form and, well, order. As her life was ordered. Which pleased her greatly. Not that she would call herself *tidy* — but dear Martha took such good care of her that it hardly mattered if one was . . . a little less enthusiastic about the niceties of broom and duster on the days when Martha didn't come. But, on the whole, an orderly, peaceful existence, blessed by a routine which was so pleasant, being one's own choice, after the bells of Mrs. Benn's school. Like living with an alarm clock permanently in one's pocket, when, after a sensible eight hours' sleep, there should be no need —

"Worn out after the night's exertions, of course. The fire," she said, delighted to have solved the mystery to her own satisfaction. "And the falling weather vane, as well. I must remember to sketch it — so unusual — before the smith replaces it. If he is anything like dear Mr. Eggleden — such a painstaking craftsman — it may have been repaired before my return, and possibly in the correct order, which would not be nearly so interesting. Whereas —"

She stopped, and looked about her for somewhere to sit, so that she could jot down a few ideas for her subsequent sketch of Glenclachan's kirk before she forgot them, with so much else to see. And what she saw was the waters of the loch, sparkling just a hundred yards in front of her, at the bottom of a gentle slope. She'd been concentrating so hard, on the uneven track and on her little self-imposed puzzle, that she'd come farther than she had thought.

She recalled hearing in the shop about the monster, and wondered if this was where it might be found, and chuckled at herself for being so foolish. "A rather improbable specimen of natural history," she said firmly, "though a romantic notion, to be sure — and, as the talk was of attracting visitors . . . one might hide somewhere with binoculars . . ."

And there was a suitable place to hide: the shelter of which the bus driver had spoken. A plain wooden hut, nestling between two clumps of low trees and tall, knotted shrubs: the perfect place, overlooking the loch, to look for its monster and (more realistically) to watch the water-fowl and other birds which frequented this quiet region.

Or — *was* it so quiet, after all? To her surprise, as she stood admiring the view, Miss Seeton thought she could hear — muffled, as if through walls — a man's voice . . .

"Moonshine," said Miss Philomena Beigg. "Hooch, firewater, rotgut — call it whatever you like, producing the stuff is still, if you'll pardon the pun, a cottage industry in these parts. Keechin's another name — peat reek, jute —"

"Keechin? Why, I thought," said Mel, "when they started muttering about the kitchen, and the white sheet, they were talking about curtains or tablecloths or something."

Philly Beigg laughed. "They talked like that — in front of you? After you'd been asking questions, no doubt."

"It's my job," said Mel at once. "But yes, it was — how did you know? Is it the traditional way of making people feel at home? Because, if it is —"

"It's the traditional warning," Philomena broke in, "for the presence of a government spy — an excise man or, in your case, woman." She ignored Mel's sudden yelp, and continued: "They used to spread white sheets out on bushes — ostensibly to air in the sun, or for bleaching — when word went round that the Preventives were in the neighbourhood. It would appear, Miss Forby, that your professional reputation isn't as great in these parts as you might have hoped. It seems probable, from what you've told me, that I'm the only person in Glenclachan who knows who you really are."

Mel was still feeling insulted. "Do I *look* like a spy, for heaven's sake? I've been called a lot of things in my time, but a government snoop, never. Amelita Bond? Forget it." She struck an attitude, and laughed. "Double-oh-eight in person, right? Wrong!"

"I," said Philomena, "know that very well, and so do you — but does everyone else?"

Mel sobered at once. "Guess they don't, if you're talking about the locals. I just turned up here and said I'd be staying a few days — but I didn't say who I was, or why I'd come. There's less chance of getting the truth behind a . . . a certain type of story if everyone knows who . . ."

Then she realised what she'd started to say — the shock of being thought a Customs officer must still be preying on her mind — and shut up at once. Miss Beigg

316

regarded her thoughtfully.

"If you're after a story, I suppose I shouldn't appear too inquisitive. But I have to deduce that it wasn't about the illicit still, was it?"

"If it exists," returned Mel quickly, trying to deflect her in another direction. Philomena's smile was knowing.

"It exists. I couldn't tell you where, or who runs it — but it's somewhere around, and not far away. Never mind what might be called other considerations, Miss Forby: doing the government down is in the blood, through uncounted generations, believe me."

"Oh, I do," said Mel with a sigh, "now I've had time to think about things. It explains why Hamish McQueest was so keen to get me sl— er, to put me out of action that first night — I'd almost for-gotten about it — and why he gave me such a funny look when he passed on the message a policeman friend of mine rang through. It convinced him I was after his pals running the still, so he did them a big favour and, well, tried to keep me out of the way —"

"No, Miss Forby." Philomena's upraised hand stilled Mel in her flight of fancy. "Or rather, yes, I am prepared to believe what you say — at least, part of it — but not for the reasons you suggest. Hamish McQueest is hardly the type to court popularity — you may have noticed — and he certainly is not on sufficiently good terms with his customers for him to wish to deflect a Customs officer when she arrives and starts asking awkward questions.

"Why on earth do you suppose," she demanded, "that they set up the still in the first place?"

"Cheap booze," said Mel, with barely a moment's thought. "I've heard all those jokes about mean Scotsmen! And when it comes to not having to pay tax, well . . ."

Philomena was shaking her head. "With the size of the operation they'll be running — a few yards of copper tubing and a kettle, no more — the tax saving isn't going to break the Exchequer. Of course, some of them might not realise they aren't running an enormous risk — apart from the risk to their health: I'd hate to have their livers in a couple of years' time — and could think they'll be in for a hefty fine, maybe a prison sentence, instead of a slap or two on the wrist and fifty or a hundred pounds maximum penalty. On the whole, though, it's not considered a heinous offence."

"Oh," said Mel. "So — unless it was someone who didn't realise that — not worth . . . killing anyone for, then?"

"Ewen Campbell, you mean? Good gracious, no. He'd have been in sympathy with the whole scheme, if not one of those who set it up in the first place — probably in cahoots with Dougall McLintie, who's our local rebel. Poor Ewen wasn't the only person in Glenclachan inclined to be hot under the collar — and he didn't like Hamish any more than the rest of them. Which will be the reason for setting up this still in the first place — sheer dislike of Hamish McQueest."

Philomena shrugged. "When Glenclachan makes up its mind about anyone or anything, it's not easy to change — not easy at all. And they seem to have decided they can't agree with the new landlord — not that I'm altogether surprised. He's annoyed me, from time to time. So, rather than give up what every Scot sees as his God-given right to enjoy the creature in congenial surroundings, they'll have a dram or two at the hotel just to lull suspicion, and then away afterwards back to someone's house for more than a few drams of what's come from the hills, or wherever. Leaving landlord McQueest to

319

worry at his falling profits, and — I know how their minds work — with luck, before long, he'll cut his losses and move on to another hotel, leaving them back in charge of their local once again."

"He doesn't strike me," said Mel, "as the sort of man to go under without a fight. There's a tough streak in Hamish McQueest, I'd say."

"And so would I, my dear. He has a look in his eye — it sounds like an old maid's fancy, I'm sure — but there are no flies on Hamish McQueest, Miss Forby. He's clever, yes, and devious enough to know when he's being manipulated — and to try to turn it to his own ends . . .

"Whatever they might be. But running a still isn't one of them, I'm sure. So, if you're right to remember that he tried to stop you asking questions — then I'd say the man has something else to hide . . ."

Chapter

24

They had come there one by one, secretly, looking over their shoulders, taking care that when they parked the vehicles in which they'd sneaked away from home, nobody would notice them among the low trees and tall, knotted shrubs, thickly green with the lush foliage of high summer. Each had been charged with taking care of some particular item; each had retrieved his charge from its hiding place, slipped it into the boot of his car or truck or four-wheel drive, and, on arrival at the appointed place, lugged it from beneath its protective sacking to join with what the others had brought.

"Now, that's a sight to gladden a Scotsman's heart," the first arrival remarked to the last, as the final component was added to the collection. "We've worked and waited for this all these weeks, and now —"

"Weeks? Man, it's longer than *weeks* we've waited — that *Scotland's* waited —

for justice to be done. Twa hunnert years or more, that's how long it's been — and now, at last . . ."

The speaker put out a hand to touch, almost fearfully, his own contribution to the strange assortment on the floor in front of him; a close observer might have seen his fingers tremble.

A general sigh went round the group. He drew his hand away, looking guilty. Nobody met his eyes.

"A grand sight," said someone — very loud, very certain. "But better to be used than looked at, any day!"

Everyone murmured their approval of this sentiment, one voice adding, "And today's the day we start putting it all to use — the culmination of all our endeavours." He paused pondering the beauty of that phrase. "All our endeavours — working together towards one end, and that the proudest and most glorious a trueborn Scot could have . . ."

"Aye, we'll go down in history, right enough. For it's to be us that achieve what has not been achieved in over two centuries — after these many woeful years, to set the House of Stuart back on the throne where it rightly belongs . . ."

There was a silence, while they all contemplated what glory was to be theirs. "And Balmoral," someone pointed out in a voice preternaturally gleeful, "up in flames . . ."

There was an even longer silence. "The symbol of Victorian oppression," somebody said at last. "What use have the Highlands for German queens pretending to be what they never were?"

"John Camden Neild," chipped in somebody else, "has much to answer for. If he hadnae left her that daft bequest, she'd never have thought of building —"

"But he did, and she did, and we've been stuck with yon . . . yon excrescence for over a hundred years. So, here's our chance to right the situation — and tomorrow the time."

"I'd not forgotten," came the reply. "Glenfinnan Day," he added, in a hushed, almost reverent tone, and everyone murmured again.

"Have we the standard ready to raise over the ashes of the castle?"

"Himself will bring it, he says, when what's needful to be done has been done." The speaker fumbled in his pocket.

"The sealed orders — you have them, Alexander? Can you be telling us what's to be done?"

Alexander nodded. "Our final instructions before we disband — before there's no more need for us, because the task will have been carried out. Death to the oppressors!"

"Death to the oppressors," came the dutiful chorus, and fists were raised in defiant gestures, and feet stamped with fervour on the wooden floor, so that the whole edifice began to rock. Alexander glowered round at his colleagues.

"Will you be having the floor give way beneath our feet, and everything dropped in the mud below and fit for nothing? Will you hush now, and listen like sensible men while I tell you how we're to do the deed, tomorrow as ever is."

"Tomorrow," echoed his fascinated audience. Alexander, conscious of his responsibilities, nodded.

"Didn't I hear him say so myself? A whispered voice on the telephone — a message, hidden under the grey stone by my front gate, wrapped in plastic against the storm . . ."

He took a piece of paper out of his pocket, followed by a box of matches. "I'm to burn this, the same as ever — no trace to be left, and the ashes tossed to the four winds." He held the paper aloft, the gaze of everyone fastened upon it where it wavered, a symbol of defiance, until he hastily lowered his shaking hand, unfolded the paper, and cleared his throat, several times.

"That's a gey host you have on you, Alexander," observed one whose own throat sounded husky. "No doubt you caught a wee bit chill last night, with fighting the fire up at the — up at MacSporran Castle," he amended swiftly. At present, "the castle" could only signify one place — and that place was fifty miles from Glenclachan.

"Aye, well, it was a stormy night," agreed Alexander, as his fingers pleated the paper of instruction open, and shut, and open again, without his seeming to notice they did so. He cleared his throat again, and turned his gaze from one conspirator to the other. "Now, gather round — and not a word from any until I'm finished . . ."

Mel was still frowning over Philomena's words when the older woman leaned forward and took the unfolded sketch from where she had placed it on the table. She held it first at arm's length, then closer, studying it with care.

"An interesting composition," she

remarked, "and locally very significant, of course. But I don't seem to recognise the style. Do I know the artist?"

"You mean because of the blackbird?" Mel answered Philomena's spoken, rather than her unspoken, question with a question of her own; she was still anxious to protect Miss Seeton's privacy as far as she could. "Does this make you think of . . . well, think that a Jacobite rising is rather more likely than you thought earlier?"

Philomena, too, could answer questions with questions. "Should it? I know of the song, of course, but this sketch is in pencil. The bird could be a rook, a crow, a raven — we have nothing by which to judge the scale. The necklace might be of any length, although the crown . . ."

Now she was taking a more detailed look at the drawing, especially at the crown where it rested at the foot of the rock on which that anonymous bird perched. "Well, now, yes. I do see what you mean, Miss Forby: that there could be some connection with the Royal House of Stuart. This crown . . . it isn't the one you see on official documents and letter boxes — it isn't King Edward's Crown. *That* is part of the English regalia — worn by the sovereign at state functions such as a coronation, or the opening of Parliament. But this . . . this looks very much like the crown that's kept in Edinburgh Castle, and has never been near England, despite all Cromwell's efforts during the Civil War. He tortured the wife of the Keeper of the Scottish Crown Jewels, Miss Forby — a Mrs. Ogilvie — and she died rather than reveal the whereabouts of the Honours of Scotland . . .

"Robert the Bruce wore it to be crowned King of Scots," said Philomena. "Oh, it's been remodelled since then, but it's stayed the same now for four, five hundred years. Did I tell you about Mary Stuart's necklace — the one of Scottish pearls set in gold, and how my fancy is it was Glenclachan gold she wore? Well, this crown, too, is of Scottish gold — and it's set with pearls — and just take a look at the cross, will you? Unmistakable. A pearl at the end of every arm, and four in the corners, too. The whole crown is rich with pearls and jacinths and white sapphires and carbuncles — to my taste rather less gaudy than the jewels your English monarchs wear. Though King Edward's cross," she had to admit, "is not so ornate as this one. Almost plain, one might s—"

"So this," broke in Mel, too excited to

bother about the common courtesies, "is the crown they'd use to crown a Jacobite king!"

Philomena stared at her. "The Scottish Crown isn't worn any longer, Miss Forby, even by the monarch at a coronation. More's the pity, some might say — but you don't want me to start lecturing you about the Act of Union, do you?"

"Is it anything to do with the Jacobites?" enquired Mel, with a wary note in her voice.

Philomena smiled. "Some might say yes; others might say no. You have Jacobites on the brain, it seems."

"What did you mean," asked Mel, ignoring this second try as she'd ignored the first, "when you said there were local connections? I thought you just meant the blackbird."

"Or rook, or crow, or raven. But no, I had in mind more the background to the bird, and the rock on which it perches so . . . so regally, yes, I grant you that. But the hills there — lightly sketched, it's true, but I'd know them anywhere."

"Scone," said Mel, as Miss Beigg hesitated, looking just once more at the drawing before committing herself. "Well, somewhere near Perth, anyway," she amended, as Philomena favoured her with a puzzled look.

"Now, what can have put such an idea in your head? This range of hills is nothing like the scenery around Perth — to say it is misleading you sorely. I've walked the moors and mountains of Glenclachan for miles around since I was a child, Miss Forby. I know them as well as anyone, or I did in my youth. But I could never forget them, no matter how long it might be since I walked them — as walk them I have, I assure you. I could take you there . . ."

She stopped, and stared again at the drawing, then, with an odd expression in her eyes, at Mel. "I could take you to the exact spot where you might stand and look at the selfsame view, Miss Forby — though I doubt if you'd find it as peaceful and still as this drawing suggests. If hordes of sightseers aren't swarming everywhere, that will only be because the police haven't yet finished their investigation — oh, yes" — as Mel jumped — "this looks to me very much like the place where the body of Ewen Campbell was found."

As a cold, invisible hand stroked a finger along Mel's spine, a shadow darkened the little kitchen of Philomena's cottage. Miss Beigg looked up. "The forecast was right," she said. "The clouds are gathering — we could well be in for another storm."

You don't know the half of it, thought Mel. For storm, read tempest — read turbulence — read turmoil — read Miss Emily Dorothea Seeton . . .

"It can't be coincidence," she said aloud, looking more worried than Philomena would have expected anyone to be on learning that her proposed sight-seeing excursion might be blighted by the presence of others. "Miss Beigg — this may sound a little odd, but . . . I wouldn't want . . . anyone at the hotel . . . to overhear . . . and I need to talk to someone in rather a hurry. Could I possibly use your telephone? For a local call," she added.

"But not for the weather forecast, I take it," replied Philomena dryly. She glanced out of the window. "There's more than a breeze blowing now, and worse to come, I'd say. Let me show you to the telephone, Miss Forby; come through to the hall, and I'll shut the door so that you can talk in private. But I hope that you'll see fit at some point to let me know what's been going on . . ."

In normal times, it was Armorel McScurrie who answered — insisted on answering — the telephone at MacSporran

Castle. These times, however, were not normal. As soon as she was warned that the builders would be coming to repair the damaged roof, Mrs. McScurrie had without words made very plain her lack of faith in the ability of her employers to superintend proceedings unaided. She was now up with Ranald and the foreman in the portrait turret, listening to every proposal the wretched man made, demanding the likely cost and the length of time it would take, and priding herself that, without her, the family would be helpless.

It was therefore Liusaidh who informed Mel that it was not possible for her to speak to Miss Seeton at present. "She's not here, Miss Forby. She must have woken up early, and gone off somewhere without telling anyone — I'm afraid I've no idea where she might be, though I'm sure she'll be back before long."

"Gone off somewhere? Without leaving a message? That's not like Miss S." The chilly trickle of anxiety which had caressed Mel's spine was turning into a steady flow. "She's the politest little person you'll meet in a hundred years. She must have told somebody!"

Liusaidh politely reiterated that she had not, and Mel found that her throat needed clearing before she could say, "But I . . . I have a — an important message for her, and . . ."

"The weather's changing for the worse, Miss Forby, and Miss Seeton's a sensible soul. I shouldn't think she's gone very far — probably down into the village for another chat with Philomena Beigg. She was quite taken with —"

"No," broke in Mel, "because that's where I am, and she isn't. I'm worried about her, Lady Glenclachan."

And, when Mel had reminded her of a few selected facts about Miss Seeton, Liusaidh was worried, too.

"Now," said Alexander, "gather round — and not a word from any until I've finished . . ."

He cleared his throat again, then swept the hut with his gaze. "Listen," he began.

"Listen!" From the conspirator nearest the door came a quick gesture for silence. "There's someone outside!"

Everyone froze. Nobody spoke.

And everyone heard — heard a cheerful, off-key piping voice proclaim, "I wouldn't leave my little wooden hut for you-hoo! I've got one lover and I don't want two-hoo . . ." Though the sun was perhaps not as bright as it had been, the day remained delightful, and Miss Seeton's delights did not always find full expression in her sketches or paintings. When there was nobody around to make her self-conscious, she would warble away to her heart's content, whether or not she could remember all the words.

There was a pause while (unseen by those inside the hut) Miss Seeton negotiated a particularly uneven portion of the track. Then, tidy-minded as ever, she began her song again. "I wouldn't leave my little wooden hut for you-hoo . . ."

She was much closer now. To the tense conspirators, her song sounded like a warning. She knew they were there.

"She's got to be stopped," said Alexander.

Chapter

25

"There's nobody with her," reported the man near the door, having peeped cautiously through a crack in the planking.

"Then she's easy enough dealt with," said Alexander. His colleagues exchanged glances.

"Mebbe she'll not venture inside," breathed someone, in a hopeful whisper.

"She will," Alexander assured him, grim-faced. "Where's the wits you were born with, man? If she knows we're here — which seemingly she must — then what woman's going to walk away? Not to mention the clouds building up, and a storm likely, and this the only shelter for miles . . ."

Everyone listened again as that happy warbling drew ever closer. Alexander was right: she was coming straight to the hut — coming to find them . . . coming to find what they'd all brought to the hut and placed in the middle of the floor . . .

"A tarpaulin," cried someone in desperation. There was a frantic scuffle as everybody tried to search for something they knew wasn't there, tripping over everybody else as they did so. They found nothing.

"She'll have to be dealt with," said Alexander. "Angus, you and Archie stand either side of the door, and when she pushes it open one of you hit her on the head and the other catch her as she falls. Alistair —"

"Hit her on the heid?" Angus was appalled. "It's one thing to set bombs to explode at a safe distance, but —"

"We've nothing to hit her with," objected Archie. With a growl of fury, Alexander bent down to snatch a length of metal pipe from the pile of miscellaneous objects in front of him. "What's wrong with this?" he snapped, and thrust it into Archie's startled grasp. "Hurry up, man!"

Archie was weighing the weapon thoughtfully in his hand as the next report came from the door. "Why, that's yon wee body who found the laird's baby!"

There was a rush to elbow the reporter out of the way; people found knotholes and cracks through which to peer, and everyone recognised the laird's visitor.

"Glenclachan will no' be pleased," someone muttered.

There was silence.

"This pipe's too heavy," said Archie, dropping it back on the miscellaneous heap. "Angus — when she comes in, I'll take hold of her while you grab for her binoculars. A wee tap from them in their leather case and she'll be out like a lamb, and no real harm done . . ."

"There'll be harm enough done if she recognises any of us," pointed out Alexander, as Angus and Archie moved to take up their positions beside the door and everyone else moved well away from them. The two ambushers glared first at the speaker, and then at their colleagues. "One wee old woman," muttered Angus, as the singing drew ever closer. "Archie, suppose I take hold of her while you —"

"Wheesht, man!" The singing, and Miss Seeton, were upon them, as her foot was upon the step, her hand upon the door handle, her eye upon the curious knotholes of the wood . . .

And as she finally pushed open the door to step inside, the last thing she saw before encountering oblivion was, to her surprise, a knothole that almost seemed to wink at her.

"Do you think," suggested Liusaidh, "that we should alert the mountain rescue people, or the police? No, surely not the police," before Mel had time to reply. "She's a very sensible little soul. I can't believe — though she doesn't realise, of course, just how quickly Highland weather can change . . ."

"Sounds as if you're trying to convince yourself as much as I'm trying to convince *my*self," said Mel, with a nervous giggle. "But she wouldn't thank us — well, she would, but she'd be so embarrassed — if we sent out the search parties when we aren't one hundred per cent sure . . ."

Then inspiration dawned. "Lady Glenclachan — Miss Beigg says she knows the area as well as anyone. How about if you drove us there, and we could, well, take a look around?"

"I'll be at the cottage within ten minutes," Liusaidh promised, and rang off. Mel stared at the silent receiver in her hand, then replaced it on the cradle with a shake of the head and went back to the kitchen to talk to Philomena.

Twenty minutes later, the MacSporrans' Land Rover had left the road and was bouncing across that uneven ground which

Miss Seeton had traversed just two days before. "She followed the track for part of the time, she told me, and then went along beside the burn towards the crag," said the countess, doing her best to steer a comfortable path. "But whether she'd take exactly the same route today — if she's even here . . ."

"It's the best we can do," Mel reminded her, "for the present. When the weather gets too bad" — staring at the sky — "or, well, whatever, we'll get the professionals in. But for now, if we keep our eyes peeled . . ."

Four plebeian eyes were peeled full-time, while another, aristocratic pair fastened on the road ahead, from time to time snatching a wider view. Whenever she looked up, Liusaidh pressed on the horn, short sharp blasts, a signal borne by the gusting breeze in all directions; otherwise, it was in a tense silence that the Land Rover arrived at the foot of the waterfall.

"This is the place," said Philomena firmly, and, though the sky was overcast now and the light grown dim, Mel knew it for the view shown by Miss Seeton in her sketch.

"Can we get up that slope?" she demanded, but Liusaidh had already thrust the lever into first gear, and with a grinding rumble and a clatter of stones they made their slow way to the top of the waterfall. It was not an easy climb — they had rocks and boulders in their path which had to be circumnavigated, and broken scree rattled under the wheels, making them skid — but they reached the top at last.

Once more Liusaidh let the engine idle. Six eyes stared round. "She could be anywhere," said Mel, looking in dismay at the scattered rocks, gnarled trees, tangles of scrub, and — worst of all — fissures in the ground which she could see in all directions. "And it's starting to rain . . ."

Liusaidh punched the horn once again — and again. There came no response; even the birds, mindful of the approaching storm, had taken shelter. "Which is maybe what she's done, too," suggested Liusaidh, hopefully.

"Or maybe she's fallen down one of those cracks and hurt herself," said Mel, wriggling her way into the oilskin Philomena had lent her back at the cottage. "If we all go in different directions . . ."

They all went in different directions, taking care never to be out of sight or hearing of one another, calling — calling Miss Seeton's name, calling their lack of success, calling encouragement through the now pouring rain, their words ripped away by the wind.

And then came the first bolt of lightning.

Mel, no country girl, yelped, though it was miles away, the thunder which followed it countable seconds later a low growl, not the sharp overhead crack which warns of immediate danger. Suddenly, she had had enough. Dripping, her shoes soaked, her voice hoarse, her hair plastered over her face, she felt she could do no more.

And the others felt the same. As she looked round, she saw Lady Glenclachan and Philomena Beigg making, as she was, for the safety of the Land Rover. One by one, they reached it and climbed in.

"I'd better not drive in this," Liusaidh shouted, almost inaudible above the rattle of rain on the metal roof. "Once the storm's blown over, I'll feel safer. No sense in taking the risk!" They had done all they could; the wind, now near gale force, was hurling the clouds across the sky in furious tatters, taking the tempest with it. And, on the distant horizon, the thin, pale herald of calmer skies to come . . .

Another javelin of vivid light ripped the heavens apart, accompanied by a doomsday clash of thunder directly above their heads. Mel yelped again, but this time not alone, and the Land Rover rocked on its springs as the ground shuddered beneath them.

In weather like this, what hope had Miss Seeton?

It was just starting to rain as the conspirators, with their captive bundled unconscious into a concealment of jackets, knew they must abandon their meeting place. They had supposed that, with the hut's being so new, nobody would remember its existence; and they had been proved uncomfortably wrong. Far better to cut their losses, and make for a safer place, there to assemble . . . the Device, as everyone referred to it in hushed tones; there also to make some decision about their unexpected captive.

"She knows too much," said Alexander. "She should be . . . should be . . . we should stop her saying aught to a soul."

"What can she say," objected Angus, "considering she was tapped senseless before she'd laid eyes on any of us?"

"Tie her up and leave her where she

could struggle free, after a while," suggested Archie. "We'll have . . . have done the deed by then, and no harm to her."

"We could telephone a message to the police where she's to be found," said Alistair. "Or — well, mebbe not to the police" — as everyone looked at him — "but to Glenclachan or his guid lady — they'll be worrying about her," and he gave the swaddled, sleeping form of Miss Seeton a pat. Alexander snorted.

"We've more to worry about this day than one auld woman, remember! We'll carry her away with us before anybody else arrives to take shelter from the rain — and, for aught we know otherwise, it wasnae the shelter she was seeking at all so much as — as us. We cannae take the risk. She'll have to be . . . silenced."

"We've no time to argue about it now," Alistair said, in a voice he tried to make firm. "We'll get everything out to the cars first, and decide then what's best to do. So long as she's not left here to bear witness . . ."

"Before the rain grows heavier," said Archie, and everyone in the hut, even Alexander, agreed. Everyone save Miss Seeton, that is. She was still unconscious, breathing with heavy, though regular, gasps

342

through several thicknesses of jacket. Whenever she gave a particularly loud snuffle, anxious glances shot towards her shapeless form and people listened hard, without wishing to show that they did, until the next, reassuring breath was heard.

"To the van with her, before it rains harder," commanded Alexander, though this proved more easily said than done. They had come to the shelter one by one, in separate vehicles; there was more than one from which to choose, and the choice was not quickly made. Explosives could leave traces — and so could a body, whether conscious or not.

"She's no' dead yet," Alexander reminded everyone sharply. "Havers, the pack of you! She's wrapped up tidy enough in there — loosen those wraps, now, so the air can reach her better — but who's to say a man cannae wear his own jacket in his own car, and a friend or two with him . . ."

Eventually, the choice was made. Miss Seeton was to go in one vehicle, the largest van: why crowd the puir woman any more than was needful? Half the components of . . . the Device would go in another, half in one of the cars, and the remaining conspirators separately. The blame — that was to say the glory, Alexander corrected himself hastily — to be shared by as many as possible.

The burden, too, was shared by as many men as could comfortably assist in the carrying of one small, blanketed form out of the hut, through the falling rain, and towards the little hollow masked by trees where the conspiratorial cars were parked. They took care that Miss Seeton remained the right way up throughout the journey, and there was almost a squabble over who should hold her head steady. It shouldn't need two, Alexander pointed out tartly; but he was ignored.

It was while they were fumbling with the van's double back doors that they received their greatest shock so far. Miss Seeton, her upturned face open to the elements — to the refreshing powers of water — suddenly wriggled, coughed, and opened her eyes.

"Oh," she said, closing them again. "Oh, my head . . ."

The former occupants of the hut gazed at one another in horror. Miss Seeton moaned faintly, and blinked. Her eyes drifted open, unfocussed, as the rain continued to fall.

"Oh, dear," murmured Miss Seeton. "My umbrella . . ."

After a paralysed silence, Alexander found his voice. "So what's the matter with you, gawping gaibies all, and the puir wee soul catching her death of pneumonia under your very eyes? Archie, man, open that door smartish and get her in the dry, while I . . ."

Without waiting to see how his instructions were being followed, Alexander turned and headed back to the hut, while the rain continued to fall and Miss Seeton to regain, slowly but surely, consciousness. Nobody cared to set her down on the ground while they fumbled with the handle of the door; they found themselves uttering apologies for the delay and similar soothing words, while Archie's hands, slippery with a combination of perspiration and rain, struggled to open the recalcitrant lock.

Inside the shelter, the now heavy rain drumming on the roof, Alexander prosecuted his search for Miss Seeton's umbrella. She'd been carrying it when she was ambushed, as he recalled, but in all the kerfuffle she'd dropped everything she carried — as anyone would have done, in the circumstances. They'd retrieved her handbag and wrapped it in the larger bundle, replaced the binoculars round her neck . . . but they'd never even noticed the umbrella, and where it had gone was anybody's guess, with people taking off jackets and putting things down and moving them around . . .

And then he saw it: black silk, metal shaft, crook handle, lying half-buried among the components of . . . the Device — lying beneath that length of metal pipe which Archie had rejected as too heavy for bludgeoning purposes. During the scrimmage of the attack — the encounter, he amended silently — it must have been set rolling down on top of the umbrella; which was a fraction its size and weight.

"And mebbe it's been damaged," muttered Alexander, as he inspected the slim, neatly furled shape for tears or snags. He whistled silently as he recognised the hallmark, and knew what the handle and shaft must be made of. "Gold," he said, and glanced out through the open door in the direction taken by the gold umbrella's owner. "A gold brolly — well, well." And his opinion of Miss Seeton rose considerably.

"She'll no grudge me saving myself a soaking," he said, as he prepared to open the umbrella before plunging out into the cloudburst. "No use for everyone to catch their death!"

He did not pause to ponder the incongruity of this sentiment, but straightway opened the umbrella, felt the spike bump on the lintel as he ducked through the doorway, and set off on a trouser-soaking dash between the raindrops . . .

Which was interrupted at just over the halfway point by a sudden, startling, psychedelic streak of lightning, drawn perhaps by the glitter of the gold umbrella but missing it, by no more than an inch, flashing out of the sky to plunge, tearing the world in two, right to the middle of the little wooden hut.

The "Whump!" of expanding air was already blowing Alexander off his feet, his ears ringing from the thunder, the umbrella bounced from his grasp by the blast, when another, fiercer blast followed just a few seconds after. Blinking, gasping, shaking his head, he finally dragged himself to his knees and turned round . . . to see the shelter he had left not two minutes earlier erupting in a gigantic fireball.

Chapter
26

"If anyone says that we've just had a narrow escape, I won't quarrel with them," remarked Liusaidh, in a voice from which the trembling could not be entirely banished.

"And if *that* isn't good old British understatement," Mel said, "I don't know what is. Guess escapes don't come much narrower. If my knees aren't knocking, it's only because they've turned to jelly. How about you, Miss Beigg?"

Philomena was shaking her head. "I thought I must have been struck blind, if not deaf as well. And that Scotland was having its first earthquake in centuries . . ."

The Land Rover's springs had stopped juddering, and the last echoes of the thunderclap had died away. Liusaidh took a firm grip on herself: noblesse oblige. "Ladies, I'm sorry to say I feel we're wasting our time. If poor Miss Seeton's out in all this, she'll be in need of better help than any we can give her. I think we should go back, and report her — report her missing."

She hardly looked at Mel as she made the suggestion, but there came no dissenting voice from the passenger seat as she started the engine and drove warily forward through what had become, since the storm, a quagmire. Although the rain had almost stopped, new-made rivulets swirled around rocks, and formed pools, and turned earth into mud: what had been loose and rattling scree as they climbed the slope was more like liquescent toffee as they started to descend. Liusaidh fought with the steering wheel, and spun from one skid into another, while stones were thrown up from under the tyres, clattering against metal or rock before splashing into the sea of thick, brown, treacly sludge.

The front wheels lurched into a pothole, and everyone was flung sideways. "Sorry," panted Liusaidh, "but I simply can't see where I'm going . . ." The wheels whirred, spitting mud and stones; the engine whined, as she ground the gears and forced them to drag the Land Rover up and out and on down the slope of the waterfall . . .

The waterfall, or rather the stream which

fed it, was spilling over its banks, making the ground even more treacherous. The lower down the slope they went, the thicker and more glutinous the ground. The rain stopped; the sun began to struggle through what remained of the clouds — but it was nothing compared to the struggle below.

They found another pothole. "Oh, no," muttered Liusaidh through clenched teeth. Mel and Philomena said nothing as she began to manipulate the accelerator . . .

And then all three of them cried out together, as there came a low rumbling from farther up the slope, and a sudden boulder, loosened by moving mud, erupted past and in front of them to smash into another, more stable rock face fifteen feet to their right — and split into three pieces.

Mel gulped. She gulped again. "Did anyone," she asked, "say something just now about a narrow escape? Because . . ."

"If we hadn't stuck in the pothole," breathed Liusaidh, "that boulder would have . . . would have . . ."

"But we did, and it didn't," said Philomena, trying hard for her normal brisk tones, and very nearly achieving them.

There was a long, thoughtful silence,

broken only by the sound of the idling engine. Liusaidh's hands gripped the steering wheel, Mel's had the whitest knuckles she had ever seen. Philomena contemplated her heartbeat, which sounded more like thunder than the thunderclap had, and stared into infinity.

Liusaidh kept looking in the driver's mirror for further horrors to come, but nothing stirred. In the end, she found her voice again. "Well, we'd better get on," she said.

"No, wait." Philomena's eyes had returned from infinity to focus on the shattered boulder. The sun, having won its battle with the clouds, was recklessly pouring warmth and light on everything within sight. Smooth puddles turned to mirrors; steam rose from rocky surfaces — from every rocky surface save those newly revealed to human gaze, untouched by rain since their first formation.

So why, then, did they glitter so very strangely?

The damage to the turret had been surveyed by the builders, and the progress of the builders had been surveyed by Mrs. McScurrie. She made them nervous. Where Ranald was affable and interested, the housekeeper was alert and clerical. She carried a stout pad of paper with her, and a pencil; she made notes of the slightest comment passed by the foreman, glared pointedly at the boots of his two companions, and cleared her throat whenever the laird looked like committing himself to some course of action which she thought deserved a longer period of reflection.

The thunderstorm came as a relief to every man present. It is not easy, nor is it altogether safe, to survey a damaged building in gale-force winds and driving rain; when the wind and rain are accompanied by the same forces which first caused the damage, it is even more advisable to desist.

They desisted, and returned to safe ground, where Ranald discovered Liusaidh's hurried note that she had accompanied Miss Forby and Miss Beigg to go in search of Miss Seeton, whose whereabouts had given cause for some concern.

"She's taken the Land Rover, and says she ought to be back in a couple of hours — but she hasn't said when she left," Ranald grumbled, looking first at his watch and then at the weather. "Or where she was going . . ."

"She kens well how to take care of herself, Glenclachan, and of those with her, never fear." The builder would have clapped the laird about the shoulders, but spotted Armorel's expression just in time and changed the gesture to one of general encouragement. "Her leddyship may not ken the hills as well as yourself, but close enough, and she's a bonnie driver — I've thought many a time she should go in for the rallying, the way she tears about in yon truck —"

Mrs. McScurrie skewered him with a look, and he swallowed the rest of the remark. His two henchmen, hitherto silent, found themselves equally lost for words. Ranald forced a grateful smile.

"You're right, of course, Calum. There's no sense in my worrying, when she'll turn up in her own good time with no worse than a soaking, I'm sure. Talking of which" — Ranald, Lord Glenclachan, remembered that *noblesse* should *oblige* — "will you have a dram to keep out the chill? The calendar may say it's August, but . . ."

But Calum and his colleagues felt the eye of Mrs. McScurrie upon them, and declined the invitation with thanks.

Ten minutes later, driving back through the downpour, they headed by silent consent for the Pock and Tang. Calum, parking the car, muttered that it was ill luck they could no longer rely on Dougall McLintie for another batch of the creature; Fergus and Finlay, sparing as ever with words, intimated that this did not matter. No doubt they considered paying the full price for a warming drink worth any reasonable expense, if it would only serve to banish from their minds the icy remembrance of Armorel McScurrie's glare.

The three men dragged their donkey jackets over their heads and ran into the bar. Calum, arriving first, asked Hamish for three Lairigighs, to be put on the slate.

"Three doubles?" Hamish raised his eyebrows as Fergus and Finlay came panting up, dripping quite as much as the foreman. While the drinks were being poured, the builders shook out their heavy blue topcoats and hung them over nearby chair backs.

The storm was passing; the sun was shining. Hamish went to throw open the door, letting in air much less humid than that into which the trio of jackets had exhaled dust and damp and waterlogged wool. Calum sighed.

"We'd best be getting back to the castle, now there's no more risk from the weather. And mebbe Glenclachan will have guid news of her leddyship and the wee

Sassenach woman."

"And if he hasnae . . ." said Fergus, thoughtfully.

"We could mebbe offer . . ." supplied Finlay.

"To help?" Calum nodded. "Aye, we could. But —"

"Help? Up at the castle?" Hamish was all ears. "Some trouble with Lady Glenclachan, is there?"

"Not necessarily," Calum told him, while Fergus and Finlay bristled. But Hamish was looking at them with a more-than-usually mellow expression, and Calum relented.

"They've a guest gone missing," he said. "Glenclachan's leddy has gone searching for her, along with the young woman who's staying here — and Philly Beigg, though heaven alone knows how *she* came to poke her neb into the business. There it is, though: the three of them vanished into the blue, and the wee auld woman with them, or so we hope, if they've only found her. She'd be washed away by the heaviness of the rain, else."

"Miss Forby, too? I see." An acute observer would have deduced that Hamish was thinking busily, for he stroked his moustache and frowned. "If you're heading back now to the castle," he said at last, "I'd appreciate a lift in your car, Calum. There are . . . a few matters I think his lordship ought to know about — being the laird, as it were."

Calum looked at him, then, with a shrug, at Fergus and Finlay. "We're no wasting time now the sun's out," he said.

Hamish nodded. "Bear with me a moment, will you?" He went to the inside door, opened it, and shouted for Shona. She came strolling in with a duster in her hand, to be told that she must take her employer's place at the bar, as he was going out. On business. "Oh, aye?" was all she said, dropping her duster on a convenient table, and Hamish was in too much of a hurry to rebuke her. He turned to Calum, and asked, "Well, are we going?" So they went.

There was no sign of the laird's Land Rover as Calum and company reached the castle. Nevertheless, he did not find it easy to park: the entire front courtyard — a gravelled area, originally laid down by the motoring Earl Allain — was cluttered with an assortment of cars, vans, and trucks, the disorder of whose disposition must have greatly vexed the methodical mind of Mrs. Armorel McScurrie. Calum scratched his head, shrugged, and reversed farther down the drive, to park under a convenient tree. Now that the sun was once more shining, it seemed like a good idea.

The four men approached the heavy front door; it was not closed. They clattered the knocker; it was not heard. They looked at one another, and walked inside.

They were not noticed. Indeed, so great was the general excitement that it is doubtful if the shade of Bonnie Prince Charlie, playing the bagpipes, wearing the kilt, and dancing a reel at the same time, would have been noticed.

Mrs. McScurrie was issuing orders: Ranald, and the indoor staff, were running to obey them; the outside staff stood in huddles, communing with several sheepish-looking men whose faces were immediately known to Calum and his friends.

"Angus! Alistair! Archie! What's to do, man?"

Mrs. McScurrie turned in a fury on the newcomers. "Will you be scaring the puir wee soul into fits with your noise? When she's had a bump on the heid, nearly deid from a bolt of lightning, and then you come caterwauling in with no more sense than — No, Glenclachan" — as Ranald came hurrying up, a hot-water bottle in his hand — "blankets for warmth, I said, and then to call the doctor. Why, a hottie's the worst you can do when a body's suffering from shock . . ."

Ranald apologised, and hurried off again, babbling of brandy, and sweetened tea. A chorus of voices volunteered to drive down to the village for Dr. Beltie, if the laird found himself too busy to telephone. Mrs. McScurrie rounded on the chorus and ordered it to keep quiet, because it was only making things even more confused.

The cause of all this confusion was lying, muffled in a selection of jackets and coats, on the old oak settle near the chest in the castle hall — a female cause, as might be observed from the wavy grey hair and neatly shod feet which were all that could be seen at opposite ends of the mufflings. Beneath the head which must have been assumed to belong to the grey hair a makeshift pillow had been placed. The two suits of armour and the figure on the settle were the only calm human forms in the place.

But then, as Hamish, Calum, and the others stood staring, the jackets and coats began to writhe as if a minor earthquake had occurred within their confines, and at once Mrs. McScurrie leaped to suppress the writhing. "Wheesht now, hen, and lie still. There's no need to go fretting yourself. You're in safe hands now."

She turned to glare round at the entire hall-full of men, and perforce her concentration drifted from the jackets. With one final upsurge, their prisoner was free, and struggling to her feet. "You're very kind," said Miss Seeton, "but really, I'm sure — Oh," and she sat down again, her hand to her head. "Oh, dear . . . perhaps . . ."

"*Perhaps* is no the word," she was briskly informed. Mrs. McScurrie's face wore a distinct I-told-you-so expression as she proceeded to rewrap Miss Seeton in overcoat layers like some wool- and worsted-skinned onion. "Warmth, and rest, and checking with the doctor, that's what you need — and no argument. Now, where's Glenclachan gone?"

Ranald reappeared — saying he had telephoned the doctor, who hoped to be here before long — and followed by one of the maids, with a cup of tea on a tray. She was followed by a second maid, with an assortment of blankets in her arms. Mrs. McScurrie took the blankets and draped them about her victim's person; she took the tea and coaxed Miss Seeton to drink. A brief spasm shook Miss Seeton as she realised how heavily the tea had been sugared, but Armorel refused to pay any heed to her plaintive suggestions that really, she felt so much better now, and would, she was sure, do very well after a little nap . . .

The tea, stronger and sweeter than she would from choice drink it, either cured her shock or gave her enough of another to be able to announce (when she had finished it), in a far firmer voice than she had hitherto used, that she felt a great deal better now.

"We're very pleased to hear it, Miss Seeton," volunteered his lordship, with one eye on his housekeeper in case she considered he was taxing the strength of his invalid guest. As Armorel merely scowled, but said nothing, Ranald was emboldened to enquire — if Miss Seeton felt able to talk about it — what, exactly, had happened.

Chapter

27

Before Miss Seeton could reply, the chorus had started up again, in a self-defeating babble. Half-a-dozen voices all speaking at once achieve a remarkably low level of communication, as well as a remarkably high level of decibels. In the echoing hall, Miss Seeton was observed to wince, and put a hand to her head.

Mrs. McScurrie withered the chorus with one look, and the subsequent silence was of pin-dropping intensity. Miss Seeton's wavering smile of gratitude did not go unnoticed.

"There, there, you puir wee soul." Mrs. McScurrie's tone was so soothing and gentle that Ranald had to look twice to make certain it was his housekeeper who spoke. "Dinna you fash yourself over anything, hen. Just bide here until the doctor comes . . ."

"The doctor's here." From the doorway came the sound of scraping feet, and a large man with a black bag in his hand strode into the hall, nodded to Ranald, allowed his gaze to sweep over everyone else until it fastened upon Miss Seeton in her wrappings, and uttered a cheerful "Ha!"

"Doctor? Oh, dear." Miss Seeton only now appeared to understand even a part of what was happening. "Oh, dear — a doctor — but I do feel rather . . ."

"Which is no surprise," volunteered Alexander, who stood farthest from Mrs. McScurrie and therefore felt less at risk. "If you were a cat, hen, you'd have barely a life left — one inch lower, and yon thunderbolt would have burned you to a crisp." He turned to his friends. "Lucky for her, was it not, lads, that we were in search of shelter too, and coming up behind her in our cars, and able to carry her back here in safety once the bolt had struck?"

"And lucky for us," said Archie, seizing his cue, "that we'd not already reached that shelter, else it would have been *us* burned to a crisp, instead. Scattered to the four winds, what's more," he made a point of adding, as his colleagues muttered corroboratively beside him. "I havenae seen anything like the way yon wee wooden hut was blown to shivereens since I don't know when — but lightning's gey powerful stuff. A body can never tell what it will do."

The conspirators tried not to look at Miss Seeton as the story they'd taken such care to concoct was presented for her approval. Since nobody else in the hall was disputing their version of events, it rested with their former victim, now their (possible) nemesis, who, while Dr. Beltie held one hand captive as he took her pulse, raised the other to her head again, blinked, and said,

"Oh, dear — I suppose — that is, I *know* I must thank you kind gentlemen, from what you have said, but I really can't — can't say — can't *remember*, I'm afraid, anything about it. There was another kind gentleman, driving the bus — and he told me about the loch, and the bird-watching shelter . . ."

As she paused, and frowned with the effort of memory, the conspiratorial chorus was heard murmuring that it, too, had harboured a desire to learn more of the loch's feathered denizens — at which Hamish McQueest, whose attention, like that of everyone else, had been focussed on Miss Seeton, put his hand thoughtfully to his moustache and twirled it. Not a hint of doubt, however, could be sensed in any other occupants of the hall.

"Amnesia," pronounced the doctor, now shining a pencil torch into Miss Seeton's eyes. "Mild concussion as well, of course, and shock — but they'll both wear off, in time."

"And what about the amnesia?" enquired Alexander, while his fellow conspirators held their collective breath. "Puir wee soul — it's to be hoped she never remembers what a gey close shave she's had . . ."

Dr. Beltie shrugged. "She might, she might not — there's always a risk, in a case of this sort. Amnesia's a funny thing — but she'll come to no harm, that's for certain. She was lucky, though, that you found her when you did. Lying out in the rain, unconscious . . ."

He clicked his tongue, and began to issue instructions concerning Miss Seeton's well-being which rendered inaudible the sighs of relief from Alexander, Archie, Angus, and their friends. That thunderbolt which had knocked Miss Seeton's umbrella out of Alexander's stunned grasp had served also to knock the nonsense out of the entire Jacobite gang, who had watched with horrified eyes the explosion of the wooden hut, to which they had been on the point of returning once their captive was safely immured within Archie's battered van; and the realisation of exactly what they had planned to do — of what they'd been urged to do by somebody else who'd done most of the planning for them — had struck them with as much force as the thunderbolt had struck the hut. It did not require Alexander's frantic words, once he had regained his sense of balance, to convince them that their revolutionary zeal had just undergone a sudden, terminal decline. Their energies would henceforth be concentrated on nothing more important than Miss Seeton's survival . . .

"Will she be all right, though, Doctor?" persisted Alexander, as Dr. Beltie drew breath and Miss Seeton murmured her repeated thanks and apologies for all his — for everyone's — trouble. "She's taken no serious harm?"

"Oh, she'll live." The doctor looked at Ranald. "I'll have to deprive you of your guest for a day or so, though. A short stay at the cottage hospital, a few tests, and —"

"Hospital? What's wrong? Who's ill?" The interruption came from Liusaidh, who, flanked by Mel and Miss Beigg, had arrived at the open door in time to catch

Dr. Beltie's final words. "Ranald, is it Marguerite? Where is — Miss Seeton!" The countess caught her breath as she observed her guest's rather woebegone appearance. "Miss Seeton . . ."

"Miss S.!" Mel ran across to the oaken bench, brushed aside Dr. Beltie and Mrs. McScurrie, and took her old friend by the hand. "Honey, are you all right? How come you're always in the wars like this? And what on earth am I going to tell the Oracle?"

Miss Seeton was seen to perk up at these words, and to look startled. Really, it was most kind of dear Mel to concern herself — but then she was here, wasn't she, so it was understandable — though she would hardly have supposed that dear Mr. Delphick needed to hear about her having had such a . . . a very remarkable . . .

As words failed Miss Seeton, so they found expression through almost everyone else. It took a while for Ranald and the rest to explain — in unison until the laird's authority prevailed — how Miss Seeton had suffered a hairsbreadth visitation from a thunderbolt, appeared to have a touch of amnesia, was otherwise unharmed, had been ministered to by all of them. Mrs. McScurrie, sniffing, then added that such excitement had so upset the bairn — who had come down from the nursery the minute before Miss Seeton was brought in — that she'd been taken straight back upstairs again in the care of the third housemaid. Who had, Armorel appended in her bleakest tones, been threatened with instant dismissal if the nursery door was opened by so much as a crack until the fuss had died down. "As I have no doubt your leddyship," she concluded, "would have said yourself. If you had been here at the time."

"Er, yes." The housekeeper was skilled at making her employers feel superfluous — and guilty. "Yes, thank you, Mrs. McScurrie." Liusaidh had retreated to the doorway while Armorel made her complaint, ostensibly to stand beside Miss Beigg, who of the three newcomers was the only one not to have moved since that first appearance. "Ranald," Liusaidh said, justifying her retreat, "just listen to what we've — to what Miss Beigg has found! You'll never guess, not in a hundred years — Miss Beigg, tell him!"

Philomena's eyes sparkled at thus becoming the centre of attention. She had been a silent, though interested, observer of all that was said and done since the return of the Land Rover's passengers to the castle — and she'd been thinking rapidly. The various attitudes of the assorted groups of men had given her particular cause to ponder. She looked from Miss Seeton to Lord Glenclachan, and from his lordship to Hamish, still hovering close to Calum and the other builders. She rubbed the tip of her nose.

"I wouldn't want to be before anyone else who has business with the laird," she said slowly. "Mr. McQueest, for instance. I'm sure you haven't taken time away from your hotel to come and help repair the castle roof, have you?"

"Oh, well, it's not important, now," said Hamish, glancing across at Miss Seeton. "Really, it's not," and he twirled the tip of his moustache again.

Alexander stirred. He looked at Hamish. "You're a wee bit nervous, seemingly," he said. "There's no need of that. There's nothing at all to worry about. Is there, now?" to the hall in general.

"Certainly not," said Ranald, who wondered why Alexander spoke with such strange emphasis, but decided that he, like Miss Seeton, was no doubt suffering from shock. "Nobody has any need to worry about anything now that Miss Seeton's safe home again — isn't that right, Doctor?"

"She'll be fine," agreed Dr. Beltie. "Although I'm not so sure about Miss Beigg, if she isn't allowed to tell us what's on her mind," he added, with a smile for Philomena. "Watch your blood pressure there, Philly!"

Ranald, after a quick look at Liusaidh, begged Philomena's pardon and asked her to expound upon what his wife had given them to understand was a momentous discovery.

"That's one word," said Philomena, with another glance at Hamish. "If you're sure?" He nodded, noticing for the first time how she was still standing in the doorway. "We have found," said Philomena calmly, "the probable motive for Ewen Campbell's death. If anyone's interested, that is."

Perhaps, she thought gleefully, she should have been an actress rather than an author. The consciousness of having made a sensation — of being the centre of attention — people staring, listening, waiting for her next word — was delightful . . . but her father, of course, would have disapproved. She sighed, then brightened, as the gasps and exclamations died away.

"I take it," she said, "that you're interested. And so will the police be, when we tell them. I'll be surprised if they came across the sort of information which helped us to solve the crime — partly solve it, that is." She'd allowed herself to be carried away — oh, Father, how shocking — and backtracked quickly. "We know why, but we don't know who, not yet — though I'm starting to have my own ideas . . ."

"It wasnae Malcolm Macdonald," said Alexander firmly, to the accompaniment of nods and mutters from the other locals. "You'll never make us believe that — he's shocked himself to his bed, so he has. Isn't that right, Doctor?"

Dr. Beltie nodded. "It's hit him hard, all right —"

"It wasn't Malcolm," broke in Philly Beigg. "At least, I doubt it. Malcolm's always preferred pearls. He wouldn't kill a man just for a share of — the gold . . ."

The uproar as she paused was tremendous. Miss Seeton's wince went unnoticed even by Mrs. McScurrie, although Mel did pat her comfortingly on the hand; but even Miss Seeton wanted to hear the rest of what Philomena had to say.

"There have always been rumours of a gold mind around the Glenclachan area," went on the historian, enjoying herself hugely. "As children, I don't think any of us didn't dream of finding it — but we wouldn't have known what to look for. Nuggets, I imagine, or seams in the rock, but without proper knowledge . . . well, knowledgeable eyes ought to be able to find it, once they know where to look. And we can tell them that all they have to do is follow the track . . ."

She narrated the Land Rover's narrow escape, and told how the splitting boulder had revealed the veins of gold at its heart. "Right where Miss Forby, for some reason, seemed to think the answer to the mystery of Ewen's murder lay . . ."

Hamish McQueest said, "But of course she'd be trying to find the answer — she's a police officer, isn't she? It's her job." And once more he pulled at his moustache.

Alexander spoke before Mel had time to deny her involvement with the constabulary. He had been staring at Hamish throughout the whole of Philomena's narration, and now said, frowning, "You aye tug at those handlebars of yours when there's something on your mind, Mr. McQueest. Reminds me of someone I once met — a heavy beard, he had, black as night, and speaking in a whisper on account of naebody was to hear us — fair-spoken he was, though. Could almost talk a body into believing the most remarkable tales . . ."

Hamish looked at Alexander, then at Ranald. "There's no law, I hope, that says a man can't finger his own moustache? And as for resembling someone else with a beard — well, one beard is much like another, in the dark."

"I never said it was in the dark," Alexander told him. Hamish stared, and shrugged.

"Black as night — the beard or the time of day? To me, there's very little difference. You're talking nonsense, Alexander — no doubt it's the shock of your own narrow escape. From the explosion," he added, pointedly. "A surprisingly forceful one, for just a bolt of lightning, I believe you said?"

But Alexander had made up his mind and was not to be intimidated. He shook his head. "That bolt of lightning destroyed all that was in the hut — but even had it not, it wouldnae matter. Ewen Campbell was one of us, Mr. McQueest, as you can never be." He glanced round at his former colleagues, who were frowning, puzzled, yet had obvious confidence in their erstwhile leader. He spoke directly to Philomena. "You found the gold where Ewen died?"

"Where his body was found, or near enough, yes."

"But it would take a . . . a specialist to know it for what it was, if yon stone hadnae shattered to pieces?"

"I imagine so. The police will probably have a horde of experts checking the entire area for traces . . ." She wasn't sure whether she meant traces of gold or traces to show the exact spot of Ewen's murder.

"There's experts," said Alexander, following her lead, "and experts, as everyone knows. History experts" — with a bow in Miss Beigg's direction — "and police experts, and mining experts — and what do you suppose that would be, Mr. McQueest, but another word for a mining *engineer!*"

At which accusation, Hamish lost his head and made a sudden run for it.

And afterwards everyone agreed that Philomena could have done nothing else, after he'd so rudely thrust her out of the way, but snatch the targe from the nearest suit of armour and hurl it after him . . .

So that there were two patients for Dr.

Beltie to take to the cottage hospital in his car. One suffering from shock, with slight amnesia, and one suffering from bruises, with severe concussion.

Chapter
28

Three days later, Miss Seeton was once more a guest at MacSporran Castle, where she found, to her delight, that Mel had joined the party. As Ranald had explained when Mrs. McScurrie began to grumble, nobody could reasonably expect Miss Forby to feel happy staying on at a hotel whose proprietor she had been partly responsible for putting in gaol.

For a day or so, Armorel continued to complain, but the discreet manner in which Mel handled her scoop, the skilful manner in which she fended off her importunate Fleet Street colleagues, and the affectionate manner in which she treated — and was treated by — Miss Seeton, all served to promote a gradual thaw. It was not long before the housekeeper was busy in the still room concocting strange herbal messes and producing new forms of liniment, poultice, and balsam which she insisted Miss Forby must use on her ankle, which, after Mel's exertions during the hunt for Miss Seeton, was slow to recover its former strength.

Ranald, being not only laird but provost of Glenclachan, was in a position to know much of the police investigations and imparted all the interesting items of news to his wife and guests as he himself learned them.

One such item he waited to impart until Miss Seeton, who had not abandoned her intention to sketch the main street as a bread-and-butter gift, was safely on her way down to Glenclachan with her pencils, sketchbook, and a small easel the laird remembered using as a boy, which he had unearthed from one of the attics. When he could be sure that she was not about to return, Ranald looked at his wife and his remaining guest and swore them to secrecy before he would say a word.

Mel had a brief struggle with her professional responsibilities, but the courtesy of a guest outweighed them, she supposed. Besides, she'd had her scoop, and she'd hate not to know the full story, even if she couldn't use it.

"Okay," she said nobly. Ranald smiled.

"Just this one matter, Mel, and you'll understand why when you hear it. The rest, you're free to use in whatever way you see fit."

"Fair enough." Mel smiled back, and pronounced herself all ears. Liusaidh seconded this sentiment, and Ranald nodded. "Remember," he warned them, "keep it quiet . . ."

And he told them of how Alexander, throwing himself and his friends on the mercy of their clan chief, had confessed everything. The duplicity of Hamish McQueest had shocked them all: his deliberate public mockery of the sacred Cause, to inflame and incite the Jacobites he'd recruited himself; the stealth and disguise he'd used to do so; the reason he'd recruited them, mere sordid gain; the way he'd tried to send Mel, the supposed police officer, chasing after them so that official attention, as well as that of the locals, would be deflected from his recently discovered gold until his claim had been duly staked; the killing of Ewen Campbell, which he'd hoped to blame on Malcolm MacDonald until he realised the Jacobites were sitting targets . . .

"If you ask me, they've learned their lesson," concluded Ranald, with a smile. "Archduke Casimir and Her Highness Clementina, or whatever they call themselves, can be away back home as soon as they like — nobody's going to miss them around here. Alexander and the others have sworn off revolution for life, they say, and I'm sure it's true. They're good lads, at heart, even if they're sometimes a little slow on the uptake, which was how McQueest managed to take unfair advantage of them. I don't honestly think it would serve any purpose to get them into trouble now. Their narrow escape was quite enough to shake them up — Alexander says the way that thunderbolt just missed the tip of Miss Seeton's umbrella had a profound effect, and not simply because it set fire to the explosives in the hut. The Highlander can be very superstitious, you know. If they set up a sect of brolly worshippers, it wouldn't surprise me! But seriously, they're all glad everything's over without their having had to hurt anyone . . ."

He turned to Mel with a guilty smile. "I'm afraid I took it upon myself to warn them they'd better not start filling the hospital with flowers and boxes of chocolates, in case Sergeant Trumpie smelled a rat — they weren't at all happy about hitting poor Miss Seeton on the head, and it's been a great relief to them to see how quickly she's bounced back. Your friend — our friend, I hope — is a truly remarkable woman. If that's what yoga can do for you" — Miss Seeton's daily routine, while of course private, was no secret; she'd been caught reading the chapter on "A Restless Body Means a Restless Mind" to the baby one evening when all the ministrations of Liusaidh had failed — "then I'm tempted to take it up for myself."

"I'm sure," Mel told him, "she'd be pleased to lend you *Yoga and Younger Every Day* for as long as you wanted — she must know it backwards by now, and if she thought you were interested — well, she's not one to interfere, of course, but she does love to be of use. She's been dropping hints about this" — indicating her bandaged ankle, from which emanated the faint effluvia of Armorel's latest embrocation — "ever since she came out of hospital. She feels it's partly her fault I strained it — looking for her, you see."

"Poor Miss Seeton," said Liusaidh, with a smile, and a sigh. But Mel shook her head.

"You've no need to feel sorry for Miss S., believe me. *She* never does. Whatever happens to her, she just — well" — with a laugh in Ranald's direction — "bounces back, every time. Mind you, she scares the life out of all her friends, because we're always afraid her luck's going to run out one day — but anyone who can survive being bopped on the head and almost blown up by a gang of anarchists is pretty much a born survivor, in my opinion. And thank goodness for that!"

Miss Seeton had been invited to take afternoon tea with Miss Beigg, and it was while she was still there that Liusaidh telephoned to invite Philomena to accompany her guest back to the castle for dinner. Ranald, it seemed, had one final piece of news to impart: the real reason for the death of Ewen Campbell.

"He found the gold mine, surely?" Philomena tried not to show it, but her disappointment was plain. "You mean those veins in the boulder were something utterly boring like iron pyrites, or copper, instead? I can't believe it!"

Ranald handed her a glass of Rainbird whisky, telling her that just because her father had been teetotal it didn't mean she had to be. Philomena chuckled — but weakly. "I'm sure I was right," she protested, and he nodded.

"In a way, yes — but there was rather

more to the veins than you thought, you know. Didn't they strike you as . . . as rather washed-out–looking, for gold?"

"Don't know," said Philomena, while Mel sat up suddenly and didn't even notice she'd jogged her ankle. She had just remembered that last still life Miss Seeton had drawn, where the gold of the pearl necklace had seemed so very pale . . .

"I've never seen gold in the raw, so to speak," Philomena said, frowning. "But it looked like gold — like gold as one imagines it to look, in its natural state . . ."

Ranald poured drinks for the others, then helped himself to whisky, and sighed. "I've had a lengthy lecture on mineral deposits from the geologist the police brought in, and I'm not sure I remember all of what he said — but the gist of it should be enough, I fancy." He cleared his throat. "When metals and minerals are found in the, um, wild — ores, and so forth — they don't necessarily occur singly. I mean they might be mixed with other metals — copper and nickel are often found together, I gather. And Hamish McQueest was smart enough to recognise that the gold he discovered didn't come, er, neat, as it were" — with a desperate sip of whisky to inspire him — "but was mixed with another metal, one that gave it a pale appearance . . ."

"Silver," suggested Philomena, in a tone of anticlimax.

"Platinum," said Ranald simply. Everyone stared.

Mel said, "Platinum's kind of valuable, right? Twice as expensive as gold, or whatever? And McQueest found it just lying around on the moor?"

"Oh, there was rather more to his discovery than that — he had to work his way up the vein from traces he'd found lower down, traces of exposed and decayed ore that signalled something worth hunting for nearby — but he'd had to recognise what they meant to begin with. Which he did. All of us, remember, had been brought up on tales of a gold *mine*, with the understanding that it was already there, and hadn't been weathered out of obvious existence. If it ever existed at all, of course. There are pockets of gold all over the Highlands, you know, and it's more than likely that a folk memory of a mine already known about was grafted into Glenclachan — Miss Beigg will know more than I do about how such things can occur. But there's a zone fifty miles long, and around twenty miles wide, from Oban to Aberfeldy, where gold has been found — still is, in small quantities. Anyone can take a pan and a pair of gum boots and start wading around in the burn to see if they'll make their fortune."

"Interesting waterways in your part of the world," said Mel. "Pearls, gold — salmon, of course . . ." Salmon was on that evening's dinner menu, in one of Mrs. McScurrie's finest sauces. "All worth money, and quite right too. But granted it's expensive, what use is it? Platinum, I mean. I guess anyone would think it was worth killing somebody for a plain old gold mine" — with a quick look at Miss Seeton, who clicked her tongue sorrowfully, but couldn't help listening with much interest — "but what does anyone use platinum for?"

Ranald cleared his throat again, and frowned. "Industrial and scientific uses mainly, I gather, because it has, er, exceptionally high resistance to corrosion, and it makes an excellent catalyst. Especially in the refining of petroleum, and in the manufacture of, um, certain important acids whose names and functions escape me. Oh, and it can be used to coat, and line, and otherwise protect, er, various pieces of equipment — optical lenses, electrodes —

oh, jewellery as well, of course . . ."

"Let's hear it for the jewellery," muttered Mel, while Philomena was more outspoken.

"How very boring," she said.

"But deadly," added Mel, then frowned. "That sketch of yours with all the birds, Miss S. — did you ever work out what they were?" And she bet herself a new hat that they'd be platinum flycatchers, or something of the sort. Otherwise, what had been the point of drawing them in the first place?

Miss Seeton looked round vaguely. "My sketchbook is in the hall," she said at last. "But, if you're really interested, Mel dear . . ."

"I'm interested. On the chest, I suppose?" But before Mel could limp along to fetch it, Philomena was before her. Miss Seeton's unique talent had been explained in a private moment, and she, too, had been sworn to secrecy.

On her return, with a quick enquiring look at Miss Seeton, she handed the book to Mel, who flipped through its pages for the she-didn't-know-how-manyth time. "Birds," she said triumphantly, as she found the sketch Miss Seeton had drawn on the day she found Ewen Campbell's body. "Ducks or something similar, and sparrows? Any idea what they really are?" And she looked at Miss Seeton expectantly.

Miss Seeton blushed, and twisted her fingers together as Mel smiled. Philomena, natural history expert, took the book when Miss Seeton made no further move. She studied the sketch for a moment, then chuckled. "Members of the duck family, without a doubt. *Bucephala clangula,* at a guess — the, er, goldeneye." At Mel's quick gasp and knowing nod, she chuckled again. "The smaller birds, I suggest, would be either gold-crested wrens or goldfinches . . ."

And everyone regarded Miss Seeton with much respect. An awkward silence was broken at last by Mel. "Guess I'll be treating myself to a new hat next time I'm in Brettenden, Miss S. A Monica Mary special, I reckon I deserve!"

Miss Seeton, relieved that the topic of conversation had so fortunately been diverted from herself, smiled absently, and murmured that she looked forward to dear Mel's visit, but then she turned to Ranald, blushing again.

"Although, as Miss Beigg says, *platinum* is rather unromantic, one has to admit, I think, that *gold* is not only far more attractive, but has even more practical applications — my umbrella, for instance . . . and also one can paint window frames with gold leaf, which needs very little maintenance, according to dear Lady Colveden." She coughed delicately. "One hesitates to interfere, Lord Glenclachan, but Mac-Sporran Castle is far larger than Rytham Hall, with a great many windows. And, as these must require painting far more often — with being so far north, you know — and as one assumes the land on which the gold was found belongs to you . . ."

"I only wish it did," said Ranald, while Mel regarded Miss Seeton with amusement. A sensational discovery, in which she'd played an important, though as usual unwitting, part — and all she could think of was somebody else's household maintenance. When they made her, they certainly broke the mould.

But it was Philomena Beigg who produced the telling, final phrase. "Miss Seeton," she said, "you really are, if I may say so, a pearl without price . . ."

The employees of Thorndike Press hope you have enjoyed this Large Print book. All our Large Print titles are designed for easy reading, and all our books are made to last. Other Thorndike Press Large Print books are available at your library, through selected bookstores, or directly from the publisher.

For more information about titles, please call:

(800) 223-1244
(800) 223-6121

To share your comments, please write:

Publisher
Thorndike Press
P.O. Box 159
Thorndike, Maine 04986